"So you don't think th[...] wanted Dexter out of the [...]

"'Out of the way'? [...] Margie stared at McLeod. [...]

"Margie, forgive me, b[...] ever a death is from mysterious causes, I can't help but ask if foul play was involved."

"That's a ridiculous idea. Dexter was highly respected...foul play—that's just not possible."

"Isn't it?" said McLeod.

"It is completely and totally out of the question. You can put that out of your mind."

McLeod switched back to condolence mode and left. Did Margie Kinkaid protest too much? Could all that grief be simulated? Was foul play ever "completely and totally out of the question"?

The
PRINCETON MURDERS

Ann Waldron

For Jeff

Ann Waldron

BERKLEY PRIME CRIME, NEW YORK

THE PRINCETON MURDERS

A Berkley Prime Crime Book / published by arrangement with the author

PRINTING HISTORY
Berkley Prime Crime mass-market edition / January 2003

Visit our website at
www.penguinputnam.com

ISBN: 0-425-18820-5

Berkley Prime Crime Books are published
by The Berkley Publishing Group,
a division of Penguin Putnam Inc.,
375 Hudson Street, New York, New York 10014.
The name BERKLEY PRIME CRIME and
the BERKLEY PRIME CRIME design
are trademarks belonging to Penguin Putnam Inc.

PRINTED IN THE UNITED STATES OF AMERICA

10 9 8 7 6 5 4 3 2 1

Author's Note

❧

LET ME SAY forthwith that while Princeton University is a very real place and I have used its campus, libraries, classroom buildings, and dormitories as a setting for this book, the people portrayed here are entirely products of my imagination. They hold positions in the Princeton University of my book—director of Public Safety, director of the Humanities Council, administrator of the English Department—that exist in real life, but they themselves do not. I made them up, and any resemblance to any living person is wholly coincidental. Believe me.

I should like to thank two doctors for providing information on poisoning. They are Dr. Judy Travis and Dr. Nick Partenope. John D. Reading, Chief of Detectives of the Princeton Borough Police, answered my questions about local police procedure. So did Jerrold Witsil, Director of Public Safety at Princeton University. Marcia Snowden was a great source of information about Princeton in general, and Kitsy Watterson let me visit her writing class at Princeton.

And to those people who valiantly read the manuscript and gave suggestions, I am forever grateful: Margaret Keenan, Amanda Matetsky (twice over), Lolly O'Brien, Marcia Snowden, Roxane Waldron, and Jeanne Norberg.

Elizabeth Frost-Knappman, my agent and friend, has won my unstinting and undying gratitude for her incredibly wonderful advice and her untiring help. As usual, she went far beyond the call of duty.

Susan Allison, my editor, was generous, keen-eyed, and keen-witted, and I'm grateful to her. I was lucky to have Joan Matthews, a Princeton alumna, for a copyeditor.

One

❧

THE PRINCETON ADVENTURE began in Tallahassee for McLeod Dulaney one day in June, when she pulled the letter with the TRENTON, NJ postmark out of her mailbox at the *Star of Florida.* When she read the letter, she was astonished and delighted. In the age of telephone, fax, and e-mail, very little information that was surprising, important, or even interesting, arrived by way of the United States Postal Service but this, by God, was all three.

The letter was from someone named Ginger Kingsley, executive director of the Council of the Humanities at Princeton University, who invited her to apply for a lectureship in the humanities and teach a class called "Literature of Fact" to twelve handpicked students for the fall semester.

"John McPhee '53 teaches this course each spring, but Princeton is delighted to invite visiting journalists of distinction to take over each fall," Ms. Kingsley wrote. She added that if McLeod's application was successful, an apartment would be made available at a reasonable cost. She knew it was short notice, Ginger Kingsley said, but she hoped McLeod's schedule would be flexible enough to allow her to come.

Assuming correctly that the application was a mere formality, McLeod swiftly updated her résumé and prepared a portfolio of clips. McLeod had never been to Princeton, but the thought of teaching, even if for just a semester, on the campus where Scott Fitzgerald had walked and where her idol among nonfiction writers, John McPhee, taught, was numbing.

McLeod had already had one astonishing piece of news the month before. She had won the Pulitzer Prize for a series of pieces she had done on a group of welfare families in Tallahassee. This news had arrived over the Associated Press news wire, however, and not by mail, and had been greeted with celebratory hilarity in the city room of the *Star of Florida*, Florida's oldest and most liberal newspaper. It was a place where a Pulitzer was such unlikely recognition that scarcely anyone on the paper had drawn a sober breath for three days. "McLeod, you have brought a touch of glory to us all," Jim "Toe Sack" Burlap, the oldest reporter on the *Star of Florida*, had said to her. "I never thought anybody from here would win a Pulitzer." (He pronounced it Puuuuulitzer.) McLeod's picture had run in the Media section of *Time* magazine and she had appeared on two network television shows, where she was a great hit, possibly because of her Southern accent, her trim figure, and her short snow white hair that always looked disheveled, even right after she brushed it. Her hair had turned white when she was thirty, more than twenty years ago. During her brief celebrity, she was often described as "an older woman journalist from sandspur country."

Everything that had happened since had been something of a letdown, but it must have been the national publicity that explained Princeton's invitation to her. (McLeod did not know it, of course, but a much more famous journalist, originally slated to fill the slot, had dropped out at the last moment—and left Ginger Kingsley desperate.) It would be wonderful to go to Princeton, McLeod thought. She trotted in with the letter to show Charlie Campbell, her boss, her friend, and the owner of the *Star of Florida.* He told her of course she had to go, and suddenly offered to pay her salary while she was gone, even though Princeton would be paying her. "We owe you," he said.

MCLEOD DECIDED TO drive to Princeton so she'd have a car to use while she was there and she picked the Southern route—not the Southern route geographically, but a route that was thoroughly in the Southern style. In other words, she took seven days to make the two-day drive, stopping off in Atlanta to see her mother, in Charlotte to spend the night with her journalist daughter Rosie, in Winston-Salem to visit her college roommate, and in Washington and Baltimore to stay with cousins. The long automobile trip alone did not bother McLeod. She was used to being alone. Her husband had died about the time her hair turned white, and left as she was with two small children, she had gone to work full-time for the *Star of Florida.* Her parents had come and stayed for two months to help her get her new life started, and then she had managed job and children with the help of a web of friends, her extended family, as she thought of them, and visits from her parents, then after her father's death, her mother alone. She had had moments of aching loneliness, and sometimes with the responsibilities of job and children, she had almost broken. But now the children were grown, and she at least had an interesting job and a circle of wonderful friends in Tallahassee. Now she would be able, for almost the first time, to pull up stakes for as long as a semester. She was excited.

•   •   •

SHE ARRIVED IN Princeton, parked at a meter on Nassau
Street, and entered the campus by what she would learn
later was the Fitzrandolph Gate. To her delight, it was the
same time of the year that F. Scott Fitzgerald had come
there in 1914, and just as Amory Blaine, Fitzgerald's fic-
tional Princeton freshman, had, McLeod "noticed the
wealth of sunshine creeping across the long, green swards,
dancing on the leaded window panes, and swimming
around the tops of spires and towers and battlemented
walls."

The sun shone on the Gothic buildings all right, but
those towers cast dark shadows, and McLeod shivered.
Searching for the Humanities Council, she was directed to
the Joseph Henry House, a Georgian yellow-painted brick
house, not one of the Gothic buildings with battlemented
walls.

She had no sooner given her name to a Humanities
Council secretary, than a large cheerful-looking woman
with a mass of red-gold hair burst into the room.

"McLeod Dulaney! Come in. Come in. And welcome.
I'm Ginger Kingsley. We're so excited you're here. How
was your trip? Come in and sit down a minute."

McLeod followed her into a spacious, sunny office and
sat down in a dark red leather chair. Ginger Kingsley sat
down in another chair and beamed at her. McLeod could
not tell how old she was—her skin was creamy and youth-
ful, but lines marked her forehead.

"I won't keep you long today," said Ginger Kingsley. "I
know you want to see your apartment, and I'll take you
down there. But you must come to dinner tonight at our
house. Then we can have a good talk. I want to hear all
about your trip. Come on, I'll ride with you to the Housing
Office to pick up your keys, and then I'll go with you to
show you the apartment. It's close enough for me to walk
back. Let's go!" She pulled herself up and seemed ready to

pull McLeod up, too, but McLeod, though dazed by all this energy, managed to stand up and follow.

"Be right back, Frieda," Ginger said to the secretary, and led McLeod on her way.

McLeod was full of questions when they got in her car. As for the official questions, Ginger told her that she'd learn everything she needed to know—"more than you want to know"—about her job at the meetings during the next week. But McLeod, ever curious, wanted to know about Ginger. "How long have you been at Princeton?" she asked her.

"Twenty years," said Ginger. "Can you believe it?"

"Do you teach?"

"Oh, no," said Ginger. "My husband teaches. I'm just a staff person."

Under McLeod's questioning—always the reporter—Ginger revealed that she and her husband had come to Princeton right out of graduate school, with a new Ph.D. each, and a new baby. "I thought I might get to teach, too, eventually," she said. "Of course, I never did. But at least I have a job, and I get to deal with interesting visitors—like you."

"What about the baby?" asked McLeod, ever curious. "Girl or boy?"

"A girl named Miranda," said Ginger. "Our only child."

At the Housing Office, McLeod gulped at the "reasonable" rent—it was astronomical by Tallahassee standards—but paid two months in advance. Keys in hand, Ginger sat beside her in the car and repeated her invitation to dinner that night.

"Cliff, my husband, is a wonderful cook," she said, "and we're having a few people in. They'd love to meet you and you might enjoy them. I think most of them are from the English Department. Cliff teaches English, but Mystique will be there. She teaches creative writing."

"Mystique Alcott?" asked McLeod.

"That's right," said Ginger.

"I've read her work," said McLeod. "I'd love to meet her."

"Well, you will—this very night," said Ginger. She gave McLeod directions to get to the Kingsleys' house on Jefferson Road, then turned her attention to directions for the present. "We're on Elm Drive right now. We'll stay on Elm to Faculty Road. Now, turn left and take the first right."

They were in a parking lot for an apartment block that faced Lake Carnegie. McLeod's small but hygienically clean apartment was on the first floor; it had no lake view. It had two bedrooms—"You can use one for a study," said Ginger—a living room, a small dining room, an ample kitchen, and a tiny balcony looking over the woods.

"Now, I can help you unload the car," said Ginger briskly.

"I loaded it myself," said McLeod. "I can unload it. Besides, my son is a graduate student at Yale and he's coming down tomorrow. He can do any heavy lifting. You've been splendid."

She walked out with Ginger to the parking lot. Ginger showed her the footpath that wound through the woods, crossed Faculty Road, and went up the hill to the campus, then she set off herself. McLeod took two suitcases out of her car and began the moving-in process.

Two

WHEN MCLEOD HAD brought everything in from the car, she unpacked the luggage and boxes and hung up her clothes. She made up the bed and even connected her laptop computer and printer, but she had forgotten the telephone extension cord for the modem.

Still, I'm settled, she thought. That was easy. She drove uptown to find a grocery store and located something called Wild Oats, offering a combination of health food and upscale comestibles. It all looked very attractive and she stocked up on organic staples and environmentally pure detergents, although she doubted that these would be as effective as faithful old Tide and Electrasol. (They weren't.)

When the groceries were put away, it was time to get ready for Ginger's dinner party. What should she wear for her first social event in Princeton? Having no idea what people wore to Friday night parties in the North, she finally settled on a long flowered skirt with a black T-shirt top, hoping that the combination of informal top and not-too-formal bottom would seem appropriate.

It thrilled her to drive up Washington Road through the Princeton campus—where I am going to *teach*, she thought. She found the Kingsleys' house—a big old shingle monstrosity on Jefferson Road—and knocked. She was among the first guests to arrive, but later it got crowded.

"Is the whole English Department here?" she asked.

"Oh, no," said Cliff Kingsley, Ginger's husband, a jolly, red-faced, bald man who was even plumper than Ginger. He had come out of the kitchen to help serve drinks and stopped to talk to McLeod. "There are thirty-six people in the English Department. This is only a fraction of them. And some of these people aren't even in English—like Mystique. She's in creative writing. But creative writing is very close to English and to the Council of the Humanities. Everybody in creative writing has a joint appointment to one or the other."

McLeod found it confusing, and turned her attention to the guests. Mystique Alcott was a novelist and playwright, whose work McLeod admired without enjoying it much. Everything she wrote was deadly serious, but everything she wrote won prizes. McLeod was surprised to find that she was very fat—even fatter than the Kingsleys—with straight shoulder-length blond hair and loose, flowing garments that tended to flap into the hors d'oeuvres.

Astonished at the famous author's appearance, McLeod blurted a question. "Didn't you write a piece for *Vogue* about how much you loved fashion?"

Mystique beamed. "Yes, I did. Did you read it?"

McLeod, realizing how narrowly she had escaped being offensive at her very first Princeton party, recovered herself and asked Mystique if she did much writing for magazines.

"I write anything for anyone," said Mystique with a swirl of sleeve. "So you're teaching nonfiction writing? What is your background?"

"A lifetime of journalism," said McLeod.

"Where?" asked Mystique.

"Mostly in Tallahassee, on the *Star of Florida*, the oldest paper in the state," said McLeod.

"Oh, you're the 'sandspur journalist,'" said Mystique. "I remember. You won a Pulitzer, didn't you?"

"Yes," said McLeod. "I believe you've won several."

"I have," said Mystique, her face relaxing at the implied praise, her eyes opening wider to reveal that they were slightly crossed. And even open fully, they weren't all that wide, thought McLeod unkindly. Then she reminded herself that this was a famous writer and she, McLeod, was lucky to meet her in person.

"What are you working on now, Miss Alcott?" she asked. She had many questions for Mystique, the only person who had started asking her questions before she could vent her own curiosity.

"Don't try to write anything about me," warned Mystique. "I detest personal publicity. I want my work to stand on its own."

"I'm sure it will," said McLeod neutrally, "and don't worry. I shan't write anything about you."

Mystique narrowed her eyes again and then, surprisingly, laughed. "You make me almost sorry that you won't. Are you thinking of doing a book?"

"I guess everybody is thinking about doing a book," said McLeod. "I've always wanted to do something about the Bartrams, you know, John and William Bartram, the father and son who collected plants all over the East Coast and brought them back to Philadelphia. They sold them all over the world—this was long ago, when botanists in England were fascinated with plants from the New World. William, the son, came to North Florida . . ." She stopped. "I'm sorry. I'm rattling on," she said. "I'm boring you."

"No, you're not," said Mystique. "I just don't know what you're talking about. But all I know is that writers have to write books if they want to get anywhere. I tell my students that short stories don't cut it. And I'm sure that journalism is the same."

"I don't know that I'm trying to get anywhere," said McLeod. "I never thought about it. I like it here."

Mystique looked puzzled.

"I mean it metaphorically," McLeod said. "I know I can't stay in Princeton."

"But you have to think about getting somewhere *metaphorically*," said Mystique, and moved away, her flowing garments flapping. "Or else."

McLeod talked next to Gertrude Sergeant, a full professor in the English Department, whom she found she rather liked. Sergeant was skinny, almost anorexic looking, but McLeod noted that she was wiry and muscular, not frail. She had straight brown hair cut short with bangs. She had written a lot of books with the word "gender" in the titles.

It seemed appropriate to ask Sergeant about her views on the status of women, and McLeod discovered that they were extreme. Sergeant believed that an evil patriarchal system conspired to strip women of all rights.

"Are you married?" asked McLeod.

"Oh, no," said Sergeant. "Marriage is a form of slavery for women." McLeod looked at Cliff Kingsley, wearing an apron and serving drinks, and Ginger chatting up the guests, and wondered.

Elizabeth Finley seemed to McLeod to be the mousiest person at the party. She was gray-haired and quiet and wore a tweed suit. She, too, was an English professor, specializing in eighteenth-century writers.

Before McLeod could launch into her interrogatory mode with Finley, a man who had just arrived rushed over to meet her. His name was Archibald Alexander. "Call me Archie," he said. He had a thick mop of curly white hair, round rosy cheeks, bright blue eyes, and he hugged McLeod when they'd been introduced.

"I'm so glad to meet you," he said. "I knew your husband when we were in graduate school at Duke. He was a brilliant scholar. I lost touch with him after he went to Florida, but I remember him well. He used to talk about you . . . You were engaged then, weren't you? I'm sorry we never met."

"Me, too," said McLeod. "I was working on a newspaper in Atlanta while he was at Duke. We were married right after he got his Ph.D."

Archie asked her about her children. McLeod told him about Rosie, who worked on a newspaper in Charlotte, and Harry, who was a graduate student at Yale, and asked him about his job. "I teach the Victorian novel to a lot of rude young people who couldn't care less," he said. "No, that's not true. They could care less. And some of them actually read the books." He knew about her Pulitzer, and congratulated her.

McLeod asked him if he was married. "Oh, dear, no," he said. "Was once, but no more. Do tell me about poor Holland. When did he die?"

McLeod liked people who said "die" instead of "pass on," and told him it was twenty years ago.

"I thought it had been some time," he said. "And you're still a widow?"

"Oh, yes," she said.

"Are you free for dinner on Sunday night?" he asked suddenly.

"I'd love to," said McLeod. "I don't have to check. I know I don't have anything going on."

"You'll soon have something on every night, don't worry," said Archie.

BEFORE THEY SAT down to dinner, she had met all twelve guests. Cliff Kingsley was indeed a fine cook and his scallop stew, endive and walnut salad, and chocolate soufflé were sublime.

"I don't think I ever had a real oven-baked chocolate

soufflé before," said McLeod over dessert. "This is wonderful."

"It's so bad for us, Cliff," said Trudy Sergeant. "Are you trying to kill us all?"

"Or just fatten us up?" asked McLeod.

"Don't even mention fat," said Mystique Alcott. "Oh, you don't have anything to worry about, Trudy. You're as thin as a chive."

"And she works out, so she must be very strong," said Dexter Kinkaid, the English Department chair, who had a stiff neck, a straight back, and a gray crew cut. "I've seen her in the weight room at the gym."

"Oh, Trudy, you're wonderful," said Ginger.

"She does it to protect herself from men," said Cliff.

"I don't care why she does it," said Ginger. "She looks great."

McLeod asked Cliff how long he'd been interested in cooking.

"Always," he said. "My mother was a great cook, but she became an invalid and I used to cook for all of us. Mother would give me directions from her bed. And after I got married, I seemed to do all the cooking." Everybody laughed, even Ginger. "Then Ginger and I went to France for the first time. And that did it. After I first tasted French cooking, I knew I wanted to learn to do that."

AS MCLEOD WAS leaving, Ginger Kingsley thanked her for coming. "You were an absolute hit," she said. "I knew you would be. You look divine—your hair is wonderful. Is it natural?"

"Of course it is," said McLeod. "I don't have the skill to do anything artificial. But it's prematurely white, you know. I hated it when it first happened, but I've gotten used to it."

"It's very striking," said Ginger. "Archie Alexander was quite taken with you. I could tell."

"It's nice to meet someone who remembers my husband after all these years," said McLeod. "And he's not married?"

"No," said Ginger. "He was, but he always ran around—with graduate students, I'm afraid—and his wife told him the next time he had an affair, she was through. He said he was sorry and it wouldn't happen again. It happened again and Eve left him and sued him for divorce and got half his retirement income, which will be important in a few years. I think Archie was totally surprised that she kept her word. Now he can run around all he pleases, but I think he misses domesticity. Those graduate students don't look after him the way Eve did."

"Maybe he thinks I'm old enough to look after him," said McLeod.

"No, no, it's not that. He's really interested. I'm sure."

It was nice to have someone "interested" in her, McLeod thought, and it had been exciting to meet all those brilliant people in one evening. Mystique Alcott was a little weird, but she was a world-famous writer. Still there had been undercurrents to the evening that made her vaguely uneasy.

Three

❦

MCLEOD WAS DELIGHTED to see Harry, her tall, curly-haired son, when he came down on Saturday to help her get settled. He led her to Radio Shack, where she could buy a telephone extension cord for her modem. Harry had been to Princeton several times during his years in the East and kindly showed his mother the hardware store, a drug-store, and the train stations in Princeton and at Princeton Junction. He spent one night and then shot back to New Haven.

On Monday, McLeod made the half-mile walk up to the campus—through the woods by the apartment building, across Faculty Road, through another patch of woods, then onto Elm Drive. It was not an easy walk, and McLeod thought with satisfaction how fit she would be by the end of the semester. She went to the Joseph Henry House to find her office. Ginger went upstairs with her and showed her how Princeton's computer network worked and how to send and receive e-mail.

"The students use e-mail instead of the telephone," Ginger said. "You have to know how to use it. You can check it from home by going through the university's home page. Here, type in your password." She discreetly turned her head.

"I always use 'Peaches,' since I'm originally from Georgia," McLeod said as she keyboarded it. "Goodness, this is fast."

McLeod went to meetings every day that week—with the board of the Humanities Council, for instance, and with the other teachers in the Council's program, where she met John McPhee face to face, and could only gabble helplessly. She received her final list of students—over the summer she had read the writing samples the applicants had submitted for the class and had found it difficult indeed to pick twelve from the hundred who applied. Now here they were in her roll book. She inspected the room where her seminar would be held.

When she wasn't in meetings, she walked. Princeton was a wonderful place to get about on foot. In Tallahassee it was almost always too hot to walk, except very early in the morning or late in the evening. But in Princeton she could walk anytime. She thoroughly explored the campus, admiring the Gothic buildings designed by Ralph Adams Cram; the Georgian simplicity of the college's first building, Nassau Hall; the classical, white-columned Whig and Clio Halls, built to house the two early debating societies; the Woodrow Wilson School with its very modern columns that nevertheless followed the classical rule determining the ratio of columns on the front to the number on the side; the modern residential college designed by Robert Venturi; and the dormitory by I. M. Pei. There was the collection of outdoor sculpture—works by David Smith and Henry Moore and Picasso and Louise Nevelson—to be hunted down and identified, and the stained glass windows in the Gothic chapel to be decoded.

At the U-Store, as the University Book Store was

known, she found little guidebooks to everything on campus—the buildings, trees, and sculptures—though nobody seemed to know why the squirrels at Princeton were black, not gray. But black they were, scampering up and down the elms and eating tidbits from their paws while their bright button eyes gazed at humans passing within inches of them.

She ventured off the campus to downtown Princeton and made forays into the nearby residential districts, where every house had pots of bright-colored chrysanthemums on the front steps. Lake Carnegie was right next to her apartment and the towpath on the Delaware and Raritan Canal just across the lake was a wonderful place for a serious walk.

She discovered a yarn store on Chambers Street and bought some brilliant multicolored wool so she could knit a sweater for herself. The weather was really too warm in Tallahassee to work with wool, and McLeod had not knitted since she had gone there to live. It would be fun to knit again, and if her sweater worked out, she could make one for Rosie and one for Harry. They both lived where the weather was cold enough for wool sweaters.

At night she went out. She was astonished at the immediate busyness of the social life that whirled her into its vortex. At her first dinner with Archie Alexander, he filled her in on the English Department and the Creative Writing Program. Cliff Kingsley was an amiable plodder, he said, but not without redeeming qualities. He just liked to cook better than to do any scholarly work. Everybody adored Ginger Kinglsey, he said, and that may be why they put up with Cliff. She had a Ph.D., too, and had wanted to teach, but she was considered a good administrator. Dexter Kinkaid, the English chair, was a Keats and Shelley scholar, stingy and conservative, but a man of absolute integrity. His books on the romantic poets were landmarks; he was always going to Oxford or Harvard to lecture and he got grants by the bushel. He was also a ladies' man. "So watch out," said Archie, leering like Groucho Marx.

Trudy Sergeant was a doctrinaire feminist but also wonderful at getting grants. "Feminism's hot," said Archie. "Notice her biceps." Elizabeth Finley was even more conservative than Dexter Kinkaid, Archie warned, and twice as mean, but was a good teacher. Guy Peyton was rather foolish, but a nice man. And so on.

When he had finished with the senior professors, Archie described the young assistant professors. All McLeod remembered at that point was that one was interested in death, one was in Queer Studies, another in pan-African literature. She concentrated on her sea bass with eggplant chutney.

Archie loved to gossip, she discovered as she saw more of him. And he knew everyone, not just everyone at Princeton. He asked her about friends of his in the English Department at Florida State—"finest Yeats scholar on this continent," he said of one. He even knew some of Harry's professors at Yale. He asked McLeod if she was interested in writing for scholarly publishers—editors had asked him for help in locating writers for various upcoming projects. "A handbook on Dickens's works, for instance?" he said.

"Good heavens, Archie, I'm not a scholar," she said.

"But you're a good writer, I'm sure," he said. "How about a brief biography of Nadine Gordimer?"

"I'd love to do a biography someday, but I'm not that fond of Gordimer's work," said McLeod. "And I'd surely have to read and reread it for a biography. Now Rosie, my daughter, loves Nadine Gordimer. If she ever has a daughter, she wants to name her Nadine."

"The editor of this series wants people who can write for a general audience, not just scholars," said Archie. "She—the editor—is a good friend of mine—she was my graduate student."

McLeod wondered if the editor had been one of Archie's girl friends when she was a graduate student.

"But we'll find you somebody else to write about," Archie went on. "Did I hear you mention the Bartrams one night?"

"It's just an idle thought," said McLeod.

"We'll have to go down to Bartram's Garden outside Philadelphia," Archie said. "It's a spectacular place on the Schuylkill. We've got lots we have to do."

SOMETIME LATER HER daughter, Rosie, called McLeod from Charlotte. "The funniest thing happened," she said. "An English professor at Queens College called me and asked me if I'd be interested in writing a brief biography—a long article, really—about Nadine Gordimer. She said her old friend and mentor Archibald Alexander had recommended me. He told her he knew you."

"That's wonderful, Rosie," said McLeod. "I'm thrilled."

Archie was too good to be true, she thought after she hung up.

Four

✧

MCLEOD WENT TO her first class with some trepidation. She worried about what to wear—and finally settled on a brilliant pink linen suit. With her white hair, she refused to dress in black like everyone else. She was afraid she would not be able to keep twelve presumably brilliant Princeton students interested for three hours. The ability apparent in all the writing samples had impressed her, and the work of the twelve she selected had dazzled her. Engaging those twelve would be—she hated the term—a challenge.

She had learned from all the meetings the past week that people who had held her post in the past had nearly always brought in friends of theirs, prominent journalists from New York and Washington, to speak to the class. Princeton paid their expenses and a small honorarium.

"How can I bring people up from Tallahassee?" she grumbled to herself. And then she remembered that the old warhorse of a reporter, Jim "Toe Sack" Burlap, had told her he was coming to New York this fall and would come out to Princeton to see her. She would make sure he came on a Thursday so he could visit her class. And a couple of cronies from the press corps at the state capitol in Tallahassee had moved to New York—John Mackintosh was at *Newsweek* and Oliver Hunt had gone to the *New York Times*—and she was sure they would come talk to her class. And there was the guy in Washington—what was his name? She would give Princeton a taste of the South!

Now on Thursday afternoon she sat at one end of a long table in a seminar room in the Joseph Henry House and looked around at the young faces lining both sides of the table. All twelve students were present.

She had watched them coming in, all carrying backpacks that they dumped on the floor and from which they extricated notebooks and ballpoint pens. They were, she thought, a nice assortment, mostly female, one African-American, one Asian, one Hispanic, and the rest humdrum Caucasian. She noticed a lot of earrings—not just in earlobes but in the upper rims of ears—and two nose studs.

She said hello and introduced herself. Some of the students smiled at her, but most of them seemed to be waiting for something. I hope they're withholding judgment on me, McLeod thought, and haven't already decided I'm a fool.

"First, let me call the roll, and as I call your name, I hope each of you will tell us a little bit about yourself," she said. "Tell us your ambitions and what class you're in." In the short time she'd been at Princeton, McLeod had learned the vast importance of the class numerals after a student's name; it was, as somebody had said, part of the "alumnization of the student body."

The young man on her left was named Ben True, blond and blue-eyed. "I'm a graduate student," he said. "I would like to be a writer in case I can't get a teaching job after I get my Ph.D. Well, I guess I really want to be a writer anyway. I grew up in Baltimore, where we worship H. L. Mencken and Edgar Allan Poe—that may be why."

The woman on his left was Daisy Wood, a redhead from New York City. "I'm majoring in English. I applied for this class because I want to be a journalist," she said.

McLeod smiled and took notes, and listened. Marcy Flowers was an attractive young woman with chestnut hair, green eyes, and a pointed chin that gave her face the shape of a heart. In a Southern accent she said she was from South Carolina and was taking the class because she wanted to know if she had enough talent to become a writer.

And so it went. They were all serious, and mostly English majors, although one, Lyle Cramer, was a computer science student who wanted to write.

"Now tell us about you," said Lyle Cramer when the others had finished. McLeod looked at him. He was sulky looking until he smiled, when he suddenly seemed charming. Even though he was sitting down, McLeod could see that he was tall and so thin he looked as though he had coat hangers instead of arms in his shirtsleeves. He wore wire-rimmed glasses and had a shock of dark hair that hung down over his forehead. She liked the look of him, and she liked it that he had asked about her, the teacher. It was not just polite, it demonstrated curiosity, a trait she much admired.

"I've already told you that my name is McLeod Dulaney and I'm a newspaper reporter in Tallahassee, on the *Star of Florida.* I do all kinds of reporting—crime, politics when the legislature is in session, conservation—but mostly I write about people, one way or another. And that, of course, is what we are going to concentrate on in this class."

"Are you married?" Lyle asked.

The question startled McLeod.

"I'm a widow," she said. "My husband died twenty years ago."

"Do you have any children?" Lyle asked.

"Two. Rosie works on a newspaper in North Carolina and Harry's in graduate school at Yale."

A gentle sigh of relief seemed to emanate from the class. Was it because talk of Tallahassee—the Boonies!—made them nervous but a nice Ivy League connection was somehow reassuring?

"Excuse me for interrupting," said Lyle Cramer. "I just wondered."

"That's all right," said McLeod. "I'm a curious person myself, and I always ask questions. I think curiosity is a noble trait for a journalist, or a writer of any kind."

Nobody laughed at this sally, but a few students smiled at her. McLeod hoped the class was warming up.

"People," said McLeod. "We're going to be talking about writing about people. . . ." She went on to explain her plan for the semester. They would read some examples of good personality pieces, or "Profiles," as *The New Yorker* had dubbed them. They would begin immediately writing their own pieces about people and for a term paper at the end of the semester would write a long article, or even a series of articles. "Right now I have handouts—three good interviews I've photocopied. One of them is Lillian Ross's famous interview with Ernest Hemingway. I'll pass these out so you can read them and we'll talk about them a little next time. After this, I think I'll be able to post all the outside readings on-line so we don't have to bother with photocopies after today.

"But I want you to get started immediately writing about people," she went on. "And the heart of writing about people, the basic tool, is the interview. That's how you get your information, either through interviewing a person directly or interviewing other people about him or her. We won't be writing about dead people in this class—that's a whole other skill. We'll be interviewing live people, and we'll start today.

"One more handout. Here are some guides to interviewing. Look them over and we'll talk about them now."

The guidelines were straightforward: Ask noncombative questions at first. Keep it simple. Ask questions about feelings, like 'What do you feel about this thing that's happened to you?' "

She admonished the students to do as much research as possible on the people before they were to interview them. "That's about it," she said. "Any questions?"

"Can we interview people over the phone?" redheaded Daisy asked.

"Sometimes you have to use the telephone," McLeod said. "But it's always best, if you possibly can, to talk in person. That way you can see the facial expression and the body language. Certainly, when you're doing campus interviews, I expect you to talk to the subject in person."

"Should we use a tape recorder?" asked the computer science student.

"I seldom use one myself," said McLeod. "I don't know shorthand, but I can take very good notes. That is—they're good if I type them up immediately. I can't make head nor tail of them the next day even. Actually, I wish I had trained myself to use a tape recorder. It's a protection for both the source and the reporter and I don't think it bothers most people you interview. And for technical language, you can't beat it. The science reporter on the *Star of Florida* always uses a tape recorder."

They discussed the drudgery of transcribing tapes, but McLeod pointed out that you didn't have to transcribe the whole tape. "Just listen to it and take out the quotes you need," she said.

They had no more questions and McLeod said, "Now for your first assignment. Divide into pairs, and one person in each pair can interview the other. Before the class is over, we'll switch so the interviewees can be interviewers.

"Do a thorough job. You may arrange to see your subject again at some point after class, but do the best you can right here. You can use a tape recorder on interviews after this, but do it today without a tape recorder. Take notes.

Dig into that person's life and find out what happened to
him or her in kindergarten, in elementary school, in high
school, and so far at Princeton. Find out what he or she
does in the summer. Find out about family, friends, ambitions, love life. Be careful with your questions about love
life—you want your subject to open up, not shut down.

"Type up your notes—if you like you can show them to
me at a conference—and I want you to turn them in to me
next week, and then extract enough from the notes to make
it into a narrative. There's nobody on earth you can't find
out enough about to write a riveting 250 words."

There was much consternation in class. "We can't just
start in and do an assignment right away," protested Daisy
Wood.

"Why not?" asked McLeod.

"It's a lot of pressure," said the preppiest-looking student in the class, who wore an Andover T-shirt.

"Come on," said McLeod. "Work on a newspaper and
I'll show you pressure. You might as well get right into it.
We only meet once a week and we only have twelve
weeks. We have to move fast."

"But I don't know him," said Daisy, waving at the student on her left. "Wouldn't it be better to pick somebody
we know, or somebody we choose to write about?"

"You'll have plenty of time to write about people you
choose," said McLeod. "In journalism, you often have to
take an assignment and write about somebody you *didn't*
choose." Her patience fled. "Just do it."

Self-consciously, they set to work. By the time everybody had been interviewed and had interviewed somebody
else in turn, it was time for the class to end. McLeod felt a
great sense of satisfaction that none of them had openly re-
belled or run out of class screaming.

Five

MCLEOD WAS PLEASED with the way her students carried out their first assignment. A few e-mailed her to arrange a conference and brought their notes to ask her advice, but most of them just turned up with finished profiles.

Some of them were very good. Lyle Cramer, for instance, had interviewed Marcy Flowers and had also talked to her roommate, two friends, and one of her professors. From his extensive notes he pulled out a lively vignette about Marcy's encounter with a pit bull when she was eight years old. "The scars, at least on her face, are very faint," he wrote in his closing sentence.

McLeod read student papers, held conferences, and went to class, but found she had a great deal of free time. In the afternoons she went to hear other visiting lecturers, which helped her get acquainted with the campus. In the theater at the 185 Nassau Street building, a smart, modishly dressed Brenda Maddox talked about her biography of W. B. Yeats. In the big Gothic-raftered upstairs lecture hall, McCosh 10, Charles Scribner IV (a Princeton alumnus) described his family's publishing firm and its relationship with Ernest Hemingway. In the auditorium in McCormick Hall, the art and archaeology building, a faculty member who was an expert on Renaissance art devoted an entire lecture to the Tivoli fountain in Rome. She sometimes took her knitting to lectures; her sweater was coming along nicely.

She went out to dinner often and met more local luminaries, including a man who was the world's foremost authority on Thomas Hardy and another who was an expert on the institution of the United States presidency.

It was heady stuff for McLeod, but as life whirled on, she sensed again the uneasiness she had felt after her first party in Princeton, an undertone that was dark, almost threatening. Nonsense, she told herself. It's just all these Yankee accents everywhere.

She often went places with Archie. With his plump rosy cheeks and curly white hair, he might look like an old gaffer in a Norman Rockwell painting, but he was by no means unfit. He liked to walk as much as McLeod did, and on bright autumn afternoons the two of them strolled along the towpath beside the Delaware and Raritan Canal. Once they saw Lyle Cramer running along the towpath. His long, coat-hanger-like limbs looked much more graceful and coordinated when he ran, McLeod noticed. He smiled at her and gave a little wave as he passed them.

She and Archie had dinners together, either in a restaurant, or in one of their apartments. Archie was not much of a cook, but could grill salmon or a steak. McLeod might offer more complicated dishes, but she hated to spend too much time in the kitchen. There were better things to do in Princeton.

She went to more parties. Dexter Kinkaid, the crew-cut, ramrod-stiff chair of the English Department, and his wife, Margie, gave a huge catered dinner party in a tent in the garden of their house on Hibben Drive. Gertrude Sergeant,

the wiry anorexic feminist, invited McLeod to a big
catered cocktail party at her house, and Elizabeth Finley,
the quiet little expert on eighteenth-century English literature, had her to dinner. With McLeod's help, even Archie
gave a small dinner party in his apartment. And the gre-
garious Kingsleys entertained often.

With all these parties, McLeod was getting to know
people quite well. She noted general characteristics of the
faculty. They were by and large liberal as far as politics
went. They exercised relentlessly, talked about healthy
food all the time, and wolfed down rich, unwholesome
meals whenever they were set before them. They drank
wine instead of hard liquor, except for the occasional martini, and except for Dexter Kinkaid, who always had a
cocktail called a cosmopolitan. McLeod thought this
sounded completely vile, and looked the part, a bright red
mix of vodka, cointreau, cranberry juice, and lime juice
served over ice in a large snifter.

"I have one every night," Dexter told her at one party.
"And only one."

"How long have you been drinking them?" McLeod
asked him.

"I fell in love with the first one I ever tasted," Dexter
said. McLeod thought he showed more animation than he
ever had before, which seemed to her a bit pathetic.

But the continual round of parties made McLeod realize that she was going to have to return invitations. And
how could she do it in her small apartment? She could handle no more than six for dinner, and at that rate, it would
take forever to catch up with her obligations.

The parties also made her realize that she needed new
clothes. People seemed to have established their individual
looks—Mystique always wore her flowing robes; Gertrude
Sergeant invariably had on a navy blue pantsuit; Elizabeth
Finley seemed to favor good tweed suits both day and
night. Only Ginger dressed up now and then, as McLeod
understood "dressing up." But everything she had brought

from Tallahassee was, unsurprisingly, too summery for Princeton in the autumn. The weather was definitely cooler. The men on the faculty marked the change in temperature by switching from khaki trousers and navy blazers to gray flannels and tweed jackets. The women turned to darker colors, if not to smarter lines.

McLeod made an unsuccessful foray into New York to look for clothes, where she succeeded only in becoming confused to the point of panic. But she seized the opportunity to invite Harry to lunch at the Plaza, the only restaurant she could think of at the time.

"Well, this is a change from Peppi's Pizza in New Haven," Harry said appreciatively. He asked his mother how she was getting along at Princeton.

"It's a lot different from Tallahassee," McLeod said. "I have culture shock. There are plenty of smart people in Tallahassee, as you know, but there's a great soft underbelly of people who aren't very smart. Up here, everybody seems smart."

"Are they nice to you?" Harry asked.

"Yes, very nice, and you'd be surprised at my social life. I go out to dinner constantly, but it's not relaxing somehow. Something about the life puts me on edge."

Harry dismissed her worry with the worldliness of a Yale undergraduate. "How's your class going?" he asked.

"It's great," said McLeod. "The students are bright and most of them work hard. A boy named Lyle Cramer is a standout and so are two of the girls."

"Mama, you have to stop calling students girls and boys," said Harry. "They're women and men."

"I know, but I do forget."

She looked at her politically correct Harry, shocked to see that his hair was turning gray. And he wasn't even thirty. He was going to be prematurely white-headed, just like his mother.

Harry saw her to Penn Station and said he would come

to Princeton for Thanksgiving. They agreed they would both urge Rosie to come up, too, for a family holiday.

Back in Princeton, McLeod found exactly the kind of clothes she wanted at a shop in Palmer Square. It seemed like a good omen.

Six

ON THURSDAY, SHE was surprised at how glad she was to see the members of her class come filing in. Daisy Wood, the redhead from New York, wore a ring in her newly pierced lower lip. She could barely talk.

"Oh, Daisy, does it hurt?" asked McLeod.

"Not weally," said Daisy. "It hurt when they firsht piershed it." As McLeod continued to stare at her lower lip, Daisy said, "It will look better when I get my shtud."

"Your what?"

"My shtud," said Daisy. "You know, they take the ring out and put in a shtud. In six weeksh."

"A stud," Lyle translated. "I thought you were a feminist, Daisy. Feminists are against mutilation of the female body."

Daisy glared at Lyle. "Conshishtency," said Daisy, speaking with great difficulty, "is the nightmare of little minds."

"Forgive my pedantry, but the correct quotation is 'A

foolish consistency is the hobgoblin of little minds, adored by little statesmen and philosophers and divines,'" said Ben True, the graduate student. "And you're none of those things, Daisy, so don't worry about that particular hobgoblin."

"Who actually said that, Ben?" asked McLeod.

"Ralph Waldo Emerson, the Sage of Concord," said Ben.

"Thanks," said McLeod. "And now, if all of you will give me your attention, I have a new assignment—to profile a professor. You've each done two stories about students, one you knew and one you didn't know. Now do a professor. Talk to him or her, talk to people who know him, other students who've had classes with her. Try to make your subject come alive for your readers, to show what motivates him, what's most important to him. You can concentrate on her teaching if you like. Or concentrate on some hobby. I know one of the English professors, for instance, has a printing press in his living room and prints beautiful little books. Or you can concentrate on his childhood in Rome, like the man in art history. Or that other man in art history who's from Yugoslavia—what does he think about what's going on in his native country now?"

They discussed this, and McLeod warned them again to do some research before the interview. "I've learned that the Communications Office in Stanhope has a publicity file on each member of the faculty, with a résumé and clips of any news stories that have appeared about him. You can certainly get the basic facts there."

They grumbled in their customary fashion that they didn't have time for such a lengthy assignment.

"You have a whole week," said McLeod. "How much do you need?"

No professor would take a student interviewer seriously, they said.

"I've been at Princeton long enough to know that professors take requests from students *very* seriously indeed,"

said McLeod. Courtney Phillips, who was, McLeod had
decided, the laziest person in the class, said she couldn't
think of a professor she wanted to interview, and McLeod
said, in that case, she would assign her one, and she could
do— Courtney hastily interrupted her to say no, no, she'd
think of somebody. Eventually they all accepted the inevitable.

"I have a treat for you next week," McLeod said. "A
colleague of mine from the *Star of Florida* will be here to
talk to us about legislative and political reporting, writing
about people in that context. His name is Jim Burlap. Of
course, we all called him Toe Sack."

Marcy Flowers, who was from South Carolina, was the
only student who had ever heard of a toe sack, but she faltered when she tried to explain it to the class. "It's a burlap
bag," said McLeod. "We also called them croker sacks.
But 'Toe Sack' seemed to fit Jim. You'll like him, and
don't underestimate him just because he sounds like a hill-
billy."

Seven

CLAD IN A new brown dress with bands of black velvet around the skirt—it looked autumnal without being woolly and hot—McLeod went off to yet another party, this one at Mystique Alcott's.

Mystique lived in a huge house on Hodge Road in Princeton's most upscale neighborhood. Every window was lit, and when McLeod walked in the open front door, the living room and library were crowded with people, most of whom she did not know.

Mystique bore down upon her, flowing garments streaming behind her, pointed toward the bar in the library, and introduced her to a very young assistant professor in the English Department named Grady Schuyler.

"I'll get you a drink," he offered. "What will it be?"

"I just drink Pellegrino or soda water," said McLeod.

"How very sensible," said Schuyler.

"I've changed my mind," said McLeod abruptly. Who

wanted to be called sensible? "I'll have a martini, if you can get one."

"How very exciting," said Schuyler.

That was more like it, thought McLeod. "Wait, I'll go with you," she said. She had no desire to stand there in the big front hall waiting for her drink. She followed him to the library, where a student from the bartending agency manned the bar.

Schuyler was nice, McLeod thought. She had been at Princeton long enough to know the unenviable position of an assistant professor. Just out of graduate school, holding down a first teaching job, each was frantic to get tenure somewhere, but always somewhere in the East. Well, Berkeley or Stanford would do, maybe even Northwestern or the University of Chicago, but none of them wanted to go to Florida or Alabama or anywhere else in the South. Duke or Vanderbilt might perhaps, just perhaps, be acceptable . . . but nothing else below the Mason-Dixon Line. Assistant professors got three-year appointments, renewable for another three years. At the end of the six years, it was either up or out. They were either promoted to associate professor and given the invaluable gift of tenure, or they had to leave—the lucky ones to start all over on some other campus and the less lucky ones to flounder in a morass of adjunct teaching positions or to go into investment banking. Consequently, all assistant professors spent their time applying for grants so they could take a year off to get their dissertations into publishable shape. The published book was essential—but no guarantee—for getting tenure.

While the bartender mixed her martini, McLeod asked Schuyler how long he'd been at Princeton.

"Three years," he said.

"Will you be here another three years?" she sked.

"I hope so," he said.

"And have you had a book published, or are you about to have one published?" she asked.

"Actually, I'm working on one, and it's going rather well," he said. "I'm doing Queer Theory and that seems to be hot just now. I'm looking at the plays of Shakespeare through the prism of homosexuality. It's quite interesting."

"It sounds it," said McLeod, just as a beaming Archie Alexander came up to the bar, his white curls bobbing.

"I need a drink," Archie said. "Where's the bartender?" The student from the bartending agency had disappeared. "I want a drink," Archie repeated querulously. He pointed to a red cocktail in a brandy snifter, which sat on the big table being used as a bar. "As I live and breathe, that's bound to be a cosmopolitan that somebody has fixed for Dexter Kinkaid," he said. "Nobody drinks them but him. And he doesn't drink anything else. And he doesn't have but one, so everybody always fixes his drink in an enormous snifter."

"I haven't seen Dexter," said McLeod.

"He's never late," said Archie. "I bet he ordered this and then left before the bartender got it made. Or maybe Mystique had the bartender make it ahead of time so it would be ready when he got here. It'll just get hot sitting here—I really think I'll have to drink it myself." He said this with the air of doing mankind a great service. "Besides, I'm dying for a drink. Somebody can make Dexter another." He sipped it.

"Is it a cosmopolitan?" asked McLeod.

"It must be," said Archie. "What else could taste like cranberry and lime?" He took another gulp and shuddered. "It's got vodka in it, all right. I can't taste the cointreau, but I can feel the kick already."

While McLeod and Archie were standing near the bar, Ginger and Cliff wandered up, then Gertrude Sergeant and Mystique herself. They all seemed to think it was terrible that Archie was drinking Dexter's drink.

"Stop it," said somebody. "That's Dexter's exclusive."

"I've done it now," said Archie, draining the snifter.

"I'll have a Scotch for a chaser," he said to the bartender, who had returned to his post.

ARCHIE AND MCLEOD joined the Kingsleys when they sat down in the library with plates filled from the buffet. The food was very good, McLeod thought. And it wasn't cheap, either—rare roast beef and divinely seasoned au gratin potatoes. Ginger introduced her to another assistant professor, John Pope, an ardent deconstructionist and worshipper of Lacan, whom he had actually met in France.

McLeod asked him to explain deconstruction to her, and his discourse barred all other conversation during dinner.

"I've learned my lesson," McLeod told Ginger when the men had gone off to fetch dessert for all of them. "I'll never ask again."

"I can't talk to any of those young people in the department," Ginger said. "Actually, Cliff can't either. The president of the university—he's an economist—said he could handle a discussion on nuclear physics, but he could not understand deconstruction."

Since Archie had walked to Mystique's, McLeod gave him a lift home. In the car, she repeated her vow never again to ask anyone to explain deconstruction.

"I should hope not," Archie said. "These kids don't know what conversation is."

"Why did the department hire them?" asked McLeod. "Was it Dexter Kinkaid?"

"Dexter was on leave," said Archie. "And Fred Harper was acting chair. He's a young Turk and it happened to be a year that six vacancies occurred. Fred went wild and hired a Queer Theorist, a deconstructionist—well, they're all deconstructionists, but it's Pope who's the doctrinaire deconstructionist. Ursula Barnes specializes in death. Bob Dewey does Marxist criticism, and Guadalupe Hutchinson

is a Pan-Africanist. She's writing a book on the samba, or
something like that.

"I was furious. Elizabeth Finley had a fit. All of us old
timers were disgusted. Now the barbarians want tenure,"
lamented Archie.

When she pulled up in front of her apartment, he kissed
her chastely on the cheek, wished her good night, and said
he felt tired and wasn't going to invite her in.

Eight

❧

"ARE YOU ALL right?" It was Archie on the phone late the next morning.

"Sure," said McLeod. "Why?"

"Well, I'm sick as a dog," Archie said.

"Did you eat something last night that I didn't?" she asked.

"I don't know," said Archie. "It seems to me you ate everything." (Good heavens, thought McLeod, I must have made a pig of myself.) "Anyway I've been throwing up since early this morning," Archie was saying. "It must be flu—I'm wringing wet with sweat. Look, I just wanted to make sure you were all right. I'm going to try to get some sleep."

"Thanks for checking on me," said McLeod. "Can I bring you anything—Cokes? Groceries? Chicken soup?"

"Not a thing," said Archie. "I'll talk to you tomorrow. Let me know if you catch this bug."

On Monday, McLeod called Archie, who was still sick.

"I guess it's a forty-eight-hour virus," he said. "Not a twenty-four-hour one."

Again McLeod offered to bring him anything he needed, but he said he wasn't really able to eat yet.

He was still sick on Tuesday. On Wednesday McLeod drove him to the emergency room at the hospital, where he was admitted. She talked to his doctor, Dr. Winchester, who said that Archie wasn't doing well at all.

McLeod had no idea how to reach Archie's family, so she called Ginger Kingsley, who said that Archie's ex-wife had moved to New York and she didn't know her telephone number. Ginger seemed very upset about Archie's illness and rattled on until McLeod asked her who would know how to reach Archie's ex-wife. Ginger finally suggested Stephanie West, administrator of the English Department. She gave McLeod Stephanie's extension number.

McLeod had to get more change for the pay phone (the hospital forbade the use of cell phones on its premises) and finally reached her. Stephanie said she'd have to go to Archie's office and look in his Rolodex—the world's largest, McLeod thought again—and find a phone number for Eve Alexander.

"But I'll call her for you and tell her," said Stephanie.

"That would be wonderful," said McLeod. "I have a conference with a student at one, and I need to get to my office and look over what he's turned in before I talk to him. It's eleven now—you forget how slowly time moves in the hospital. And somehow I think somebody ought to be here."

Stephanie said she would send someone from the department to the hospital as soon as she could.

McLeod gave her Archie's room number and went upstairs. Archie looked frail and pale in the hospital gown. A parade of people came in to collect samples of blood and urine, take his temperature and blood pressure, and peer at the bottles and tubes of IV liquid.

McLeod waited anxiously. Dear Archie, she thought. She had known him only a little more than a month, but she was already extremely fond of him.

Nine

❧

IT WAS ALMOST noon before Cliff Kingsley arrived and McLeod could hurry back to campus, picking up a sandwich and a cup of coffee on the way to her office. She had managed to choke down a few bites of sandwich and a few swallows of coffee before Lyle Cramer, the computer science major, appeared for his conference.

When students came for conferences, they often whined, thought McLeod. They always had some excuse for not doing the assignment. Their roommate had had a heart attack or their mother had come to visit or their best friend had had a bad trip on drugs.

McLeod was not inclined to sympathize. "Too bad," she would say briskly, "but you realize I must count off for late assignments. Journalists have to meet deadlines. That's all there is to it." She was not sure how the students felt about this real-life insistence on timely submissions, but didn't much care. At first she thought Lyle Cramer was going to be another whiner.

"I thought and thought about the assignment and then I decided to write about an English professor I had last year. It was a course in Victorian literature and I think I registered for the class by mistake. I don't know what I thought I was doing—with Dickens and Thackeray and Trollope I was reading a thousand pages a week. But the professor turned me on to them. I got so I could hardly keep up with my other courses, I was spending so much time on all these three-volume novels. The professor's favorite is Trollope, and he told us how Trollope worked out his novels while he rode a horse around Ireland inspecting post offices. I'm a computer science major, but I want to write novels, and I decided I could be like Trollope—get up early in the morning and write, and then go off to earn a living."

"I love Trollope, too," said McLeod. "Do you like the Barchester novels best, or the Parliamentary series? I always like the Parliamentary ones because I spend time around the Florida legislature. You'd be surprised at the similarities between British politics and Florida politics."

"He's amazing, isn't he?" said Lyle.

McLeod liked Lyle Cramer; it was marvelous to find a computer science major turned on to Victorian literature.

"And so I wanted to write about Professor Alexander and find out how he got on to those old guys," Lyle was saying. "But guess what? He's been out sick. I never knew a professor to miss a class at Princeton, but he's missed two days of classes or maybe more. So I can't interview him. I'm really disappointed."

"I know about Professor Alexander," said McLeod. "He's in the hospital. He went this morning. I'm afraid he won't be able to be interviewed for some time. Can you do somebody else?"

"What's wrong with him?" asked Lyle.

"I'm not sure," said McLeod. "He got sick after a party the other night and he's just gotten sicker and sicker. And finally he was so weak he had to go to the hospital."

"Are you a friend of his?" asked Lyle.

McLeod thought that Lyle Cramer might actually be *too* curious, if anybody could be too curious. "I only met him after I came up here this fall," she told him. "I get invited to a lot of English Department parties—they try to include us Humanities Council people. Professor Alexander was in graduate school with my husband, so he came over and introduced himself—I had never met him before."

"And you and Professor Alexander became friends?" asked Lyle.

"Well, yes," said McLeod. "We're both single, and he's very open and outgoing. It was nice to make a friend like that." She decided the conversation had gotten personal enough. "At any rate, you need to pick somebody else to write about," she said briskly. "There are tons of interesting professors here. Mystique Alcott—"

"She never gives interviews," Lyle said. "Everybody's always trying to talk to her."

"Gertrude Sergeant," said McLeod. "She publishes all over the place. And she's not married. Why not?"

"Of course, she's not married," said Lyle. "She's a lesbian. All those rabid feminists are."

"They may be and they may not be," said McLeod. "Don't leap to conclusions before you interview somebody."

"But I'm not going to interview her," said Lyle.

"Look, you have to interview somebody," said McLeod.

"Can I have more time?" he asked.

"No," said McLeod.

"I talked to Professor Alexander once," protested Lyle, "but that was just the preliminary interview. I don't want you to think I didn't do anything."

"No. You people have got to learn about deadlines. The newspaper isn't going to wait. If you can't do one story, do another," said McLeod.

"What a concept," said Lyle. "It doesn't matter who you

write about just so you write something? That's what's
wrong with publishing today."

"It may well be," said McLeod. "But it's the way it
works. The newspaper, or the magazine, has to be filled up.
And you'd be surprised how often the story you didn't
want to do turns out to be the most interesting one you ever
did. That's life. And that's the way this class is.

"Now let's talk about the student interview you turned
in last week."

McLeod, who had suffered the sting of editors' unbri-
dled criticism many a time, always tried to temper her advice for young reporters, and she tempered it even more
for these students. She tried always to end on a positive
note, and she suffered for that now, as she and Lyle chatted—endlessly, it seemed to McLeod—about Lyle's piece.

It was the middle of the afternoon before McLeod could
get back to the hospital, retrieve her car, and drive home.

Ten

❧

ON THURSDAY, ARCHIE was no better. The capable Stephanie West had not been able to track down Eve Alexander, Archie's ex-wife, who was traveling in France with friends. She did reach Archie's daughter, Laurie, who said she'd come right down to Princeton from New York.

McLeod, busy that day with the arrival of Jim Burlap and then her class, did not get by the hospital to see Archie. Before lunch she walked down the hill to the little railroad station on the campus. She had told Jim what train to take from New York, to buy a ticket to Princeton, to get off at Princeton Junction, changing from the main line to the Dinky, the little one-car train that shuttled back and forth from the Junction to Princeton. Jim had managed it perfectly, and pleased to see him, she took him to Prospect, the faculty club, for lunch.

"This is wonderful. I haven't seen autumn leaves in years," said Jim, looking at the trees just beginning to turn.

"In Tallahassee, you forget what happens in the rest of the world when the seasons change."

"I know," said McLeod. "And I love the way you see pots of chrysanthemums everywhere, massed on everybody's front steps. It's so truly autumnal."

As they approached Prospect, the Italianate house set in lavish grounds, she began to talk like a tour guide. "This was where Woodrow Wilson lived when he was president of Princeton," she told him. "All the university presidents, in fact, lived here for years."

Inside, she showed him the library where Wilson had interviewed students who needed discipline. "Wilson's daughters used to sit in this little parlor here," said McLeod. "They'd watch and giggle at the students who came in to see their father. Of course there were only men students then."

Jim was suitably impressed with the house, but more impressed with his lunch, with which he had a bourbon and water and two glasses of wine, causing something of a rustle in the Garden Room at Prospect. In class, though, he was at his very best, recounting anecdotes about the Florida legislature and the capitol press corps. He told about the time the *Miami Herald* reporter decked the governor's press secretary in the capitol corridor and was hauled off to jail until he could raise bail. He described the time the president of the state senate passed out while he was out drinking with other legislators and a couple of newspapermen; whereupon his buddies whisked him off to the funeral home and bribed the undertaker to lay him out on a slab in the mortuary. When the senate president awoke, he took one look at his surroundings, screamed, and shot out. "He never took another drink," said Jim, "and everybody agreed it made him meaner than ever."

Most of the class loved the stories, but McLeod, who had discerned a puritanical streak in many well-fed Princetonians, was not too surprised that one of the stuffier students came to her after class and complained.

"That was very amusing, Ms. Dulaney, but what has that kind of stuff got to do with writing about people?"

"Maybe not much, maybe everything," said McLeod. "Toe Sack Burlap does a good job when he writes about people. Part of his secret may be his zest for life—and his pleasure in everything odd, or the eccentric, or flamboyant."

MCLEOD POPPED BY the hospital Friday afternoon to check on Archie. "Laurie's here," Archie said. "And I've had tons of company. The Kingsleys have been faithful. Mystique came—she seemed very upset that I was sick. I was surprised. I never knew her to notice anybody else's problems very much. And Trudy Sergeant—she seemed concerned, too, and furious that all the nurses are women. 'But the doctors are women, too,' I told her. That didn't satisfy her. Liz Finley talked about diseases and cures in eighteenth-century England. The esteemed chairman came, of course. He's worried about who's going to teach my courses while I'm out."

"Who is teaching them?" asked McLeod.

"Grady Schuyler is doing my Dickens course—I'm sure he's giving the students a gay perspective on Little Nell. Dexter himself took the graduate seminar this week. I hope I'll be back next week."

McLeod did not think it likely, but she didn't say so.

A young woman came in, kissed Archie on the cheek, and looked at McLeod.

Archie, seeming very tired, introduced his daughter to McLeod.

"Oh, I want to thank you for getting Dad to the hospital," said Laurie Alexander.

"I was glad to," said McLeod. "Your father has been terribly nice to me since I got here this fall."

"You're new?" said Laurie. "Dad does like new faces."

"I'll only be here one semester," said McLeod, "so he can find somebody newer next spring."

Laurie looked at her ruefully and said, "I'm sorry." She appeared relieved when McLeod smiled.

"I'll be on my way," said McLeod. "Call me if you need anything, but I guess you're more familiar with Princeton than I am. You grew up here, didn't you?"

"Oh, yes," said Laurie. "I know it like the back of my hand."

She walked toward the elevator with McLeod, who asked her if the doctors had decided yet what was the matter with Archie.

"Blood tests and all the other tests have come back perfectly normal," said Laurie. "The doctors don't know what's going on."

"That's hard," said McLeod.

SHE WENT BACK to the hospital again on Saturday and found Archie alone. The head of his bed was raised to prop him up, but he looked white and weak. He managed a feeble smile.

"One of your students came to see me," he said.

"Who?"

"Louis or Lyle somebody," said Archie. "He was in my Victorian novel class last year. Marvelous student. He wants to write a profile of me for your class."

"It does look like he could wait until you're out of the hospital," said McLeod.

"Oh, that's all right," said Archie. "Anything for one of your students. But I'm afraid I couldn't tell him much. I did tell him something important, though. I forget what it was now." He sounded vague. "But I told Lyle."

"Don't worry, Archie. Where's Laurie?"

"She said she'd be back," said Archie. "I had company and she said she'd go home to see about some things. She doesn't need to stay here all the time, you know. I'm well looked after." He paused and closed his eyes.

"You're tired," said McLeod. "Do you want me to crank the bed down?" He didn't answer, so she cranked it down anyway. She went to the nurses' station and asked a nurse to come look at him. The nurse came, took his pulse, held his hand a minute, and shook her head. "He needs the rest," she said. Reluctantly, McLeod left.

ON SUNDAY, OVER soup at lunch at the Kingsleys, Ginger told McLeod that Archie was in a coma and that there were signs of terrible liver damage—but from what cause no one could say.

"A coma!" said McLeod. "Good heavens! When I went to see him yesterday, he was talking. "But he did seem terribly weak."

"Well, Margie Kinkaid saw Stephanie West at church, and Stephanie told her," said Ginger. "Margie called us."

"It was just a week ago today that he got sick," said McLeod.

"Was it?" asked Ginger.

"He called me on Sunday after Mystique's party to see if I was sick, too. It's been downhill ever since. Poor Archie. I do hope he'll be all right."

Cliff brought in a cheese soufflé that looked like an illustration in *Gourmet* magazine, puffing over the sides of the casserole, lightly browned on top, and smelling like heaven.

"Cliff, you're wonderful," said McLeod. "Will you marry me?"

"All the girls say that," said Cliff. "Oh, if only they'd said it thirty years ago."

"And just whom would you have married?" asked Ginger grimly. "Tell me that, Romeo."

"Call me Escoffier, not Romeo, if you're looking for a foreign pet name," said Cliff. "I would have married no one but you, not even McLeod. And you have to admit it's a very good marriage—you laugh at my jokes and you eat my cooking."

"I've grown fat on your cooking," said Ginger. "I just wish it wasn't the ruling passion of your life."

"I know. I know," said Cliff. "You want me to work harder at teaching, write a book, go forward in academia. Academia is not nearly as interesting as food."

"Oh, if only I could teach," said Ginger. "You don't appreciate your luck, Cliff."

"Who wouldn't get fat on this cooking?" asked McLeod cheerfully, attempting to quench the incipient matrimonial brushfire, and picking up on Ginger's earlier remark. "I'm glad I know you both. Even if you won't marry me, Cliff." She took a huge bite of soufflé. "I don't suppose there's any use going by the hospital, if Archie is in a coma," she said.

"Unless Laurie needs some support," said Ginger. "I wonder if anybody has gotten hold of Eve Alexander? Stephanie must know. Cliff, we ought to go to church and we'd get the news, too."

"They call it the Good News," said McLeod.

"That's the essential message, I'm sure," said Cliff. "But I think Ginger meant more useful news. She meant gossip."

"Of course, I did," said Ginger.

THE NEXT MORNING Archie was dead.

McLeod felt surprisingly bereft. I'd known him such a short time, she mused, but I liked him. He was warm and funny and lively and very nice to me. I'll really miss him. Each time you dealt with death, she thought, it was a new experience, a new grief, a new and final loss. I didn't know Archie long enough to know his faults, she thought, and maybe that's a good thing.

Eleven

✦

ON MONDAY THE university lowered the Princeton flag that flew over East Pyne to half staff, but McLeod was interested to note that Archie's classes were not canceled. Classes were sacred.

After conferring, the president, the dean of the college, the dean of the chapel, and Dexter Kinkaid met with Laurie and a jet-lagged Eve Alexander. Burial would be private, they decided, after cremation. A memorial service in the chapel was scheduled for a week later.

McLeod went to the service and sat toward the back. She noticed that Mystique Alcott was weeping openly. What had gone on between Mystique and Archie? McLeod wondered. Why such a display of emotion?

But many people were weeping openly, it seemed. Elizabeth Finley, her gray hair untidy, was almost sobbing at one point. Even cool Trudy Sergeant looked distraught. Ginger Kingsley was frowning fiercely, apparently in an attempt not to cry.

After the service Laurie was the official hostess at a buffet lunch at Prospect, but Eve was there, wearing a smart black outfit, and receiving condolences.

"Look at her swanning around," said Ginger. "They were divorced, after all. Did you hear about the meeting Eve had with the dean and the president? Laurie—you know, the daughter—wanted a gospel choir from the black Baptist church to sing. But Eve said, 'Dearest child, it would be most inappropriate,' and tried to line up the dean of the chapel on her side. The dean refused to outlaw the gospel choir, but conceded that the student Chancel Choir was the usual choice. Laurie insisted that she knew what Archie would have wanted. Eve said things like, 'Dear Heart' and 'Sweetest child' and simply wore everyone down. Personally, I'm sure Archie would have liked the gospel choir."

"I thought the student voices were very nice," McLeod said. She looked around Prospect—the reception spilled over from the garden room into the drawing room, the library, and the small parlor. She saw a group of assistant professors in English—she was beginning to think of them as the Hungry Ones—clutching sherry glasses in earnest consultation in the library. She recognized John Pope, the deconstructionist; Bob Dewey, the Marxist; and Grady Schuyler, the disciple of Queer Theory. A couple of others had joined them, but McLeod couldn't remember their names.

She dutifully introduced herself to Eve Alexander and told her how nice Archie had been to her, a stranger in Princeton. Eve shook hands, nodded, smiled glassily, and looked past McLeod to see who was coming up next.

Sadly, McLeod went home. She would miss Archie, she thought, with his rosy cheeks and white curls, his affectionate knowledge of the Victorian novelists, his boundless generosity with jobs and information and help for everyone. It had been wonderful to have an attentive and nice gentleman friend as soon as she got to Princeton. Yes, she would miss Archie very much indeed.

Twelve

❧

ON TUESDAY, MCLEOD went to her office for conferences with first, Marcy Flowers, the chestnut-haired young woman from South Carolina, and then Tina Martinez, the pretty, dark-skinned Latina.

When Tina left, Lyle Cramer was waiting in the hall and poked his head in to ask if he could see her.

"Sure," said McLeod, "but you're not due until tomorrow."

"I know, but I wanted to turn in my piece on Archie Alexander before we met tomorrow."

"Great," said McLeod. "But I thought you didn't have enough to go on."

"I went to see him in the hospital," said Lyle. "And I went to the funeral yesterday."

"He told me you came by the hospital," McLeod said. "Could he talk to you at all?"

"A little," said Lyle. "He answered most of my questions. Read it, will you, before our conference tomorrow?"

"I'll read it right now," said McLeod. "See you tomorrow."

When she read Lyle's piece, she was shocked. It had its good points, as everything of Lyle's did. But it wouldn't do. She would have to tell him. He was certainly one of the brightest students in her class—and one of the nicest. But this wouldn't do.

In her office the next day, she looked at Lyle. "The assignment was to do a personality story," she said, "not a sensational first-person piece."

"I think the material warrants a sensational approach," said Lyle.

"I don't think so," said McLeod. "You write, 'Was Archibald Alexander, Booth Tarkington 1898 Professor of Literature at Princeton University, murdered?' "

Lyle looked at her in silence, expectant.

McLeod returned his look thoughtfully, then turned back to his manuscript. " 'Professor Alexander, a professor popular with Princeton undergraduates and graduate students, died suddenly a few days ago after a brief, mysterious illness that was never diagnosed.

" 'I visited Professor Alexander two days before he died at Princeton Medical Center. He was just strong enough to tell me a bit about his first encounters with the work of the novelists he would later acquire a worldwide reputation for teaching and writing critically about, the Victorian giants Dickens, Trollope, and Thackeray.

" 'But the story of his death would be more suitable for another Victorian novelist: Wilkie Collins, master of the Novel of Sensation.' Lyle, that's a beautiful line, but you don't substantiate it, and you don't substantiate your lead sentence. Just because the doctors couldn't diagnose his illness doesn't mean it's a crime."

"Wrong. Wrong. Wrong," said Lyle. "Read on."

" 'Just before he died in Princeton Hospital, he told me he thought he was poisoned,' " McLeod read. "Oh, he didn't. He wouldn't say such a thing."

"Well, he didn't say it in so many words," said Lyle. "But he said something about a drink. And you know there's bound to be something funny about a mysterious illness that can't be diagnosed in this day and age."

"What do you mean? Do you think it was a terrorist who let loose a biological drug? A murder? Come on. Who would have murdered Archie Alexander? You point out yourself that he was one of the most popular professors who ever walked the earth."

"His wife?" said Lyle. "His daughter? A crazy student?"

"His wife was somewhere in France," said McLeod, "and she's his ex-wife anyway. His daughter was in New York. And when and how was it done? When did a student have access to him? With food or poison, I mean?"

"His girl friend?"

"I think I was the closest thing he had to a girl friend right now," said McLeod.

Lyle looked at her with new interest. "Well," he said, "did you kill him?"

"I did not," said McLeod.

"There's something funny about it," said Lyle doggedly.

"Be that as it may," said McLeod. "We'll leave it for the time being. The rest of the piece is very good indeed. It could be an elegy for dear Archie. I wish you hadn't hammed it up."

"I didn't ham it up," said Lyle stubbornly. "It was already hammed up. There's something weird about the way he died."

"I'm going to ask you to rewrite it slightly, so that it's a personality piece that meets the assignment instead of a sensationalized something else. I can't give you an A on this, no matter how well you write."

McLeod knew how important grades were to Princeton students.

"Don't worry," said Lyle somewhat bitterly. "I'll do it over for the grade, but I'll sure keep this version. Maybe somebody will publish it."

"Publish it?" said McLeod. "You wouldn't?"

"If I could," he said. "Look, I'll bring in a new version tomorrow."

McLeod stared at the door after Lyle left, then opened the phone book, looked up a number, pulled the phone toward her, and punched in the digits. She wanted to talk to the coroner.

Thirteen

❧

MCLEOD SCUFFLED THROUGH fallen leaves on the sidewalks on her way to the Kingsleys' house, for a party ostensibly in honor of a friend of Cliff's from Yale who was lecturing that night on Emerson. The truth was, of course, the Kingsleys liked to give parties. This one would end promptly, because the lecturer would have to attend an official dinner before his lecture at eight o'clock.

Ginger greeted McLeod enthusiastically. "But I'm sorry your name's not on the list for dinner at Prospect," she told her. "It's just a few people from the department."

"Oh, Ginger, don't worry, I'm happy to go home and go to bed. Believe me."

"I believe you," said Ginger. "You look tired."

"That really cheers me up," said McLeod.

"You know what I mean," said Ginger. "I was being sympathetic. Come meet the guest of honor."

McLeod shook hands with the guest of honor, tried vainly to think of some intelligent question to ask about

Emerson, gave up, and asked him if he got to Princeton
often. She didn't even hear his answer to her vacuous
question and left him reaching past her to greet an old
friend. She made for the dining table, where some of
Cliff's finest *hors d'oeuvres* were laid out. She had a particular fondness for his figs stuffed with gorgonzola and
wrapped in prosciutto, and managed to scarf down several
before she was shoved aside by Mystique Alcott. Fair
enough, she told herself. She'd had her share. She moved
on to the more prosaic stuffed mushrooms and smoked
salmon.

She greeted some of the young assistant professors.
"Are you going to the dinner?" they asked her.

When she told them that she had not been invited, they
looked relieved. "I told you so," a young woman said to
Grady Schuyler. "I told you it was a very small dinner."

"I'm glad I wasn't invited," said McLeod. "I'm tired of
eating at Prospect, and if I went to the dinner, I'd feel like
I had to go to the lecture. And I think Emerson is a big old
bore."

"Emerson is very hot right now," John Pope, the deconstructionist, said reprovingly. McLeod shrugged.

"She doesn't have to *network*," said the young woman.
"She doesn't have to make contacts."

The young woman's skin was very dark, her hair hidden
by a yellow turban, and she was resplendent in an orange
dress. "You look beautiful tonight," McLeod told her.

She looked startled. McLeod was having a hard time
getting it through her head that none of the young women
in Princeton—or older women either, for that matter—
seemed to care much about the way they looked. McLeod
had decided that she cared about clothes because she was
not an intellectual and was a Southerner besides.

She gazed at the women and marveled at their looks.
There was Mystique in her flowing robes, Trudy Sergeant,
rail-thin, with her brown bangs and wearing, as usual, a
pants suit. Margie Kinkaid in an odd quilted jacket. Drab

little Elizabeth Finley in a tweed suit that must be forty years old if it was a day.

Thirsty after all she'd eaten, McLeod sought the bar, set up in the hall and manned by the ubiquitous students from the bartending agency. Club soda in hand, she was surprised that Dexter Kinkaid ordered the same thing.

"You're not drinking a cosmopolitan?" McLeod asked him.

"Not today," said Dexter. "I have to introduce the lecturer tonight, so I thought I'd better be abstemious."

"Too bad," said McLeod. "I liked it that the chairman had his special drink. A perk, sort of. The chairman should get special attention. Shouldn't he? I'm always making these rash judgments on academia and ninety percent of the time I'm wrong."

"Of course, I'm human—I'm inclined to seek all the special attention I can get," said Dexter. "But then chairing the English Department is a thankless task. It's not a department that the development office raises money for, not like molecular biology, or something that industry subsidizes, like engineering. I fear I'm not a popular chairman, so I'm lucky to get my cosmopolitan from time to time. That's about all the special attention I get. Excuse me, McLeod, but I've got to start moving the dinner guests over to Prospect."

McLeod went home, changed into a bathrobe and slippers, and deciding she had had enough to eat, made herself a cup of hot chocolate for her supper and sat down to reread *Barchester Towers*. She would be doing a lot more reading, she thought, now that Archie was dead.

Fourteen

❧

MCLEOD WENT TO campus early on Thursday for a student conference. Then she met George Mackintosh from *Newsweek*, who was to talk to the class that day, and took him to lunch at Prospect. She thought George looked very prosperous and very East Coast in his tweed jacket, dark shirt, and striped tie. His brown hair was neat and he looked fresh and bright-eyed.

They talked idly about people they both knew in the press corps in Tallahassee, about George's wife and children, and his life in Montclair, where he lived now.

"Are you happy on *Newsweek*?" McLeod asked him. "Or do you ever miss Tallahassee?"

"I never want to go back to the South again, not to live, not to visit," he said. "I've had it up to here with the Bible Belt—the racism, the provincialism."

McLeod was astounded at the strength of his rage.

"Well, we miss you," she said.

"How about you?" he asked. "Now that you've seen Paree, are you going back to the farm?"

"Oh, sure," she said. "I don't really belong up here. Frieda, the woman who works in the Humanities Council, has made that clear. She told me how I was a last-minute substitute after the star they had lined up for my job backed out suddenly. She said, 'Poor Ginger had to take what she could get at the last minute.' But I'm glad they got me, even if I was second or even third choice. It's fun, even though they scare me."

"What do you mean, 'they scare me'?"

"I don't know," said McLeod. "Every now and then I shiver."

"It's the climate, honey," said George. "It's cooler up here."

"I know," she said. "I guess we'd better get over to Joseph Henry House—it's time for class."

When class started, she gave the students an assignment to be done over fall break—find a friend or family member at home with a problem, and write about the person and his or her problem. And the solution, or lack of solution.

George, an outspoken iconoclast, was a hit with the class. He was urbane and funny and had interesting things to say about writing about people. He even talked about their assignment to write about a person with a problem and pointed out that if the problem was insoluble, the story might be more interesting. "It might have more shape if there's a solution, but it might be more realistic if there's no solution," he said.

When class was over, Lyle came up, paper in hand.

"I have to walk George to the Dinky," she told Lyle. "I'll be right back."

"McLeod, deal with your student," said George. "I can walk myself to the Dinky."

"Thanks. I really appreciate your coming," McLeod said. "You were wonderful."

"Thanks for asking me. I like your students." He hugged her briefly, smiled at Lyle, and departed.

LYLE HANDED HER his article. "Well, here it is," he said. "The conventional version."

"Lyle, I'm not trying to get you to be conventional, for heaven's sake," said McLeod. "I love rebels and unexpected writing. But you can't just fling wild charges around like confetti. As a matter of fact, you got me thinking, and I decided to do some checking. They did an autopsy on Archie Alexander, and it showed nothing that indicated foul play. The cause of death was listed as hepatic failure, or liver failure, which can be caused by many things, apparently."

"How did you find that out?" asked Lyle.

"I made some telephone calls," said McLeod. "I am a reporter, you know. In Mercer County, the coroner does all autopsies. And the coroner is a woman and so is her assistant."

"And they told you the results?" asked Lyle.

"Actually, they're not allowed to divulge results, so I called Archie's doctor, old Dr. Winchester."

"And he told you?"

"He didn't particularly want to," said McLeod. "I'm afraid I exaggerated my relationship to Archie so he'd tell me."

"Well, well, so you dissembled!" said Lyle in pretended horror.

"Sort of," said McLeod.

"Well, what did old Doc Winchester say?"

"He said it was liver damage, with no evidence of drugs or narcotics. And I said, 'That means it can't have been poison?' and he said, 'Poison! What do you mean?' and I said, 'Poison ingested accidentally or otherwise,' and he said, 'Absolutely not.' So I think that's final."

"Wow!" said Lyle. "I'm impressed. But I'm going to find out what can cause liver failure."

"Drugs and alcohol can," said McLeod. "But Archie was not a drug user—and not an alcoholic. And besides, there was no sign of drug or alcohol damage. It's apparently just one of those things."

"Well, at least I got your attention," said Lyle.

Fifteen

❦

MCLEOD RESOLVED TO do something about her social obligations. She rejected the idea of a series of small dinners—too much work—in favor of a brunch on a Sunday, a week from the next day. Brunch was simpler than dinner. She would serve mimosas and cook her ham, cheese, and egg casserole, even if it did have enough cholesterol to pack everyone's arteries. She would serve baked grits to go with it.

When she started on the invitation list, she realized how much she missed Archie. She missed him for many reasons, of course, but he would have been a perfect guest at a party given by a single woman—he would have helped with the drinks, would have helped with everything. But Archie was in heaven, bound to be—his Rolodex was as good as a golden ladder. She had to soldier on.

She would invite the Kingsleys, of course, and she owed Mystique, the Kinkaids, and Elizabeth Finley. Gertrude Sergeant had invited her only to a cocktail party and McLeod was not sure whether she owed her an invitation. But these were all women. She had to have more men. Grady Schuyler, of course, the nice guy who did Queer Theory, and Bob Dewey, the Marxist critic. Bob was deadly serious, but they were all serious. And Bob Dewey missed his girl friend, who was in Rome for the academic year. He had told McLeod all about her at some party or other.

Ginger, when called, pointed out that the brunch would be on Halloween.

"That's fine," said McLeod. "Mimosas are orange."

"And fall break starts the next day," said Ginger. "A lot of people may be out of town."

"Good," said McLeod. "I've invited too many people anyway. Maybe a lot of people can't come—and I will have halfway paid them back with an invitation. Do you have Mystique's telephone number? It's apparently unlisted."

Ginger gave her the number.

Alas, everybody could come. Mystique didn't accept right away, and wanted to know who else was coming. When McLeod, surprised, told her, Mystique hesitated before she said she guessed she could come.

Bob Dewey was leaving for Rome that Sunday night, he said, but he'd love to come to her party that morning. McLeod allowed herself the unworthy thought that she was wasting credits; she didn't owe Bob a meal.

Now she was committed to having what seemed like a huge crowd—two or three of whom she didn't even like—to a meal in a small, furnished apartment.

Sixteen

HALLOWEEN DAWNED BRIGHT and clear. The leaves were spectacular, McLeod thought, looking out her sliding glass doors that morning. From her living room she could see every shade of orange and yellow and red and scarlet and pink. A few trees were still emerald green, and here and there, providing contrast, were somber brown ones. The whole thing added up to an autumnal palette that astonished McLeod every day. At home the live oaks and the pines and palmettos never changed color. It was worth coming to Princeton for a semester just to see this, she thought.

The last couple of days had been packed with feverish activity: shopping for groceries, liquor, two big new casseroles, and extra plates. She had had to clean the apartment and she had prepared the ham and egg casserole and the baked grits. They were ready to pop into the oven.

And now she had to actually bring it off.

Why did I do this? she groaned to herself as she wrestled with the last-minute preparations. But I always think that before a party, she told herself. It was just part of the territory and it would pass.

She had just set the champagne and orange juice for mimosas on the cabinet that was to be the bar along with the vodka and the Bloody Mary mix, when the doorbell rang.

The first arrival was Bob Dewey, his dark curls brushed, his dark eyes sparkling, who cheerfully began tending bar, mixing mimosas, pouring Bloody Marys or plain tomato juice, and generally making himself useful. He told McLeod that he was excited to be going to Rome that night, but was glad to be diverted by a nice party that day. A well-brought-up young man, decided McLeod, and very helpful too, for a Marxist.

Dexter and Margie Kinkaid were the last guests to come, and there was a small stir at their arrival—Dexter was an important man and he had an imposing presence. McLeod had assumed that he wouldn't drink a cosmopolitan so early in the day, but had decided to be prepared anyway and had laid in cranberry and lime juice and cointreau to go with the vodka she had on hand.

When she saw Dexter go to the bar and ask Bob Dewey something, she trotted over and brought out the cointreau and cans of juice.

"Thank you so much, McLeod," Dexter said. "That's very thoughtful of you." He bowed to Bob Dewey. "I'll fix it myself. I certainly should know how by now."

"Good enough, sir," said Bob.

"This is lovely, McLeod," said Margie Kinkaid. "Such a nice time for a party—right after church."

McLeod was sure Margie was the only one at the party who had been to church. "I'm so glad you could come," said McLeod. "I was afraid everybody would be gone for fall break."

Dexter had deftly mixed his cosmopolitan, added ice, and moved toward the nexus of the party, drink in hand.

McLeod left to take the Kinkaids' coats to the bedroom.

When she heard a shriek, she went flying back to the living room. Dexter's drink was running down his shirtfront and he was scrubbing at it frantically with a crumpled paper napkin. McLeod got a dish towel, poured club soda on it, and handed it to him.

"Wipe it with this," she said. "Club soda works wonders."

Dexter mopped until McLeod brought him a dry towel with which he tried to blot himself. "You need another drink, if only to cheer you up," she told him.

"And here one is," said Bob Dewey, appearing suddenly with a new cosmopolitan in hand. "A guardian angel saw your need and stirred this up."

Dexter looked grateful and gulped at it.

People drank quite happily until the food was ready and then they ate heartily. The party was working, McLeod thought contentedly. It was working. Everybody was eating her delicious, fattening, cholesterol-filled, artery-clogging, Southern-style food, and they were loving it.

"You cooked all this yourself, didn't you?" said Mystique accusingly.

"Yes, I did," said McLeod.

"When I give a party, I have to have it catered," said Mystique. "I don't really know how to cook for more than two. And I can't really spend my time cooking. I seem to have one deadline right after another."

"My time's not as valuable as yours," McLeod said. "I just take the time to cook. Besides, I don't think I could really afford caterers."

"Your food is very good," said Mystique grudgingly. "It would be a pity to hire caterers when you cook so well. What is this casserole exactly?"

"I just think of it as 'My Mother's Egg Thing,'" said McLeod.

"Is it a Southern recipe?" asked Liz Finley, who had come up.

"I guess it is," said McLeod. Liz, her short gray hair

tousled, wore a battered-looking gray wool dress with a wide belt.

"It's quite tasty, rather like a Welsh rarebit, except for the country ham," said Liz. "The British are good at simple dishes that go a long way like that. You're very clever to do a big party like this all by yourself."

"I couldn't do a party like this if I spent two whole days on it," said Trudy Sergeant, who was looking taller and thinner than ever and wearing pants with big black-and-white checks.

"Sure you could," McLeod said automatically, thinking that she had spent more than two days on it, all told, but if these women thought she could just produce a meal like this with a flip of a wrist, let them.

"I'm not sure women ought to cook like this," Trudy said. "In a sense it's capitulating to the male hierarchal hegemony." At least that's what McLeod thought she said. "Of course, you come from that exploitative Southern tradition that trains women to be good cooks."

"Cooking is not intrinsically subservient work, is it?" McLeod asked. "So many of the great chefs were men."

"If a woman cooks for pay, it's honest work," said Trudy. "If a woman cooks at home, she's a servant."

McLeod, who had borrowed an extra coffeemaker from Ginger, mentally dismissed this argument and started serving coffee. After a while, she began to fear that no one would ever go home, that she was stuck with these people in some existential trap. *No Exit*, she thought. Liz Finley was talking intently, almost angrily, to Dexter about, McLeod thought, declining standards in the language of footnotes in eighteenth-century English studies. Mystique seemed to be coming on to Bob, who was rolling his eyes frantically. Trudy was haranguing Grady Schuyler about the way male writers had portrayed women as school teachers in fiction. "Shocking unfairness," McLeod heard her say, and "as though they were all sexless automatons."

At four o'clock, when the last guest left, she sank down

on the sofa, totally exhausted. It had been a pleasant party on the surface, but there had been the usual lines of tension that left her uneasy, and the sensation was worse when she had taken on a hostess's responsibility.

Seventeen

❧

DURING FALL BREAK, McLeod drove down to Bartram's Gardens near Philadelphia, to see where John and William Bartram had lived and gardened. She also finished the sweater she was knitting for herself, and bought the wool to make one for Rosie. She chose a shade of lilac—Rosie had always been partial to purple and lavender. McLeod herself avoided those colors because of her hair—she thought the combination of her white hair with lavender would be too old-lady-like. But Rosie was safe from such an illusion—nothing could make *her* look like an old lady—and the lavender was lovely.

On Friday she picked up the Trenton *Times* and learned that Dexter Kinkaid had died, "after a brief illness," as the newspaper put it.

She called Ginger for details and learned that he had collapsed at home last Sunday night, gone to the hospital, and died a few days later, on Thursday.

"What was wrong with him?" asked McLeod.

"I don't know," said Ginger. "It was kind of like Archie. He just got sick, but it seemed to go faster. They couldn't do a thing."

"Oh, dear, right after my brunch," said McLeod. "You don't suppose it was something he ate? Did anybody else get sick?"

"No, not that I know of," said Ginger. "I'm worried that some odd germ is going around and we're all going to get it."

It was a very odd germ that struck two members of the English Department, two people she knew, McLeod reflected.

"When is the funeral?" she asked.

"One day next week, at the Presbyterian Church. Margie is an active member, you know, and she wants it there instead of the chapel," said Ginger. "I'm not sure exactly when. They had to do an autopsy—that's why it's so late. Stephanie will know. I'll let you know as soon as I find out."

McLeod was impressed again by how much everybody in the English Department depended on Stephanie West. She had met Stephanie once and liked her immensely. She had a nice irreverent streak that McLeod found refreshing.

McLeod was sorry about Dexter, who had been unfailingly courteous to her, but of course her feelings were not the same as when Archie died. It was simply astounding that two senior members of the English faculty had died a few weeks apart. And during term. Who would teach their classes? Who would chair the department?

She decided she was really getting the Princeton point of view, if she could worry about who would teach Archie and Dexter's classes before she really faced the facts. Lyle, of course, would say it was murder. And was it? Was someone killing the great professors of English? It was unthinkable—but she couldn't stop thinking about it.

• • •

HER STUDENTS TRAILED in one by one for conferences the week after fall break. They were all working hard on the assignment she had given them the week before: to interview someone with a serious problem, and write a story about the person's solution, or chance of a solution, or lack of a solution. It had taken her so long to explain the assignment that she had had very low expectations, but the students brought in rough drafts that delighted her.

Lyle, for one, was on time for his conference on Monday.

"Did you find out anything about liver damage?" she asked him when she had gone over his draft of his very good piece about his uncle, the alcoholic.

"I got so interested in this project, I forgot it," said Lyle.

"Did you know that Professor Kinkaid is dead now? They're not sure what he died of; apparently it was a mysterious liver disease," she said.

"What!" Lyle stared at her. "When? Where? How?"

McLeod told him all she knew. "He and his wife came to my house for brunch last Sunday—along with a bunch of other guests—and then he went home and got sick and died in the hospital a few days later."

"Did they have an autopsy?"

"They did. They have to if the cause of death is not obvious," said McLeod.

"What did it show?"

"I don't know," said McLeod. "And I don't even know who his doctor is. I don't know how we can find out."

She was surprised to hear herself saying, "I don't know how *we* can find out." It sounded as though it was settled that she and Lyle were going to investigate further.

"Let me think," said Lyle. "I wish I had interviewed Professor Kinkaid before he died! Wouldn't it be cool if I had?"

"If you had, you might have come to be regarded as Death's Messenger," said McLeod.

"Yeah," said Lyle. "This opens up a whole new world. Is there a mass murderer loose? Is it random? Is someone wiping out senior English Department people?"

"I have to say that something did occur to me after I got the news on Friday," said McLeod. "You know I truly couldn't understand why anyone would want to murder Archie Alexander. But maybe Dexter Kinkaid was the real target? Maybe Archie got killed by accident. Oh, my God!"

"What is it?" asked Lyle.

"I just remembered something really hideous . . . Archie drank a drink intended for Dexter at that party, before he got sick!"

She tried to recall every detail of Mystique's party. She told Lyle about the cosmopolitan that had been sitting on the bar. "Everybody knows that Dexter drank nothing but cosmopolitans and this one was obviously waiting for him. Archie picked it up and drank it." she said.

"So?" said Lyle.

"You don't understand about mixed drinks," said McLeod. "You're too young. Nobody else would normally touch that dreadful drink. It's made with cranberry juice and lime juice and cointreau and vodka."

"Why did Professor Alexander drink it then?" he asked.

"I don't know," said McLeod. "I didn't know at the time. It was just a whim, I suppose. A *fatal* whim, as it turns out."

"And you think somebody intended to poison Professor Kinkaid?" asked Lyle.

"Somebody must have," said McLeod, "I saw Archie drink that cosmopolitan with my own eyes."

"We need to find out if Kinkaid had a cosmopolitan before he died," said Lyle.

"He did," said McLeod. "He certainly did. That's what made me remember the one Archie drank."

"What happened?"

"It was at my house last Sunday," said McLeod. "The brunch. And Dexter had a cosmopolitan. I saw him."

"You think cosmopolitans kill people?" asked Lyle.

"I think they do if somebody puts something in them," said McLeod. "And that awful drink would kill the taste of any poison."

She brooded a minute while Lyle stared at her.

"Did you fix the cosmopolitan for Kinkaid last Sunday?" he asked.

"No," said McLeod. "I can't remember who fixed it. I honestly don't know. I saw Dexter himself mix the first one. And then he spilled it down his shirtfront, his always-immaculate shirt front."

"What happened then?" said Lyle.

"Bob Dewey was acting as bartender and he appeared with another cosmopolitan and handed it to Dexter."

"Did he mix that one?" asked Lyle.

"I'm not sure," said McLeod. "I don't think Bob knew how to make one. He said something about a 'guardian angel' and handed it to Dexter."

"You don't think Dewey made it?" asked Lyle. "I know him. He teaches English."

"It was my impression that he didn't know how to make one. But who mixed it? Did somebody have the wit to make one quickly, put poison in it, and hand it to Bob to hand to Dexter? It doesn't seem likely, does it?"

"It does to me," said Lyle. "Somebody could have realized this was a golden opportunity—that Professor Kinkaid was going to drink a cosmopolitan, but a harmless one. That person could have nudged Kinkaid so he'd spill his drink and made another drink real quickly. Or he could even have had the drink ready and then made Dexter spill his."

"Oh, somebody would have seen all those shenanigans," said McLeod. "My apartment is tiny. There isn't room to hide a scenario like that."

"I think we better do some investigating," said Lyle.

"You know we can't do any real investigating," said McLeod. "If there's really a murderer on the loose, the police will investigate. Mark my words."

"I'm not so sure," said Lyle.

"Don't do anything rash," said McLeod.

"I won't," said Lyle. "See you Thursday in class."

After he left, McLeod again reached for the phone and punched in a number.

Eighteen

❧

MCLEOD WAS GLAD to see her old friend Oliver Hunt, the *New York Times* reporter who had once worked in Tallahassee, when he arrived in Princeton. Ollie was good looking, tall and thin, with his dark hair growing in a deep widow's peak on his forehead. The students looked at him with the air of neutral interest they gave all visitors.

All except Daisy. "Look," she said to McLeod. "Look." She pointed to her chin.

"You got the stud in place of the ring," said McLeod. "Good."

"I love it," said Daisy. "I can talk."

"Daisy, I think you'd always be able to talk." McLeod smiled at her, and set about introducing Ollie Hunt. He had switched from politics and government, which had been his beat in Tallahassee, and now covered crime. He talked with the students about writing on law enforcement officials and criminals. "I've found over and over again it's wrong to believe everything law enforcement people tell you," he said. "I don't mean they're all dishonest. They're not, but they're overworked. And sometimes you have to listen to the accused."

The class was fascinated. Even Daisy quit looking at her chin in a small pocket mirror.

"I read a book you wrote about that wife murderer," said Lyle. "How did you gain his confidence the way you did?"

"That so-called wife murderer," corrected Ollie. "That man was ready to put his confidence in anybody at all who would believe that he wasn't guilty or even anybody who had an open mind. The police know that ninety-nine percent of all murders are committed by the spouse or lover and sometimes they just don't look beyond that."

"He certainly told you everything," said Lyle.

"I'd like for you to think it was my reporting skills, my interviewing skills, that did that," said Ollie. "But that man was desperate."

When Ollie had finished and left to catch the train, the students began to all talk at once. "Sssh!" said McLeod, rapping on the table with her mechanical pencil. "I can't hear what anybody says when you all talk at once."

"What we're saying, y'all, is this—" said Lyle with a sly look at McLeod, when she interrupted him.

"How many times do I have to tell you that you never say 'you all' or 'y'all' when you're talking to one person? 'You all' is a collective noun and fills a great need in the English language."

Lyle grinned and went on as though she had not spoken. "We want to do something different, and I know what it should be. We should investigate these murders in the English Department. As a class, I mean, like that journalism class at Northwestern did. You know they managed to dig up the evidence to free that man on death row. They could do it because there were lots of them and they were young and eager and bright."

"They also had help from private detectives," said

McLeod. "I read that story. Do you know somebody on death row who shouldn't be there? I believe the lawyer for the accused came to the teacher and asked for help."

"So?" asked Lyle. "There's murder right here on campus—well, almost on campus—and *two* of them, that we could investigate. The English Department Murders."

Some of the students were obviously eager to get started.

"The police don't think it's murder," said Lyle. "They won't do anything."

"How do you know?" asked McLeod.

"I just know," said Lyle.

To be honest, McLeod agreed with him. Stephanie West, the invaluable administrator of the English Department, had told her that Margie said the routine autopsy report showed liver damage, but nothing suspicious, no evidence of drugs. McLeod's natural curiosity had impelled her to make a few more inquiries.

"You may be right," she said, almost adding, "this one time." "I found out that in Mercer County, when the nature of the fatal disease is unknown, the coroner sends the autopsy report to the prosecutor's office. Somebody in the prosecutor's office looks at it to see if there is anything suspicious about the death. It's usually a pro forma exercise. I believe it was so in this case, as the prosecutor's office said it had no plans to investigate nor to ask the Borough Police to investigate."

The class began to talk excitedly again.

"But we have no real reason to suspect anything," she said.

"I think we do have reason," said Lyle. "You told me that both Professor Alexander and Professor Kinkaid drank this weird drink. And we think"—he turned to the rest of the class—"Ms. Dulaney and I think that Professor Alexander was killed by mistake." He quickly outlined the imbibing of the two cosmopolitans.

McLeod had to concede that it sounded very persuasive.

"You were at both parties," said Marcy Flowers. "Tell us everything about them."

Students were very adept at getting teachers to talk about anything at all besides the lesson, thought McLeod. But why not? She went through the details of both scenarios—Mystique's party and her own brunch.

The students hung on every word.

"We assume a cosmopolitan killed both of them, so the question is: Who did it?" Lyle summed it up. "The two best suspects are Mystique Alcott and you," he said. "The parties were at your houses. Alcott could have put the poison in the drink that Professor Alexander drank at her house and fixed another to take it to your house. You could have taken one to her house and had another handy at your house."

"But why?" said McLeod. "That's what I can't get around. Especially why me? Why would I want to kill them? Or kill Dexter, if he's the one we agree was the intended victim? I had only met him six weeks before and saw him only a few times before he died."

"I'm relieved," said Marcy. "You know I didn't want a murderess for a teacher."

"Marcy, murderess is a sexist term." Daisy Wood reproved her. Daisy never let a word she deemed sexist go by unremarked.

"We'll eliminate you, Ms. Dulaney," said Lyle. "But what about Alcott?"

"Why on earth would she want to kill Dexter Kinkaid?" asked McLeod.

"That's what we need to find out," said Lyle.

"What about the other people at the parties?" asked Ben True. "How many were at both parties?"

"Mystique's party was much much bigger than mine," said McLeod. "And I think everybody at my brunch was at Mystique's."

"Then who was at your house?" asked another student. "Let's make a list."

McLeod rattled off the names. "Cliff and Ginger Kingsley, Margie and Dexter Kinkaid."

Ben interrupted her. "You know what Ollie Hunt said. 'It's almost always the spouse,' so we have to consider Mrs. Kinkaid very seriously."

"True," said McLeod, "but wouldn't she have had more opportunities—wouldn't it have been easier for her to do it at home?"

"Then all suspicion would have fallen on her for sure," said Lyle.

The class agreed and urged McLeod to go on with the list of people at her party.

"Mystique Alcott, Elizabeth Finley, Gertrude Sergeant, Bob Dewey, and Grady Schuyler," she said.

"All those English professors! Imagine," said Marcy.

"And they were all at the first party—the one where Alexander drank the cosmopolitan?" asked Ben True, the graduate student.

McLeod nodded.

"This class is ideal. We can each take one person and investigate him or her, find out what motives they'd have for killing Kinkaid," said Daisy.

"That's a great idea!" said Lyle. "We can pretend we're interviewing them for this class."

"This sounds all very well and good," said McLeod. "But let's be sensible. What motive could anybody have for killing Dexter Kinkaid? He was a sound scholar, a sterling department chair, a good teacher, an orderly man who never, I'm sure, had a messy affair."

"Maybe somebody thought he was too good," said Daisy.

"He was chairman of the English Department," said Lyle.

"Chairperson," Daisy corrected him.

"Maybe somebody else wanted the job," Lyle went on.

"Maybe somebody in the department was really pissed off with him."

"Look," said McLeod, "I'm sure this is all very unorthodox. I'm certainly not going to assign each of you to go interview a possible murderer."

"Why not?" said Lyle. "Remember that Northwestern class."

"It's not the same," said McLeod. "I told you: The wrong man was accused of the crime and was on death row. His lawyer asked the class to investigate it. Nobody's asked us to do this."

"We'll do it on our own," said Lyle stubbornly. "Won't we?" He turned to the class. "How many want to take on this project?"

Four other students held up their hands. The rest looked stubborn and sat quietly.

"Okay," said Lyle. "That's fine. I'll take Mystique Alcott. Daisy, who do you want?"

Daisy wanted to interview Trudy Sergeant because she was a feminist.

Marcy chose Elizabeth Finley. "She looks like such a proper little old lady that I'm sure she's a serial murderer," she said.

Ben True said he'd be happy to do Bob Dewey—he could see him the next day.

"You might as well take Grady Schuyler, too," said Lyle. "They're both in English."

Ben said okay, he'd do both.

Tina Martinez volunteered to talk to the Kingsleys.

Five students had actually taken on assignments, Lyle noted. "And what are you others going to do?" he asked the rest of the class.

"They can do whatever they please," said McLeod. "This is not a class assignment, remember. It's purely voluntary. You all have assignments for next time: Rewrite your 'problem' papers, and bring in two ideas for your final paper, your lengthy personality piece."

"How lengthy?" was the inevitable question.

"Twenty-five hundred words is the absolute minimum," said McLeod.

Groans greeted this announcement, but McLeod was adamant.

"Okay, okay," said Lyle. "Twenty-five hundred words is nothing. Let's get on with this Murder Project. Somebody ought to talk to Mrs. Kinkaid."

Nobody volunteered.

"You'll have to take Mrs. Kinkaid," Lyle said to McLeod. "And that's the lot. Let's report back at the student center on Monday, shall we? We don't want to wait until Thursday."

"I'm not committing to anything," said McLeod. "I have real reservations about this. Be careful, all of you. Whatever you do, don't barge up to these people and ask them if they killed Dexter Kinkaid. I think you should interview them for a very short piece, and if you can work Dexter Kinkaid into the conversation, you might do so. But do be discreet."

"It's a crazy scheme," said a student who was not participating.

"No, it's not," said Lyle. The other students shrugged. "It'll be fine. Good experience. What time Monday shall we meet?"

It took forever to agree on a time to meet on Monday because of everybody's schedules of labs and seminars, but finally they settled on four forty-five at Frist Student Center.

McLeod looked at her watch. It was after five o'clock. The class had stayed late—an unheard-of phenomenon.

Nineteen

SHE HAD NOT committed herself to doing any investigation, McLeod thought, but she would go and see Margie Kinkaid just the same. She hardly knew Margie and thought her rather dull, but still, she needed to make a condolence call. So on Saturday, bearing a whipping-cream pound cake, she went to the Kinkaids' big house on Prospect Avenue to pay a sympathy call. Now you don't have to ask her about her husband being murdered, McLeod told herself, just because a student told you to.

"I'm sorry about Dexter," said McLeod, after Margie had her sit down in the living room. "Can I do anything for you, Margie? Answer sympathy notes or anything. I'll be glad to help."

"Thanks," said Margie, who was dressed in a black sweater and black slacks, her gray hair looking surprisingly untidy to McLeod. "I want to do it all. It's the last thing, or nearly the last thing, I can do for Dexter."

"I understand," said McLeod. "But call on me if you need anything."

"I will, and thanks for bringing that beautiful pound cake. You made it, I'm sure."

"I did. It's an old Georgia recipe. My mother used to make it when her church circle met at her house. It was famous in the congregation."

Margie changed the subject back to her plight. "Life is pretty horrible right now. It was so sudden. Dexter was going to retire soon and we had all sorts of plans for travel. I can't get used to Dexter not being here. I keep thinking he's just gone over to the library and he'll be right back." Margie looked away, but her head was high. She turned back. "You know I'm not wearing mourning," she said. "Well, not really. I just pulled these out of the closet this morning. I must say I don't see much point in getting dressed these days. You look very nice, McLeod, as always."

McLeod, who had on a bright red turtleneck sweater, thanked her and said energetically, "I know how you feel, Margie, but life does go on."

"That's right, McLeod. You've been through this, haven't you?"

"Yes, but it was twenty years ago, and it's never the same for any two women. For instance, I had two young children and not enough insurance to live on. I *had* to go to work. That turned out to be the best possible therapy."

Margie looked at her. "Maybe so, but I don't need money and I'm too old in any case to go back to work."

"Will you stay here?" asked McLeod.

"Of course, I'll stay right here." said Margie. "We've lived in this house for a long time." She paused and looked around the big living room filled with upholstered furniture, the windows dimmed with curtains and venetian blinds. "The children are all gone now, and I suppose I'll rattle around in it, but I'll stay. I don't know what I'll do with my time. My life revolved around Dexter, you know.

It always has. Dexter and the children. But mostly Dexter. When we were young, I used to type his papers and I've always seen my role as an enabler, enabling a brilliant man to get on with his work. I took care of the children so he wouldn't be bothered with them. And as his career advanced, I did everything I could to help him socially—entertaining and being entertained."

"Maybe it's time," said McLeod, "to do something just for yourself."

"Everybody says not to do anything for a year, anyway," said Margie.

"Yes, that's the conventional wisdom," said McLeod.

"Then, after a year, I don't think I'll want to leave this house, or do anything different."

"You never know," said McLeod. "You could go around the world. Take up horseback riding. Learn to play the piano."

Margie looked startled. "I hadn't thought along those lines, I must say." She actually looked interested, then sank back into her pit of self-pity. "Why? That's what I keep asking. Why did Dexter have to die?"

"The whole thing is mysterious," said McLeod, deliberately misunderstanding Margie, "especially the nature of Dexter's illness."

"Yes, it was odd, wasn't it?" said Margie. "The autopsy showed nothing, and the doctors can't explain it."

"It was so similar to Archie's illness, wasn't it?" asked McLeod.

"I guess it was."

"Tell me one thing, Margie. Did everybody know that Dexter drank cosmopolitans and only cosmopolitans?"

"Cosmopolitans were his trademark, you might say. It was very amusing sometimes, because once in a while a graduate student would try to curry favor with Dexter and would say he, too, liked cosmopolitans. But I think nobody but Dexter really liked them." Margie actually managed a smile. "When we first came to Princeton, Dexter used to carry a little bottle with one in it because nobody had the ingredients, but as the years passed, everybody learned about them, and everywhere we went, they had cranberry juice and lime juice and vodka and cointreau. It was a tribute to Dexter, I think, that people would go to such trouble."

"Of course it was," said McLeod.

It was now or never, thought McLeod. "So you don't think there's any possibility that anybody wanted Dexter out of the way?" she asked.

"'Out of the way'? What on earth do you mean?" Margie stared at McLeod.

"Margie, forgive me, but I'm a journalist. I always ask the next question. And whenever a death is from mysterious causes, I can't help but ask if foul play was involved."

"That's a ridiculous idea," said Margic. "Dexter was highly respected. Everybody loved him—except some of those awful assistant professors and—" She broke off.

"And who?" asked McLeod, holding her breath.

"No, no," said Margie. "Oh, you know, there were always little upsets in the department. Mostly because Dexter had high standards and he was very firm about seeing that everyone adhered to those high standards. But foul play—that's just not possible."

"Isn't it?" said McLeod.

"It is completely and totally out of the question," said Margie Kinkaid. "You can put that out of your mind."

McLeod switched back to condolence mode and left. Did Margie Kinkaid protest too much? Could all that grief be simulated? Was foul play ever "completely and totally out of the question"?

Twenty

❧

MCLEOD KEPT TELLING herself she had no intention of
going to the Murder Project meeting at Frist Student Center on Monday afternoon. When Lyle e-mailed her Sunday
to remind her, she replied that she didn't think she should
come.

"If I'm there," she wrote, "it makes it look as though
I'm leading students in the investigation of a crime. I don't
want to make this Murder Project official."

"You'd better come," Lyle replied. "Everybody's got
lots of new information. Did you talk to Mrs. Kinkaid?"

"I had to pay a condolence call anyway," said McLeod.

At four-forty-five Mcleod, intrigued, of course, by the
idea of "new information," walked down to Frist, which
was basically a huge addition to the south side of Palmer
Hall, a classroom building. Architect Robert Venturi had
made the interior lower floors like streets, with shops and
cafés opening off corridors. McLeod went down to the
main dining floor and found five of her students gathered

at a table by the window. She got herself a Diet Coke and joined them.

Neither Lyle nor anyone else seemed surprised to see her. "Well, what did you find out, guys?" asked Lyle. "Who done it?"

The chorus of answers was unintelligible.

Lyle rapped on the table with the metal napkin holder. "I'll go first," he said. "I went to see Mystique Alcott."

"How did you get to see her?" asked Daisy. "I thought she was never in her office."

"I went to her house," Lyle said. "Her home phone number is unlisted, so I looked her up in the Register—that gives the addresses of faculty members—and just walked over there Thursday night after dinner.

"The Communications Office was closed, so I got some biographical data off the web. She came to the door. She looked rumpled. And my God, she's fat. I introduced myself and told her I was a student and I wanted to talk to her for a paper I had to write and she didn't ask me in. She said, 'What kind of a paper?' and I said, 'It's about the creative writer and his or her relationship to the academic bureaucracy.' I thought I could segue from there into questions about the department chair. She sounded surprised and she invited me to come in.

"I followed her into her library—it's enormous—and I said, before I thought, 'Creative writing must pay very well,' and she said, yes, she had had a certain amount of success. I said I believed she had published thirty novels in all, and she said, 'Thirty-one,' with a new one to come out in January." Lyle paused to look at his notes. "She said it should have been out for Christmas buying, but publishers were so stupid she didn't see how they stayed in business."

Lyle then told how he had asked routine interview questions—"The way our teacher taught us," he said, with a mock bow to McLeod. He had asked Mystique if she had always wanted to be a writer? (She said yes, what else could she do?) Did she grow up in a bookish family? (She said there was not one single book in her family's house in Oklahoma where she grew up.) Did she write at home or at the office? (She said always at home, that she only went to the office for office hours and conferences with students—when she had to have them."

"I told you," said Daisy.

"I asked her if she used a computer for her writing, and she said, of course she did, didn't I? I told her I was a computer science major, but it seemed to be something people wanted to know about writers, so I'd asked it. She said it was a silly question and she had thought I wanted to talk to her about creativity and academia."

"She's right," said Daisy. "Cut to the chase. What did you find out about the murder?"

"I asked her if teaching interfered with her writing.

"She looked at me. She said back when she used to give interviews to students she used to tell reporters from the *Prince* or the *Princeton Weekly Bulletin* that teaching fed the writing, and writing nourished the teaching. The president of the university loved that—you know the way Princeton emphasizes undergraduate education. So I asked her what she told other interviewers, and she said, 'I told them the truth, that teaching takes up precious time that could go into my real work, but I told them it was off the record.' And she glared at me and said, 'And it's off the record for you, too.' I had to promise not to quote her in any publication. I crawled and said of course I wouldn't.

"Here, I'll play the tape." He pulled his tape recorder out of his backpack and set it on the table and fiddled with it. "Just a minute," he said. "Just a minute." Finally, he was ready. "Listen."

They heard Lyle's voice, somewhat scratchy, saying that he absolutely would not quote her in any publication.

"I appreciate your talking to me," he said. "I don't want you to be sorry you did."

"I'm sure I won't." Alcott sounded coy.

"Well, how about other duties connected with a teaching job?" Lyle asked. "Like committees?"

"I won't serve on committees," she said. "The dean knows that, the director of the creative writing program knows that. So that's not a problem."

"How about the English Department? What exactly is your connection with them?" asked Lyle.

"I nominally hold a joint appointment to the Creative Writing Program and to the English Department. But I really have nothing to do with English, except socially, thank God."

"That's a good thing, is it?"

"It certainly is. English professors—bah! I really have very little use for them. Except one or two."

"What about Archibald Alexander and Dexter Kinkaid?" Lyle asked on the tape.

"The late greats?" she asked. "Archie was better than most of them. Dexter was a horse of another color."

"What was wrong with him?"

"He was too straitlaced," said Mystique. "He was awful. He was prudish and stingy with department funds and too strict about everything. I disliked him intensely."

"Can you give me an example?" he said.

"I can give you a hundred," she said. "For one thing, he didn't even believe in teaching creative writing! He tried to sabotage the program at every opportunity. Also, he was so unreliable about writing recommendations for people. I'm sure he kept me from getting a Guggenheim Foundation grant one year when I really needed it. I understand he wrote a distinctly cool letter for me. That's the kind of thing I hate. I'm sure I would have gotten the Guggenheim if he had given me a good recommendation. And I deserved it. He was always doing that kind of thing. He had such 'high standards,' you see." The last few words sounded like a bitter snarl.

"Did he do that to anybody else around here or just you?"

Alcott paused. "Why are you interested in this kind of thing? I don't want you to quote me on any of this."

"I guess I have an overactive imagination," said Lyle, "but I wondered if anybody, well, you know, might have been really angry with Professor Kinkaid. Angry enough to do him harm."

"I don't think anybody really *liked* Dexter," Alcott said. "But what is all this about? What do you mean, do him harm?" She sounded mad.

"Don't worry," Lyle said nervously.

He shut the tape off. "I had to change the subject," he explained. When he turned the tape back on, they heard him ask, "Tell me what some of your former students who went on to become writers are doing now."

She was off. She babbled on about former students who had won short story competitions or had published novels—and given credit to their former teacher, Mystique Alcott. "That part of teaching is very satisfying," she said.

"This has been most interesting, Ms. Alcott," Lyle said.

"Oh, must you go?" said Mystique's voice, "Can't you stay and have a drink now that you've finished the interview?"

"I need to get back and write my paper while it's fresh," Lyle's voice said. "Thank you so much." The tape recorder was silent.

The class was fascinated. "Man, it sounds like she was coming on to you," Ben True said.

"But she really hated Dexter Kinkaid," said Daisy. "And she told a student all that stuff. Wow!"

"I always said she let herself go," said Marcy Flowers, "and I meant the way she looked—all that fat and those clothes—but she really let herself go over that letter of recommendation, didn't she? Still, nobody would kill somebody because of that, would they?"

"I don't know," said Lyle. "She basically hates Kinkaid. When I left, I thought to myself, 'That woman could commit a murder without turning a hair.' But what about the rest of you? What did you find out?"

Twenty-one

✣

"IT WAS A lot easier for me to see Bob Dewey and Grady Schuyler than it was for you to go see Mystique Alcott," Ben True said. "I caught Dewey in his office in the basement of McCosh on Friday and asked him if he had gone to Dexter Kinkaid's funeral.

"He said, 'Of course. I had to go,'" said Ben. "Then Dewey leaned back and folded his arms behind his head." Ben paused, looking at McLeod. "You always tell us to notice body language," he said.

"That's right," said McLeod.

"So I said, 'You didn't care much for old Dexter, did you?' and he said he hated his guts. Dewey knew that nobody with Dexter's background would have any sympathy for a Marxist critic. He said he should have known from the beginning that he wouldn't get tenure here. But then when his book was accepted for publication, it got his hopes up. When Dexter told him he had no chance of getting tenure, it was a shock. I guess it always is when you don't make it," Ben added. "The figures were clear enough—at Princeton ninety-nine percent of the assistant professors don't get tenure. But everybody always thinks he's going to be the one percent.

"I asked him if Dexter had already told him. He said it wasn't official yet. He said the Gang of Three hadn't acted on it."

"The Gang of Three?" asked Daisy. "What's that?"

"It's the committee that has final say on tenure," said Ben. "The department votes first, and if they approve, it goes to a committee that they call the Gang of Three. I've heard that there are more than three people on it, though. Maybe seven. But it's been called the Gang of Three since it was the president, the provost, and the dean of the college. But he said he didn't even get the department's approval. Kinkaid told him this 'to be helpful,' so Dewey 'could begin seriously looking for another job immediately.'

"I sympathized with him, and asked him how the job market looked for a Marxist critic. He said not too good, even if he had a book under his belt. He said Archie Alexander had gotten him one nibble. And that was it."

"Archie was a sweetheart," said McLeod.

"Yeah, but the nibble was from South Georgia State down in some godforsaken town in the Okefenokee Swamp, I think. He's going down there for an interview. Can you believe it? South Georgia State? When he's spent fifteen years in Ivy League schools—undergraduate, graduate school, and teaching?" (McLeod had already privately decided it would be good for every single person at Princeton to live for at least one year in Texas or South Georgia. Then they wouldn't be such provincial Northeasterners.) "I asked him if they knew he was a Marxist at South Georgia," Ben continued. "Dewey said probably not. I sympathized some more and then I asked him if now that Kinkaid was dead, was there a chance the department here might approve him after all.

"He's ever hopeful. He said he was a good teacher. A couple of senior faculty told him they were all for him but that Dexter was adamant.

"I told him maybe it was a good thing Dexter had died, and he said maybe it was."

Everyone agreed that Bob Dewey was the perfect suspect: motive and opportunity all over the place, even more likely than Mystique.

"What about Grady Schuyler?" asked McLeod.

"I was lucky," said Ben. "I ran into him here and we had pizza. I asked him what was going to happen to the department now that Kinkaid was no longer with us. He said he'd heard that they might ask Liz Finley to take it on. He said that was Nassau Hall's policy: Get a woman out front whenever you can, or a black, or best of all, a black woman.

"I asked him what that would mean for faculty and graduate students and he said it would be just the same. Professor Finley is really Dex in drag."

Ben kept talking through the general laughter.

"I asked him how he felt about that, and he said, 'What do you mean? How do I feel about it? Are you a therapist?' "

The class laughed again and Ben grinned. "I told him I guess I meant I wondered if he'd get tenure. And he said he thought he might, that he'd kept his nose clean. He said he had never propositioned any of his students, male or female. He has a book coming out. It's a gay reading of some of Shakespeare's plays. You know Hamlet loves Laertes, not Ophelia. And Celia and Rosalind are an item in *As You Like It*.

"I kind of envy Schuyler," Ben said to the class. "He's carved himself a niche in a super-crowded field. But back to Bob Dewey. I asked Schuyler about him, and he said it was supposed to be a secret that Dewey wasn't going to get tenure but everybody knew it. He said Bob made people mad, always shouting his extreme views and complaining that the left never gets a hearing in this country, that nobody from the real left is even on the Jim Lehrer show. Princeton's liberal and all that, but it's not exactly *left*. Besides, Marxist interpretation sounds really old hat now, and Queer Theory is still hot."

Ben looked at his notes. "Oh, yes, now that Kinkaid's out of the way, Schuyler really thinks he—I mean Schuyler—might get tenure. He said Dexter was so 'incredibly, boringly, relentlessly *straight*' and never told Schuyler he was against him, but he never told him he was for him. He just feels much better with him gone. And then he told me to forget everything he'd said. But I didn't."

The class was quiet. As undergraduates, they had not realized how grim the battle for tenure could be, how hopeless the odds, how great the spoils for the victor, how dismal the prospects for the loser.

Everyone seemed to agree that both Dewey and Schuyler were possible candidates for murder, if not for tenure, Bob Dewey especially.

"Let's not forget Alcott," Lyle warned. "Anybody else have anything to report?"

Twenty-two

❧

IN THE ENSUING quiet, Marcy Flowers (McLeod always thought of her as the Southern belle) spoke up.

"I do," she said. "I talked to Elizabeth Finley in her office. I really enjoyed this project—I felt like a real detective." She looked at her notes.

"I had checked her biography in the Communications Office and learned that she had been hired years ago as a full professor, one of Princeton's first tenured woman professors. She teaches eighteenth-century literature, and specializes in Jonathan Swift. Her office has a French-looking rug on the floor, a nice chintz-covered chair for visitors, and she had a copper jug of chrysanthemums on her desk."

Marcy paused to look at McLeod. "You always say to notice details and be specific." She went on with her report. "She is a small-framed woman with straight, short gray hair and no makeup. She wore a gray skirt and a brown sweater. She has nice eyes. If she'd get a good haircut and put a little gel on her hair and a little blusher on her cheeks and wear a better, brighter, more flattering sweater—"

"Marcy, don't be such a moron!" said Daisy Wood.

McLeod started to reprimand Daisy, and then decided to let the students run this meeting.

Marcy, undeterred, looked at Daisy witheringly, and went on without a pause. "—she wouldn't be bad looking. I told her I was interested in writing a piece about her for a class I was taking. I told her I wanted to write about a woman who's made it in a man's world, a woman who had mastered academia without being strident. And she said she thought no one ever mastered academia, that one just lay down and let it master one."

Ben True and Daisy, for very different reasons, were outraged at this sentiment.

"So I asked her what had drawn her to the eighteenth century," continued Marcy, "and she said she had read *Gulliver's Travels* when she was a little girl and been fascinated by it. When she got to college, she read more Jonathan Swift and the plays of John Dryden. She said Dryden was Swift's cousin. She read William Congreve, who was Swift's schoolmate. And after that, she didn't think that nineteenth-century writers could compare with what she calls 'my boys.'

"I asked her if she had written a biography of Swift, and she said she had done several critical books about his work, and she has just finished a book that sums up all her work—on Swift, Pope, Fielding, Boswell, Sterne—and how each one's work affected the others.

"She's been working on that book ten or twelve years. In fact, she said it was all her life, really, since it was a synthesis of everything she'd learned.

"So then I asked her something that Lyle suggested. Did it take her so long to write the book because she had to teach? Was there a conflict, and she said that teaching and writing support each other."

"That's the party line all right," said Lyle. "That's what the administration likes to hear them say."

"But she said some of her best ideas have come from undergraduates, from the questions they ask," Marcy said. "And besides that, she pointed out that a university nurtures professors' writing. You know, with leaves and grants and stuff like that—even free xeroxing.

"And then, Daisy, you'll be glad to know I asked her if the administration—it's usually mostly white males—had been as helpful to her as it has to male scholars."

Daisy silently raised both thumbs in salute. McLeod, too, was impressed with Marcy's spunk. I didn't know she had it in her, she thought.

"Finley said she began to make her way in academia when there were very few women teaching except at women's colleges. She said she was very glad things had changed and she now taught at Princeton. She said that lots of the older male professors were secretly glad when Princeton went coed. A French professor told her that women were the first students he ever had who understood French poetry. But she said she enjoyed having young men in her classes. She thought they understand Swift better than the women. But she told me not to tell anyone she said that."

"You two had quite a little chat," said Lyle. "Did you ever ask her about Kinkaid?"

"Of course," said Marcy. "I was working up to it." She studied her notes. "She said she had no objection to white males, that she wrote about white males, that she didn't have the same sense of grievance that some of the younger women professors have.

"So then I asked her about Dexter Kinkaid. And she said he was her friend. He brought her to Princeton. She said he was a first-rate scholar and had no tolerance for the second rate. And she said he had extremely high ethical standards."

"I asked her if people got mad at him, and she said the

enforcement of his high standards could cause monumen-
tal rages on the part of a great many people. So I asked her
if she thought one of those people in a rage could have
wanted to kill Professor Kinkaid. She didn't like that question and she glared at me. 'What do you mean, want to kill
Professor Kinkaid?' she asked me.

"I told her some people thought his death was suspicious," said Marcy. "So then she asked me who thought it
was suspicious and what did they mean by suspicious? I
told her some students in my writing class thought it was
suspicious and wondered if it was murder. I didn't tell her
I thought so myself.

"We talked about it and she said that anything was possible, but that it was highly unlikely that a disgruntled professor—or anybody else—killed Professor Kinkaid. She
said he died of a strange liver disease. She was handling
this sharp-looking letter opener, running one finger along
the edge, and looking at me in a weird sort of way, you
know, and I thought, I hope she doesn't plunge that thing
in me.

"She asked me if that was all I wanted to know and so
I left."

Everyone stirred and began to talk.

"But wait!" said Marcy. "I learned something really interesting about her. I have this friend—he works at Princeton University Press as sort of a student intern—he wants
to go into publishing. And he's sort of an office boy for the
director. So he knows what's going on. Anyway Finley had
a book turned down by the Press not long ago."

"Lots of people get turned down by Princeton University Press," said Ben True.

"I guess so," said Marcy. "But her book was accepted at
first. It went to outside readers and they liked it and the editors voted to publish it. Then the board vetoed it. The
board has to approve every book the Press publishes and
it's usually a formality. But it wasn't this time. She was

upset. That book was important to her—you know, the sum total of all her work."

Everybody looked at Marcy, puzzled.

"But I guess I didn't make it plain," Marcy said. "It was Professor Kinkaid on the board that vetoed it. Kevin, my friend who's an intern, saw the memos about it. The director asked Kinkaid if he didn't want to reconsider. Kevin told me about it in strictest confidence after he found out I was investigating Finley."

"That's incredible," said Ben True.

"What a motive!" said Lyle.

"Poor Liz Finley," said McLeod.

"When did this happen?" asked Lyle.

"Over the summer sometime," Marcy said.

"Could she have killed Kinkaid?" asked Lyle.

"I think she could kill somebody if she wanted to," said Marcy. "She's tough as nails. Those old women that went to those women's colleges and got the first Ph.D.s— they're tough. I thought she was the murderer from the beginning and I still think so. But you know, she acted a little scared."

I think I'd be scared, too, if Marcy Flowers came to interview me, thought McLeod. She's improbably terrific.

Twenty-three

❧

DAISY WOOD, RED curls bouncing, was next to report.

"I never thought Gertrude Sergeant was the murderer," she told the group. "But I wanted to talk to her. I took her class on Gender in Literature, Culture, and Theory last year and I thought she was so smart she might know all the answers."

"To everything?" asked Ben True.

"To everything," Daisy said firmly. "So I went to see her in her office in McCosh—and told her I wanted to talk to her about what it's like to be a feminist in an English Department like Princeton's, a department that is, as Marcy said, mostly white men in suits.

"And she said, 'It's hell. Even if they all think they're coming around.' She said it was more bearable since they got all these young assistant professors—you know, Marxists, and Queer Theorists, and African culture enthusiasts. That was a bright spot, she said. But she has to spend a lot of time battling—I wrote this down—to get women writers included in the syllabi, to get their work taught with the same respect that men's work is taught, to expose the dreadful gender bias of most teaching in the academy, to stamp out the conspiracy that has kept women writers unknown and unsung through the ages. That kind of thing."

"What did she have on?" Marcy asked.

"I'm not writing a fashion story," said Daisy. "But she had on a navy blue pants suit, I think. What's great about her is the way she was frank with me. I asked her how the battle was going, who was winning, and she said she won a few, lost a few, but she said we may lose a battle here and there, but we'll win the war.

"So I asked her what about a new chairman? Would that be good or bad? And she said it depended on who it was. She said Kinkaid was not a feminist, of course, but most people thought he tried to be fair. But how could a man of his age, brought up the way he was brought up, be fair? It's impossible, she said.

"I asked her if he ever tried to prevent her adding courses on women's issues and she said he was satisfied with the canon the way it was. She said he was not a man who welcomed change, but he saw what was happening in the world and he gave in a little at a time. Politically, she said, he couldn't do anything else. But there were dozens of courses on gender she'd like to see added."

Daisy paused. "Then I switched, like Marcy did, and asked her if she didn't think it was kind of suspicious the way Kinkaid died. I said some of us had wondered if anybody in the department was really mad at Professor Kinkaid.

"And she got kind of flustered, I must say. She said, 'Really mad? Daisy, what are you talking about? You're not writing a story for the *Prince*, are you?' And I told her, of course not, I was just asking her woman-to-woman if she thought anybody could have murdered Professor Kinkaid. She was shocked. She said, 'Murdered! He wasn't murdered, any more than Professor Alexander was murdered. What gave you that idea?'

"So I said some of us had been kicking it around—and we thought it was very odd that two senior English professors died mysteriously so close together. And she said, 'Is that all?' and I have to say she sounded relieved. She said it was probably some weird virus that would kill us all off.

"She said it could sometimes be dangerous to talk about murder. So there it is. I'm sorry. I thought she'd really open up and tell me everything," Daisy said.

"I guess we need to find out if Professor Kinkaid did anything that would really antagonize Sergeant," Lyle said.

Twenty-four

❧

VALENTINA MARTINEZ, WHOM everybody called Tina, had coal black hair, big black eyes, and a trim figure. McLeod thought she also had a huge crush on Ben True. She seemed to throw admiring glances his way, and McLeod suspected it was this crush that had led Tina to join the Murder Project. She didn't have much to report on her talks with Ginger Kingsley in the Humanities Council Office and with Cliff Kingsley in the English Department.

"Mrs. Kingsley asked me more questions than I asked her," she said. "She asked me where I was from and what I was majoring in and what I wanted to do in life. She sounded really interested. She offered me a Coke." Valentina looked at Marcy and said Mrs. Kingsley wore a pair of gray slacks and a printed blouse.

"I told her I was writing an essay on Professor Kinkaid for a writing class and I was asking his friends for details about him. She said she thought I had a difficult subject, that he was no Mr. Chips. So I said he certainly wasn't chummy with students, but that I did take his Byron class and it was quite an experience."

"What was that class like?" asked McLeod, curious about this famous course.

"Professor Kinkaid concentrated on the work, but I read that new biography of Byron and I must say he had quite a life," said Tina. "Actually, I liked Byron's poetry a lot, but Professor Kinkaid was as dry as dust.

"Mrs. Kingsley said she was surprised, that she thought that Archie Alexander was the kind of professor students would want to write about. So, I said, maybe I'd do him, too, and what did she think of them? I think she was trying to divert me and that was the best thing I could think of to say."

"You did well," said Ben. "What did she say?"

"She said they were colleagues of her husband, and that she didn't know either of them very well. But she said everybody loved Archie Alexander, and everybody respected Dexter Kinkaid. I asked her if she had any anecdotes about Professor Kinkaid and she said no. So I asked her if she thought somebody could have killed either one of them and she said certainly not, that that was an absurd idea. I tried to ask her why it was so absurd and she stood up and said she had to go to a meeting. So I left. I guess I didn't get anything out of her."

"I think we can safely say that Ginger Kingsley is not a murderer," said McLeod.

Nobody said anything, and Tina flipped a page in her notebook. "I hoped I'd get more information out of Mr. Kingsley and I decided to abandon the essay-on-Kinkaid ploy. I looked through his file in Stanhope and found out that he had done his dissertation on Mark Twain. It was published, but he hasn't published anything since.

"When I got to his office, I asked him to tell me about Dexter Kinkaid. I told him I had a class assignment. And I remembered how you told us to ask easy questions first in interviews and so I told him I needed to know more about the English Department. I told him I knew it was a good department and I asked him what made a good department.

"He said it needed good teachers, good scholars, a good chairman, and good support from the administration. He went off into a rant about how Nassau Hall favored science and economics over the humanities, especially English. 'English doesn't need supercomputers or cyclotrons or laboratories with expensive equipment,' he said. 'We just need the library. The library is our mine, our factory, our laboratory. It's the only thing we need, all we ask. Except more money for salaries, of course, and more money for copying machines. But then we don't always get what we need.'"

Again nobody said anything when she paused.

"So then I asked him if he could tell me any stories about Professor Kinkaid and he said he couldn't. I asked him if Kinkaid was a good chairman and he said, very good in some ways. He said he was calm, maybe too calm, economical, maybe too economical. He was conservative, maybe too conservative. But yes, he was a good chairman.

"So I asked him if everybody got along with Kinkaid, and he said he thought so, then he changed the subject and asked me where I was from. When he found out I was from South Texas, he started asking me about Tex-Mex cooking. He wanted to know if you could make tamales at home. I told him it was easy if you used a food processor. I tried to switch it back to Kinkaid and asked him who did not get along with him.

"He said nontraditional assistant professors, feminists, sloppy scholars, slipshod teachers. They didn't get along with him. But they don't get along with anybody in academia, he said. I asked him if any of those people would have tried to—well, get rid of Professor Kinkaid. And he said, what do you mean, get rid of? How could they? He was a tenured professor.

"I said I meant get rid of physically, and he said this was

Princeton, not Chiapas. Then he apologized. So I thanked him and left."

Again silence greeted her—until McLeod said, "You know I never thought you'd get anything incriminating out of them. They're the nicest, most harmless couple in the whole world."

Twenty-five

❧

MCLEOD REPORTED LAST, on her talk with Margie Kinkaid. "I asked her bluntly about the possibility of foul play. She was absolutely aghast at the thought that anyone would harm Dexter. But you know something, I planted the idea in her mind. I think she may begin to ask herself questions. In fact, I bet all these people are somewhat stirred by your inquiries."

"My money's on Mystique Alcott," Lyle said. "She has a motive, and the first cosmopolitan was served at her house."

"Listen, I thought I had the best suspect, until I heard Marcy's report," said Ben True. "Still, Bob Dewey hated Kinkaid and blames him for the fact that he didn't get tenure. He's the most likely person to have fixed the second cosmopolitan. I pick Dewey. He's my man. Except Liz Finley looks good, too."

"I can't believe either one of the Kingsleys had anything to do with a murder," said Tina. "She's too nice and he's too interested in food."

"I think you're right," said McLeod.

"Who does that leave us?" asked Lyle. "Mystique Alcott, Liz Finley, Bob Dewey, possibly Gertrude Sergeant, possibly Grady Schuyler."

They talked a few minutes about what to do next.

"I think somebody different should go talk to each of these people," said Lyle. "Marcy, or somebody, could talk to Mystique. Maybe ask more pointed questions about the murder."

"I'll bet you anything Mystique Alcott would open up more to a man than a woman," said Marcy.

"Wait a minute," said McLeod. "I'm not going to be like Miss Jean Brodie, and send students off to their deaths. What if one of these people really is a murderer, and your questions rouse him—or her—to action. It could be very dangerous."

"I don't see anything to worry about," said Lyle.

"The murderer, whoever it is, couldn't know what we're doing," Ben True said.

"Everybody knows about the Murder Project by now," McLeod said. "You've interviewed all these people and each of them has told ten people and each of those fifty people has told ten others. Gossip is exponential."

"But we can't stop now," said Lyle.

Finally they worked out a plan. Each of them would reinterview a suspect, but not the same one they had talked to before. As a concession to McLeod's misgivings, they agreed to conduct each interview in a public place, like the student center. And if the suspect was the least bit threatening, then the student must report immediately to McLeod so she could arrange for protection.

"In fact, I would say that when you schedule the interview—in a public place—let me know when and where it's going to be. I'll be nearby. If it's here, I can be at another table close by. Will you all promise to do that?"

They all promised faithfully, and agreed to e-mail her or call her and tell her the time and place of their appointments. McLeod gave them her home telephone number, just in case.

They worked out the assignments. Ben True would question Mystique Alcott this time and would think up some excuse for asking to see her. Everyone agreed it would be impossible to persuade Mystique to meet anybody at the student center. Ben said he would think of something.

Marcy would do Bob Dewey.

"And be sure to ask him who made that drink for Professor Kinkaid at the brunch," said Lyle. "That's important."

"I can see that," said Marcy.

Lyle said he would have a go at Gertrude Sergeant. "I hate feminists," he said.

"Good," said Daisy. "Maybe she'll show you what a rotten sexist you are."

"That leaves the Kingsleys, Elizabeth Finley, and Mrs. Kinkaid for Daisy and Tina," said Lyle. "Daisy, you'll have to do Mrs. Kinkaid, and Tina can talk to Finley. That still leaves the Kingsleys."

"I'll talk to the Kingsleys," said McLeod.

"Okay," said Lyle. "Now let's discuss how we're going to proceed.

"I'm not sure I can lure Mrs. Kinkaid to the student center," said Daisy.

"We'll all put our heads together and figure out what excuses we'll use and what questions we'll ask," Lyle said.

As McLeod left them, she still felt uneasy about the project. Should she call it off? Could she stop them if she tried?

Twenty-six

❦

IT WAS VERY late when the project meeting broke up, and McLeod hurried home, looking forward to dinner at the Kingsleys' house. Not only was the food bound to be sublime—unless Cliff was sick or had left home—but she wanted to talk to Ginger. She thought she had better let Ginger, who was technically her boss, know what her class was up to.

When Cliff asked her what she'd like to have to drink, she asked for a martini. Sipping the cold, dry drink, she relaxed utterly.

"This is a good time for you to give up being a teetotaler," said Ginger with satisfaction. "We have something to celebrate. I propose a toast to Cliff!" She raised her own martini glass.

"Sure," said McLeod. "But what happened? Tell me."

"Cliff has been named acting chair of the English Department," said Ginger, who looked ecstatic.

"Congratulations, Cliff!" said McLeod.

"You may be pleased, but I'm not," said Cliff morosely. "And I'm not going to be any good at it. Dexter ran a tight ship."

"Come on, Cliff," said Ginger. "It's long overdue and I just hope they make it permanent."

"Good God! I'll slit my throat," said Cliff.

"Don't be silly," said Ginger. "You know you want to get ahead. Everybody does."

"You want me to get ahead," said Cliff. "I just want to cook."

Over Cliff's extraordinary scrod in horseradish meringue, they talked about the state of the English Department. Cliff had to arrange—quickly—for someone to fill in for Dexter.

"It was hard enough when Archie died," he said. "Schuyler and Dexter jumped into the breach like good soldiers, but now Dexter's gone. He was only teaching one class of his own, but who can substitute for Dexter Kinkaid on Byron? And I'll have to call on everybody in the department to take over the seniors who were writing theses for Archie and Dexter, not to mention the juniors who were doing junior papers for them. And the graduate students they were advising."

"Does every senior have to do a thesis?" asked McLeod.

"Princeton is one of about three schools in the country that still require a thesis from every senior. Yale and Harvard have made it optional, and give honors for doing one," said Cliff.

"And I suppose every thesis-writing student has to have an advisor?" asked McLeod.

"That's right," said Cliff. "And there doesn't seem to be a spirit of 'all hands to' abroad in the English Department right now. It's not like an old barn raising, I'll tell you. You wouldn't believe the excuses I've heard."

"Like what?" asked McLeod, always curious.

"Oh, they already have too many advisees," said Cliff, "or they absolutely cannot take on one more thing because they're editing this collection of essays and it was due at Cambridge University Press two years ago."

"Editing a book of essays takes years?" asked McLeod.

"Some people can stretch any piece of academic work out for centuries," said Cliff.

"Like a medieval cathedral," said McLeod.

"That's right, except the end result around here is far less impressive," said Cliff.

Ginger asked McLeod how her class was going.

"I'm afraid they've rather gone off on a tangent," said McLeod. "You know, Lyle Cramer, one of my brightest students, is convinced that Archie was murdered, and that Dexter was, too. And I'm afraid I see his point."

"What are you talking about?" asked Ginger.

"You know Archie and Dexter each had that weird drink just before they got sick and died, a cosmopolitan," said McLeod.

"What makes you say that?" said Ginger.

"Archie had his at Mystique's party and Dexter had his at my brunch," said McLeod. "Then they both got a mysterious liver disease and died. No sign of drugs or poison in the autopsies, but still."

"I didn't know Archie drank cosmopolitans," said Cliff.

"I don't think he did ordinarily," said McLeod. "But I saw him pick up one that was already mixed at Mystique's. It was waiting for Dexter, I guess. Archie drank it and got sick that night."

"My God!" said Cliff.

"My students are investigating it," said McLeod. "It was all Lyle Cramer's idea. He got them steamed up after Oliver Hunt—he's the *New York Times* reporter who writes about crime—came out and talked to the class about crime reporting. And they had all read that story about the journalism class in Chicago that found the real murderer and freed a man on death row."

"How on earth are students investigating these bizarre allegations?" asked Cliff.

"They made a list of people who were at my brunch and at Mystique's party, too," said McLeod. "Each student took one of the guests, or two, and went to see them to ask them how they felt about Archie and Dexter or whatever."

"You mean that's what Valentina Martinez was talking to me about?" asked Ginger. "I didn't have a clue. I thought she was crazy—talking about an essay on Dexter."

"She was awfully nice," said Cliff. "I asked her about Mexican cooking."

"I wondered what made her tell the class that you were too interested in food to murder anybody," said McLeod.

"I should hope so," said Cliff.

"What did she say about me?" asked Ginger.

"She thought you were too nice to be a murderer," said McLeod.

"I have to say, McLeod, if the others aren't any better interrogators than she was, they didn't find out much," said Cliff.

"Tina may be the least assertive of the students involved," McLeod said. "Lyle Cramer, Daisy Wood, Ben True, and even Marcy Flowers are all much more aggressive. But then they had more likely suspects to work with."

"You mean we're suspects?" asked Cliff. "And people we know?"

"Somehow I didn't think of it like that. We—they—just wanted to find out more about it. I guess, though, if there's a murder, then there's a murderer."

"That's right, McLeod," said Cliff. He got up to clear the table and they could hear him rattling around in the kitchen.

"You know, I don't think it was murder," said Ginger. "Not at all. It must be some strange liver disease. And the cosmopolitans had nothing to do with it. Don't let your students go overboard, McLeod."

"They won't do anything rash," McLeod assured her.

Cliff brought in salad and a plate of cheese. "Good

heavens, Cliff, this cheese is good. What is it?" McLeod asked.

"I got it at Wild Oats," said Cliff. "It won first prize for cheese at the international exhibition. French, of course."

"It really is good," said McLeod. "Ginger, you're probably right that it was liver disease, but I'd still like to know who made those two cosmopolitans. Do either of you have any idea who fixed the cosmopolitan at Mystique's house, the one that Archie drank? And who made the second one at my house? Dexter made the first one and then he spilled it down his shirtfront and Bob Dewey brought him another and said, 'Your guardian angel sent this to you.' Did Bob make it? And if he didn't, who did?"

"I don't have a clue," said Cliff. "I didn't even know about Archie and that cosmopolitan until you just told us. I have no idea who made Dexter's second cosmopolitan, either."

"It might well have been Bob Dewey," said McLeod. "He could have just made it up about the 'Guardian Angel.' Or meant he was the 'Guardian Angel.' And he certainly had a motive."

"He sounds like an assistant professor desperate for tenure. Do you ladies want dessert?" asked Cliff.

"What is it?" asked McLeod.

"Getting choosy, are you?" said Cliff.

"Actually, I want dessert whatever it is," said McLeod. "You know that."

"Good, because it's crème brûlée," said Cliff.

"He has this darling little blow torch he brûles the sugar with," said Ginger. "Cliff, let's have some champagne, and really celebrate?"

"Certainly," said Cliff. "We've got some in the fridge." He brought out the bottle and three flutes, filled them, and took his own glass back to the kitchen.

"I do believe I'm a little drunk," Ginger said while she and McLeod waited at the dining table. "I do wish Cliff were happier about being chair. I don't understand him."

"He's a teacher, not an administrator, maybe," said McLeod.

"I don't think he really cares anything about teaching," said Ginger. "I always wanted to teach. Both my parents were teachers. But I never got the chance. I got my Ph.D. and Cliff got a job here—I don't quite understand how— and we came here and I had this little new baby. And they wouldn't let me teach. But if they had let me teach, I would have left Miranda with a sitter in a second. Like *that*. Nobody would ever hire me to teach, but they gave me administrative jobs." She drank her champagne and poured some more. "I guess I'm lucky to have the Humanities Council job."

Cliff came in with three custard cups and a tiny blowtorch and proceeded to burn the brown sugar on top of the custards. He put one at each place with a flourish and sat down before his own.

"I hope Mystique is the murderer," he said. "At least she's not in my department." McLeod noted the proprietary way in which Cliff said "my department."

"It's probably not a murder," said McLeod, not believing it for a moment. "But just for the record, where were you when Dexter spilled his drink at my house, Ginger?" she asked.

"What record is that?" Ginger asked.

"It's just that I'm curious," McLeod said. "You know that."

"I didn't know he spilled his drink," Ginger said. "I must have been in the bathroom. I missed the spilled drink episode."

"Cliff?" asked McLeod.

"Actually, I was in your kitchen," said Cliff. "I was interested in what you were cooking so I peeked in the oven. It certainly smelled good and looked good. I saw the pans of biscuits all ready to go in, too."

"So neither of you saw who mixed that drink?"

"I didn't," said Cliff. "If anybody murdered Dexter, it probably wasn't Mystique. It was one of his girl friends."

"Cliff!" said Ginger.

"Old Dexter was quite a womanizer," said Cliff.

"Cliff," said Ginger again.

"What does it matter now?" asked Cliff. "He's dead. What did it matter anytime anyway? He got away with it because he acts so damned proper in public."

"Was it with students?" asked McLeod.

"An occasional graduate student," said Cliff. "Women on the faculty, women staff members. Dexter was—"

"Cliff! Stop!" Ginger was beating on the table with clenched fists. "Don't talk like that."

"Oh, Ginger, you know it's true. He had an ongoing affair with Elizabeth Finley, for instance."

"Elizabeth Finley!" said McLeod, almost shrieking. "Liz Finley! I can't believe it! She looks completely sexless."

"Hardly," said Cliff. "I think that may be why she got hired as the first tenured woman at Princeton—nearly thirty years ago."

"What did she look like thirty years ago?" asked McLeod.

"Not too different from the way she looks now," said Cliff. "Dry and plain. But under those good gray tweeds, hormones were coursing like mad things, apparently. Banked fires."

"How do you know all this?" asked McLeod.

"I think it was common knowledge," said Cliff. "If I knew it, it certainly was."

"Is this true?" McLeod asked Ginger.

"Can't take my word for it?" asked Cliff.

"I don't see why Cliff wants to spread gossip," Ginger said. "But it's true enough."

"It's just so hard to believe," said McLeod. "As old as I am, I'm always shocked to learn about couples like Dexter and Liz. And yet I know it happens all the time. But trying to visualize them making love is hard, isn't it?'

"McLeod, you have a dirty mind," said Cliff. "Don't visualize."

WHEN MCLEOD GOT home, she checked her e-mail and found messages from Ben True, Lyle, and Tina. Ben had gone over to 185 Nassau Street to find out when Mystique Alcott held office hours. They were from 5 to 6 P.M. Wednesdays, and Princeton was strict about faculty office hours. "I think that's the only time and place I can catch her," Ben wrote. "It's not a public place, but I don't think I can ever get her on the phone and then pin her down to an appointment at the student center. It's the best I can do. Don't worry. I'm fit and she's fat. I can look after myself. Really."

McLeod e-mailed him that a deal was a deal. No interviewing suspects alone. He'd have to take someone with him. "Why not Tina?" she asked, remembering Tina's rapturous looks at Ben.

She had several reasons for not wanting Ben to see Mystique alone in her office. For one, Mystique was a suspect and she really did not want to see her students in danger. For another, she worried that Mystique might become annoyed and do something underhanded, such as accusing Ben of sexual harassment. She didn't mention this to Ben, however.

Lyle's e-mail said he was to meet Gertrude Sergeant at Small World for coffee at ten on Wednesday. How clever of Sergeant to pick Small World, where the coffee was a thousand times better than the student center's, McLeod thought.

But Tina said she was going to meet Liz Finley in the Café Vivian, a small dark room at the Frist Student Center, at the same time. What to do? wondered McLeod. Somehow she thought Lyle would be safe enough at Small

World with Trudy Sergeant, since the place was compact and crowded. She would do better to keep an eye on Tina at the student center.

She e-mailed Lyle to explain the situation to him.

He replied immediately that her plan was fine. "I'll be all right. I just let you know because you made us promise," he wrote.

"Do be careful," she answered. "And whatever you do, keep your eye on your coffee at all times. Don't let anybody have a chance to slip anything into it. I know I sound hysterical, but I want to be assured that you'll be careful."

"I will," he said.

She e-mailed Tina and said she'd be at Frist. She also told her about Finley's affair with Dexter Kinkaid. "I don't imagine you can ask her about it, but I thought you ought to know," she wrote.

By this time, Ben True replied that he would do as she said and get somebody to accompany him.

McLeod gave him her cell phone number and said she would be at the bagel place next door to 185 Nassau Street from five o'clock on.

THE NEXT MORNING, she had an e-mail from Marcy, who said she had an appointment with Bob Dewey at Frist at ten o'clock on Thursday morning. "He couldn't do it before then. He has to finish up some article for a learned journal. He wanted me to come to his office. Daisy Wood would say I was sexist, but I call it using feminine wiles. I said I wanted to talk to him informally, over Cokes or coffee. And I made it sound interesting."

"Good for you," McLeod e-mailed back. "I'll be there. I'll be inconspicuous, but there."

"Thanks," was Marcy's succinct reply.

Twenty-seven

❧

ON WEDNESDAY MORNING at ten o'clock, Café Vivian was doing a flourishing business, with faculty, staff, and students wandering in for coffee.

Why do they come here? wondered McLeod. Café Vivian was okay, but Small World and Starbucks were both right across the street and they both had better coffee, and better pastries. She sipped some hot tea and knitted away on Rosie's sweater. For all the world like Miss Marple, she thought.

When she saw Liz Finley come in, get a cup of coffee, and find a seat a few tables away, Cliff's news about Finley's affair with Dexter popped into her mind; she looked at Finley in her drab duffel coat and thought, You never know who's going to turn out to be a sexpot. Women who looked completely sexless, who appeared to be entirely cerebral, often turned out to lead secret lives that positively sizzled.

It was long past ten o'clock before Tina arrived. Ten

o'clock was, McLeod supposed, early for most students. Tina waved cheerfully at McLeod, got a coffee and a doughnut, looked around, found Finley, and went to join her.

McLeod knitted, glancing up occasionally to keep an eye on Tina and Liz Finley.

Some time later, McLeod saw Finley rise magisterially, put on her coat, and leave. Tina, still seated, stared after her, then got up and joined McLeod.

"Well, how did it go?" McLeod asked her. "Tell me about it while we walk over to Small World and watch out for Lyle." She put away her knitting and put on her coat.

"It didn't go very well at all," said Tina as they walked across campus to Witherspoon Street. "I must be the world's worst investigator. I got off on the wrong foot by being late. I told her my alarm didn't go off and she said it was funny that students' alarms never seemed to go off. What could I say? I thought of asking her if Professor Kinkaid had a happy marriage, and I couldn't do that either. Oh, I don't know what's the matter with me. But in some ways she's scary."

At Small World, Lyle and Trudy Sergeant sat at a table next to the big window that looked out on Witherspoon Street. They could not be in a more public spot, and McLeod sighed with relief. Started a few years ago, Small World had been the first coffee house in Princeton, Archie had told her, and had earned far more in its first year than all the business projections had indicated that it would. Half a dozen other coffee shops followed quickly, but Small World had a cachet of its own. Its walls served as a gallery for the works of local artists, with exhibitions changing monthly, and its coffee was superb. McLeod and Tina ordered lattes at the counter and took them to a table in the back.

"Then she complained about Frist," Tina went on with her report on Finley. "It wasn't nearly as nice as the old student center, with its Gothic windows, or whatever.

"Finally, I said I wanted to talk to her about Professor Kinkaid, and she asked me why. I told her I took his Byron course and I went to his funeral. She said Professor Kinkaid did more than any man alive to keep Byron in the canon. Byron fell terribly out of fashion, she said, but Kinkaid felt that no poet appreciated physical love more than Lord Byron.

"I said I'd learned enough in that course to be sure Professor Kinkaid was right," said Tina. "Byron appreciated physical love all right. I tried to push on with the Project. I told her our class was asking questions about the way Professor Kinkaid died, and I explained about the cosmopolitans, but she refused to understand it. She wouldn't even listen. She said that's what we pay policemen for—to investigate things that needed investigation. And she was sure this didn't need investigation. And if it did, she said, why should students be interrogating Professor Kinkaid's colleagues? Didn't we know that murders—if this was a murder—were committed by wives and lovers?

"Somehow I got up my courage to ask her about her book on the eighteenth-century guys and she said it wasn't appropriate to talk about it at this point. Then she just left."

"I think it's very interesting that she thinks if there was a murder, it was probably committed by his wife. At least, that's basically what she said," said McLeod. "Don't be too hard on yourself. You may have gotten something else out of her that you've forgotten, that will come back to you later."

Tina had to leave for class before Lyle finally came to join her. McLeod had expected him to complain about her watchdog activities, but he surprised her. "I was glad to see you come in," he said. "It's cozy, all of us gathering here and there. Sergeant is a tough broad, but pretty interesting, let me tell you."

"Why, what did she say?" asked McLeod.

"She said men have exploited women for centuries," he said.

"Of course they have," said McLeod. "I could have told you that."

"But you never did," said Lyle, "whereas Gertrude Sergeant told me three times."

"Is that all she said?" asked McLeod. "If it is, it sure took her a long time."

"No, actually, she was pretty forthcoming. She has no idea who made the cosmopolitan at Mystique's house, but she thought Bob Dewey made the one at your house. She said she wouldn't be at all surprised if Dewey killed Kinkaid."

"Bob Dewey, your favorite suspect," said McLeod.

"She said his fury knew no bounds when Kinkaid told him he wasn't going to get tenure."

"How did she know this?" asked McLeod. "I thought it was a secret."

"It seems everybody knew about it," said Lyle. "She happened to see a memo on Bob's desk when she was in his office to talk about a precept or something. She said she was sorry about Dewey not getting tenure—she liked him and would be sorry to see him go. But there was no way the department could overrule Kinkaid."

"Did you talk to her about how she felt about Archie and Dexter?" asked McLeod.

"A little bit," said Lyle. "But she didn't seem to have strong feelings about either one of them."

"This is fascinating," McLeod said. "Look, it's time for me to go to the Annex to chaperon Daisy and Margie Kinkaid. Want to come along?"

"Sure," said Lyle. They walked down Nassau Street.

Twenty-eight

✥

DAISY HAD HAD a terrible time deciding where to meet
Mrs. Kinkaid. She consulted Lyle and McLeod about how
to lure a recent widow to a public place for a talk with a
student. Lunch seemed the best bet. But where? Daisy's
eating club was too noisy and offered no chance for conversation. Lahiere's was too expensive; it would have to be
the Annex.

The Annex, as Archie had told McLeod, was like an
English pub. "Everybody goes there for a drink and, incidentally, eats the food," he had said.

"If the food was any good, you couldn't get in the
place," someone else had said.

The Annex's ambiance, however, was delightful. Down
a flight of stairs from the sidewalk, it was warm and
cozy—and cheap. It had been run by the same family for
fifty years and was often very crowded. Right across Nassau Street from the campus, it was convenient for faculty
who couldn't face the faculty club. Students didn't eat

there often—they preferred the sandwich and takeout shops farther down the street—but Daisy had been there once when her parents visited.

"How did Daisy persuade Margie to come?" McLeod asked Lyle as they hurried toward the Annex.

"Daisy invited her to lunch and told her some students were interested in a memorial to her husband and she wanted to talk to her about it. What widow could resist?"

"That was clever," McLeod said.

They went down the stairs to the Annex and were seated before Daisy came in with Margie Kinkaid. Daisy, her red curls combed neatly and tied in a bun, wore a skirt and tights instead of blue jeans. When the two women were seated nearby, McLeod could see that Margie seemed happy and animated. Daisy was very serious, but it wasn't very long before Margie departed and Daisy brought the remains of her Student Special sandwich over and joined McLeod and Lyle.

"She's loco," Daisy said. "I told her that some of the students were heartbroken at Professor Kinkaid's untimely passing, and she nodded and said that Dexter lived for his students—undergraduates as well as graduate students. She asked me which of his courses I had taken. Well, I never would have taken one of his stupid courses. I have no interest in romantic poetry and he didn't teach any women poets." She paused and took an enormous bite of her Student Special (a chicken club with bacon and tomato). She rolled her eyes. "Although what Tina told me about Byron was certainly rather interesting. Anyway, I decided just to lie to Mrs. Kinkaid. I told her that I took the Byron course, and I said it was just wonderful." She swallowed the last bite of her sandwich and Lyle reached over and grabbed the slice of pickle off her plate.

"So of course she asked me if I liked *Don Juan* best," said Daisy. "Somebody might have warned me that they pronounce Don Juan like 'Don Joowan.' I was totally bewildered. And she was nattering on about *The Corsair* and *Childe Harold*.

"I had to read parts of *Childe Harold* in high school, but I remembered nothing about it, *nada*. In fact, I remembered nothing a day after we finished with it."

"'Oh, what a tangled web we weave, when once we practice to deceive,'" said Lyle sagely. Daisy glared at him.

"Ben True would probably correct that quotation," said McLeod, who was hugely amused. "What did you say?"

"I told her I liked them all," Daisy said. "She said Dexter would be delighted to hear me say that. I actually began to feel bad, you know, about what I was doing. Here was this poor woman looking at me so expectantly. But I got over that brief attack of conscience and told her it was so awful that Professor Kinkaid passed away so suddenly. I said that was why some of us were thinking about a memorial for him. I asked her what she thought would be appropriate, and she suggested a scholarship fund, or a fund for library books. She said they put a special bookplate in books bought with memorial funds. I thought it was all going very well indeed, but when I tried to bring the subject around to possible murder, I lost her. She said flatly that murder was not a possibility and she went back to the memorial. She had decided by now that a show in Dexter's memory in the Rare Books Gallery would be lovely."

When Daisy paused, they all ordered coffee.

"What could I say?" Daisy said. "Students don't have anything to do with arranging shows in the Rare Books Gallery. I tried to think of a way to bring up cosmopolitans and mixed-up drinks and grudges and murder, but Mrs. Kinkaid was running wild. She said it could be a show of the holdings in first editions of Byron and Keats and Shelley, the poets that Dexter loved. So I interrupted her and asked her what about Professor Alexander. I said wasn't it weird that they had similar diseases and died in similar ways so close together.

"And she said, 'But Archie taught the Victorian novel,' as though that made it okay. She said dear Archie had had nothing to do with the Romantic poets.

"She was wolfing down her omelet, and I asked her about the cosmopolitans. She said, 'What cosmopolitans?' She said she was still thinking about the exhibition. She said she could see it now in the glass cases in the gallery, with a big portrait of Dexter opposite the door as you come in."

Lyle and McLeod were both laughing now. Daisy soldiered on with her account. "She said it was so noble— that's what she said—'noble'—of the students to think of an exhibition. She said she was so proud of us. Then she thanked me for lunch and said she really had to run and that I had made her very happy. Me and what we're planning.

"She got up and left and I had barely started on my sandwich. She polished off her omelet, let me tell you, and I didn't find out one single thing."

"She's crazy, or else terribly clever about changing the subject and avoiding questions she doesn't want to answer," said Lyle.

"Tina didn't have much luck with Finley," McLeod said. "Don't feel bad."

McLeod picked up everybody's check and they left for individual destinations. In her office that afternoon McLeod received a call from Liz Finley protesting the invasion of her privacy by members of McLeod's class.

"Two students have been to see me, at two different times, and I have tried to help them since they told me they were doing this for a class," she said. "But I begin to wonder if this is an appropriate class project."

"I'm sorry, Liz," said McLeod. "I don't think they mean to invade anyone's privacy. It's not really a class project. I didn't assign it. Some of them wanted to investigate these mysterious deaths. I reluctantly agreed, because I thought it would provide extremely good experience at interviewing people for something other than puff pieces. I'll try to see that they don't bother you again."

Was this a good sign (that things were getting stirred up) or a bad sign (that she was going to be in trouble for letting her class run wild)?

Twenty-nine

AS SOON AS McLeod had finished her phone conversation with Liz Finley, she realized it was time for her to get over to Nassau Bagel to wait for Ben True. What a day! She was spending the whole time acting like a mother hen to students doing interviews. At least, she could take her knitting with her to Nassau Bagel. Rosie's lavender sweater was growing apace.

She ordered hot tea, and it wasn't long before Ben True and, to McLeod's delight, Tina Martinez appeared. They got bottles of fruit juice and joined her.

Ben shook his head. "Didn't get much and made Mystique mad besides," he said.

"He was wonderful," said Tina. "Ben, I mean."

Ben beamed.

"Tell me about it," said McLeod.

"I have to say I never saw an office so cluttered," said Ben. "It was the messiest place I've ever seen. And she certainly wasn't particularly glad to see us."

"Especially me," said Tina. "She never took her eyes off Ben."

"We introduced ourselves," Ben said. "And I told her how much I admired her writing. I laid it on."

"He was terrific," Tina said.

"I told her that nobody in America is writing about the working-class world the way she does," said Ben.

"And she asked him which of her books he liked the best!" said Tina.

"I said it was hard to say," said Ben. "That's the truth, but you know I really do admire her work. I said I guessed I would choose *The Paymaster's Downfall*, or maybe *The Foreman's Fire*."

"She was loving it," said Tina. "She flicked that long blond hair over her shoulder and beamed. And Ben didn't stop there. He said it was an honor to meet her at last."

"I thought that surely I had been sufficiently generous," said Ben, "that she must be softened up by now. But no, she wanted more. She asked me what I thought of *Rutabaga or Swede* and I told her I loved it."

"You did?" asked McLeod. "I disapprove of mixing fiction and fact." *Rutabaga or Swede* was a fictionalized biography of Greta Garbo, a change of pace for Alcott.

"I enjoyed reading it enormously, but I didn't take it seriously," Ben said. "Anyway, I told her I was so glad it won the National Book Critics Circle Award!"

"Mystique was wriggling with happiness," said Tina. "And when she wriggled, she's so fat that the office shook."

"She has an insatiable appetite for praise," said Ben, "but I thought I'd better get on with my business, or we'd be there all night discussing the fine qualities of each of her books. So I said, 'You're such an acute observer, so good at details, at specificity. It's quite impressive,'" he said.

Tina was laughing. "And so she asked him what his name was and she said it was really nice of him to come and see her, and she asked him what year graduate student he was and then she asked him what his field was, and Ben said, Modern American Literature."

"So she asked me who I was going to do my dissertation on," Ben said.

"And he said he wasn't sure, but then he said he was thinking of doing it on *her!*" Tina took over the narrative.

"Alcott said she was very flattered," Ben said.

"She ought to be," said McLeod.

"I tried to give myself some wiggle room and said I wasn't sure yet, but if I did do it on her, I hoped I could talk to her about her work. And she said, of course, she would talk to me as much as I wanted. And I said, but right now because she was such a good observer, some of us wondered if she could help us."

" 'How?' she said, and I plunged in and asked her if she remembered a big party she gave about six weeks ago. And she said she gave a big party every fall and every spring. I told her we were doing a kind of survey to see what people remember," said Ben.

"I thought that was brilliant, and she was happy. She said, 'Oh, I love things like this,' " said Tina. "And Ben went on."

"I said that Archie Alexander drank a cosmopolitan at that party," said Ben. "I said it was standing on an untended bar, waiting, everyone supposed, for Dexter Kinkaid. I asked her if she knew who made that cosmopolitan. She said she supposed it was the student bartender. She said she always hired the Student Bar Tending Agency. And I came right out and asked her if she was sure she didn't mix it herself. She wasn't wriggling and beaming anymore. She said, 'Of course I didn't,' and she asked why we were so interested in this. I said it was just a memory test," said Ben.

"She said it was a preposterous test and she didn't want to talk about it. So I said that Archie Alexander had died after drinking that cosmopolitan, which was probably intended for Dexter Kinkaid, didn't she think? I asked her then if she knew anybody with a grudge against Professor Kinkaid. And she said every assistant professor probably hated him. She mentioned Bob Dewey and 'even that sweet Grady Schuyler.' I asked her what he had done to Grady Schuyler, and she said she understood he had given Schuyler a bad job recommendation."

"Then a student knocked on the door and peered in, and she told us students came first at Princeton and we'd better leave. She had sure changed," said Tina. "I wanted to tell her I was a student."

"Talk about mercurial," Ben said. "And I think she's guilty, guilty of something. She's so weird."

MCLEOD HAD WALKED up the hill from her apartment to Frist that morning, to Small World, to the Annex, and to Nassau Bagel, but still she felt as though she'd spent the whole day sitting, eating, and knitting. She decided to head down Washington Avenue and walk on the towpath a bit before she went home.

She reflected on the information from the interviews that day: Trudy Sergeant thought Bob Dewey was the murderer; Liz Finley implied that Mrs. Kinkaid must be the guilty party; Mystique was edgy about the murder and had implicated Grady Schuyler. Margie Kinkaid was still in never-never land as far as Dexter's death was concerned. It was not a lot, but still interesting. She walked past the Woodrow Wilson School and Frist Student Center, past the Armory and some woods to Faculty Road, and crossed Lake Carnegie—built with funds from Andrew Carnegie so Princeton could have a place for a rowing crew to practice. She turned down the towpath and walked along the canal, but the light was fading, and before she had gone far, she turned back.

As she recrossed the lake, she realized that cars had their lights on. It was dark.

She turned left on Faculty Road, which had no sidewalks, and walked on the road's shoulder, heading home. She was walking on the lefthand side of the road, facing oncoming traffic. A car came toward her and seemed about to stop, then moved past her toward the bridge. Tramping along, tired now, for some reason McLeod turned around and saw the car turn into the Boat House driveway before it got to Washington Road and the bridge. It backed out, turned around, and came out onto Faculty Road, heading back the way it had come. Someone lost, she decided, and turned back to resume her walk home. Then she could tell from the lights of the car that it was coming toward her, very far over, on the wrong side of the road. She turned to see it coming straight, exactly—no mistake about it— straight toward her.

Alarmed, McLeod scrambled off the shoulder, into the scrubby woods between Faculty Road and the boathouse. She was tired, but fear made her as quick as one of her students.

The driver of the car came after her, crashing into the woods, but seemed to realize the car couldn't make it through the trees. It reversed loudly back through the bushes to the road and went on its way. McLeod sat on the damp, cold earth, feeling shaky, and contemplated what had happened. Was it a drunk driver? Or had someone tried to kill her? And where was her knitting bag with Rosie's sweater in it? She got herself up, found the bag, and walked slowly home. She stayed very far over on the shoulder indeed.

Should she call the police? What good would that do? She had no idea what the license number of the car was, or even what the car looked like. She only knew it was a car, not an SUV. The police would laugh at her, a middle-aged woman with too much imagination. When she got home, she drew a hot bath and soaked a long time, still feeling the chill of the night, and of sudden terror.

Thirty

❧

WHEN MCLEOD GOT to the student center at ten o'clock on Thursday morning, Marcy was already there, perfectly groomed, sitting at a table by one of the big south-facing windows. McLeod waved at her, sat down at a table nearby, but not too near, and got out her knitting. Marcy began reading a textbook, studiously underlining passages.

Time passed, and Bob Dewey did not show up. More time passed. It was ten-thirty when Marcy got up and came over to McLeod. "I don't know where he is," she said. "He said he'd be here."

"Call his office," suggested McLeod.

"Good idea," said Marcy, and went upstairs to use the campus phone. She was back in a few minutes. "No answer," she said. "I left a message on his voice mail."

"Call him at home," said McLeod. "I'm sure he doesn't have an unlisted number."

"I wish I had a cell phone. I'll have to use a pay phone," said Marcy. "I hope it has a phone book."

"You could have used my cell phone," said McLeod, "but I didn't bring it. I just dropped my billfold in my knitting bag. Oh, shoot. Do you have change? Here's some."

"Oh, thanks so much," said Marcy.

When Marcy came back, it was a quarter to eleven. "No answer there either," she said. "Should I wait any longer?"

"Let's wait until eleven," said McLeod. "Then I have to leave, and I don't want you interviewing him by yourself. I think maybe Ben True is right and he's our best suspect."

"Do you think so, really?" asked Marcy.

"I do," said McLeod.

At eleven, McLeod stood up. "We might as well go," she said.

"Well, shoot, as you said," replied Marcy. "I'll keep calling him and try to schedule another meeting. Thanks for your help."

THAT AFTERNOON MARCY and Lyle arrived early for class. When Marcy reported that Bob Dewey had not shown up for his interview and that she had still not been able to reach him, Lyle was dismayed.

"We have to ask him about the 'Guardian Angel' who gave him that cosmopolitan for Kinkaid," he said. "That's the key question."

The class went well. They talked about revisions, and several students read first drafts to the group. But McLeod had to fight to keep her attention from wandering. Talking to Bob Dewey was absolutely essential, she decided, and she had better try to see him herself.

After class, McLeod walked to McCosh Hall hoping to find him in. She stopped in the outer office of the English Department and asked one of the secretaries behind the big counter if she knew where Dewey would be.

The woman looked at the others and they all shrugged and shook their heads.

"He didn't tell us anything," said one, "and he hasn't

picked up his mail." She gestured at his mailbox among the pigeonholes that lined the wall opposite the counter.

"Is Stephanie West here?" asked McLeod, who remembered that the English Department administrator always seemed to have the answers to everything.

"She's in her office," said one of the secretaries, and waved McLeod toward an open door. Stephanie, who wore her graying hair in a French twist and was clad in one of her extremely handsome dress-for-success outfits, looked up when she tapped on the open door.

Not sure Stephanie remembered her, McLeod introduced herself.

"I know who you are," Stephanie assured her cordially. "How are you, McLeod?"

"I was just wondering if you know where Bob Dewey is," said McLeod. "He doesn't answer the phone, he broke an appointment with a student, and he hasn't picked up his mail."

"I don't know," said Stephanie. "Let's ask Cliff."

She got up and, followed by McLeod, went next door and knocked on Cliff's office door and asked him if he knew anything about Bob Dewey.

"I was just about to ask you if you knew anything," said Cliff. "He didn't meet his class yesterday or today. I've tried to call him at home and in his office . . ."

He and Stephanie dithered for a while. "I'll go check his office and make sure he's not there," said Cliff. "Maybe he left something to tell us where he is." He got up and came around his desk. "Hello, McLeod. Pretty grand office I have here, isn't it?" It was indeed a grand office, spacious, many-windowed, and paneled, McLeod could see, but she had other things on her mind.

"I'll just go with you," she said. "I want to see Bob, too."

"Come on," said Cliff. "His office is downstairs."

As they went through the departmental outer office,

McLeod noticed the secretaries had all left. It was just after five o'clock.

The basement corridor was bleak and the offices opening off it were like cells. Cliff stopped at a door that bore a card with ROBERT F. DEWEY printed on it, and knocked. No answer. He knocked again, louder this time. No answer. He tried the door. It was locked.

"He's not here," he said.

"Have you got a key?" she asked.

"Key?" he asked.

"Yes, to Bob's office," she said.

"We do have master keys," he said. "The cleaners have them, too. Stephanie will know." He turned away. McLeod trailed back upstairs with him, and waited while he got a master key from Stephanie.

When they went back downstairs, the key turned in Dewey's office door; Cliff pushed it open and turned on the light. Craning to look around Cliff, McLeod saw Bob Dewey—Bob Dewey with a livid, swollen, distorted face—slumped across his desk. He did not move.

Numb with shock, they moved toward the desk. McLeod could see two ends of bright fabric at the back of Bob Dewey's neck. Cliff felt his forehead.

"Good God!" he said. "He's dead. Stone cold dead." He turned and started pushing McLeod toward the door.

"Wait a minute," she said, shaking off his hand. "Are you sure?"

"You don't want to look at him, McLeod," said Cliff. "Yes, I'm sure. We shouldn't disturb anything. Come on." This time he got her out the door, closed it, then reopened it, turned off the light, snapped on the lock, and closed it again. Silently, they climbed back up to the English Department offices.

"He's dead," said Cliff to Stephanie West.

"Murdered," said McLeod. "Strangled, I think."

Stephanie stared at them.

"Should we call a doctor?" asked Cliff.

"Call the police," said McLeod.

"We'll call Public Safety, the campus police," said Stephanie. She reached for the phone as calmly as though she were calling to reserve a table at Prospect.

"You're white as a piece of sole," said Cliff to McLeod. "Come sit down in the big chair in my office." Stephanie brought a glass of water.

In a matter of seconds, it seemed, Sean O'Malley, the freckled-faced director of Public Safety, arrived with a deputy. "Borough Police are on their way," he said. Then they heard the siren. It was the first of many they would hear that night, as official vehicles would continue to arrive.

The Borough Police took over, roping off the basement corridor and the steps leading to it with yellow tape. Cliff formally identified Bob Dewey.

John Ives, the chief of the Borough Police, and Captain Nick Perry, chief of detectives, took over Cliff's office and asked Cliff preliminary questions about Bob Dewey—his work, his habits, his social life, his family.

McLeod went in next and answered the few questions they asked her—she had barely seen the body, she told them.

They ascertained that she had been in Princeton less than three months and that she had known no one there before she came.

"What did you want to see Mr. Dewey about?" asked Captain Perry, who was totally bald and had piercing blue eyes.

"I was worried about him," McLeod said. "He had missed an appointment with a student of mine and nobody could get him on the phone, and I guess I'm a busybody— I wondered what was the matter."

The police questioned Stephanie briefly and let her go home. They asked McLeod to stay. She sat down in the outer office, wishing she had brought her knitting. The president of the university arrived, followed closely by the

provost. The vice president for public affairs came next.
The three of them talked with Chief Ives and Captain Perry
in Cliff's office. When they came out, the president was
saying, "I'll have to call his family myself. This is dreadful, dreadful. Was he married?"

"No, he wasn't married," the vice president told him.

"Does anybody know who is the next of kin?" asked the
president.

"We'll have to get his file from the dean of the faculty,"
said the vice president. "And you should make a statement
to the crowd outside, tell them you can't release any information until the family is notified."

"And ask them to go home," said Captain Perry, coming out of Cliff's office.

The three administrators went into Stephanie's office
and closed the door to work jointly on the statement.

McLeod and Cliff sat in the outer office and waited. She
could not see who went downstairs, but the medical examiner and a police photographer checked in with Ives and
Perry before they went down. The two policemen interviewed the few people who had still been in McCosh when
the murder was reported. The medical examiner came
back.

Nick Perry came out, beckoned McLeod into Cliff's office, and asked her what she had done on Wednesday.

"Wednesday?" she said stupidly. "I can't think. Oh, yesterday. I was with students all day. I met a student for coffee at the Frist Student Center. Then I went to Small World
with another student. I had lunch at the Annex with two
students. I went to my office and then met two more students at Nassau Bagel. Then I went for a short walk on the
towpath. Then I went back home and I was alone in my
apartment all evening." She brushed aside an impulse to
tell him about the car that had swerved and almost hit her.
It seemed so small and petty after what had happened to
Bob Dewey. She couldn't bring herself to go into it.

"You spend a lot of time with your students," said Perry.

"Yesterday was unusual," she said.

"Did you come to McCosh at all?" asked Perry.

"No," said McLeod.

Perry told McLeod she could go home but not to leave town. She promised to comply. "Mr. Culkin will take you to the door so you can get out," he said. "Professor Kingsley, would you come in, please."

Mr. Culkin was a proctor, a plainclothes officer in the Public Safety Office. "Public Safety is helping with the investigation?" she asked him as they walked toward the entry door.

"We're just here to assist the Borough Police," he said. "We don't do murder."

He told the uniformed policeman guarding the door that Ms. Dulaney could leave. And McLeod went out, blinking, as floodlights blinded her. The courtyard outside McCosh was full of police cars and ambulances. A hearse was pulling out. She was astonished at the size of the crowd standing outside the area bounded by yellow police tape. Mr. Culkin walked her past the tape and said he'd drive her home if she liked.

"I'm fine, thanks," she said. "I need the fresh air."

"Sure?" he asked.

"Sure," she said.

Shivering—it was cold for November—she started walking home. "McLeod! Ms. Dulaney!" she heard someone calling. It was Lyle, who came panting up to her, looking wild, his glasses askew, his elbows sticking out more than ever.

"What's going on?" he asked.

"What are you doing here?" she asked.

"I was going home from the E-quad when I heard the sirens and saw the lights flashing," he said. "So I stayed. I thought you would applaud my curiosity. What were you doing behind the police lines? What's going on?"

"Bob Dewey was murdered," she said, trying to keep

her voice level for Lyle's sake. "Cliff Kingsley and I found him. In his office."

They stood stock still, staring at each other.

"Now we'll never know who made that cosmopolitan at your house," Lyle said.

Thirty-one

✦

THE NEXT MORNING, McLeod read about the murder in the Trenton *Times*. Bob Dewey had been strangled with a woman's silk scarf; the medical examiner had tentatively set the time of death as sometime Wednesday. A more accurate time would be established after an autopsy, the story said. McLeod had already figured out that the murder must have taken place on Wednesday, since that was the day that Captain Perry had asked her about. Poor Bob—lying there all that time.

She read Bob's obituary—he had grown up in Lowell, Massachusetts, graduated from Harvard, done a stint of union organizing in Detroit, and earned his Ph.D. at Yale. His survivors included siblings and parents. No mention of a girl friend. Did the young woman in Rome know? His parents would call her, no doubt.

McLeod sat quite still for a long time. She felt somehow responsible. If she and the project students had not asked so many questions, Bob Dewey would not have been killed. She was sure of it. But you had to ask questions, didn't you? Especially when it was a question of murder.

She wondered if she should have told the detective why she had been with her students all day Wednesday. But she had been so stunned by the actuality of Bob Dewey's death that she hadn't really grasped that he must have been killed because he knew who had mixed the fatal cosmopolitan.

Feeling very gloomy, she decided to go see Ginger. McLeod felt the need to talk to a friend, and Ginger was always cheerful.

Frieda, the cross dark-haired secretary, waved her toward the door of Ginger's office. Ginger was standing at the window looking out. She turned and greeted McLeod. She looked tired, but she summoned up something like her usual ebullience and came across the room to clasp McLeod in her arms.

"Isn't it awful?" she asked.

"Yes, it is," said McLeod.

"Sit down," said Ginger. "I'll get some coffee."

"I walked around to look at McCosh before I came in here and police cars were still there," said McLeod while they drank coffee. "And all that yellow police tape."

"Yes, and no telling how long the police will be here," said Ginger. "And they are going to interview everyone in the English Department. Everyone. Professors, associate professors, assistant professors, instructors, lecturers, secretaries, and even graduate students. And they plan to talk to every student who ever had a class with Bob Dewey. It's the worst thing that ever happened at the university. The police are demanding an office in McCosh where they can set up an on-site headquarters. It's a terrible situation. And Cliff has to find somebody to take Bob's classes. He had a hard enough time filling in for Archie and Dexter. Now he has to find somebody to take *his* classes. Poor Cliff. He didn't get home until one o'clock this morning. We're both exhausted. You were there, too, Cliff said."

"Not as long as Cliff," said McLeod.

"It just doesn't seem fair," said Ginger.

"Fair's fair, fair's in October," said McLeod. "That's what this old woman I know in Tallahassee always says about things being fair. Nothing's fair, is it?"

"That's great," said Ginger, but she said it flatly, without the usual glee she showed for Tallahassee aphorisms.

"What did the police ask Cliff?" McLeod asked, changing the subject again.

"McLeod, you kill me," said Ginger, managing a faint smile. "You never rest, do you? You have so much energy and you're so curious. They asked him everything. Everything you can think of. Everything about Bob Dewey. How long had he been here? What did he teach? How did everybody feel about him? Did he have any enemies? Who were his friends? It went on and on, he said. And today he has to get word to everybody that the police want to talk to them. I'm sure that Stephanie will be too upset to come in and Cliff will have to cope alone. Great hunks of McCosh are closed off to everyone but the police, and Cliff has to find rooms for classes to meet in."

"I'm sure Cliff hates all this administrative work," said McLeod, realizing that the pressures on Cliff—and Ginger—must be enormous. There were no precedents for such a situation. "I'm sorry."

"Not your fault," said Ginger, smiling at her.

"I'm afraid it is," said McLeod. "I'm sure Bob Dewey was murdered because of all those questions we asked about Dexter's cosmopolitan."

"Nonsense," said Ginger. "That theory of yours about the drinks—what are they? cosmopolitans?—is too baroque."

"Who else would go down and strangle an assistant professor?" asked McLeod. "What's the motive for that one?"

"Who knows?" said Ginger. "Some lowlife from Trenton looking for money for drugs." McLeod thought she was being inordinately dense, but Ginger went on, "Well, at least now you can stop those students from asking all their questions, since the police are working on it."

Thirty-two

❧

IN HER OWN office, McLeod sat down and wished that she knew more about what was going on in the investigation. She had an inspiration: She would volunteer her services to Cliff since the incomparable Stephanie West, according to Ginger, wasn't there. That would get her back inside McCosh.

To her astonishment, Stephanie answered Cliff's office phone. "Of course, I'm here," she told McLeod. "I don't know what Ginger's talking about. I left before you did. It would take a lot more than mere murder to make me leave Cliff here alone to manage. Besides, I wanted to know what was going on."

"I don't blame you," McLeod said. "I'm dying to find out more myself."

"I'll keep you informed," Stephanie said cheerfully. With this crumb, McLeod had to be satisfied.

Then her office phone rang. It was Oliver Hunt; he was

coming down to do a story about the murder for the *New York Times*. Would she be available to help him?

Would she! McLeod ecstatically agreed to do anything he wanted her to.

"Good," said Oliver. "I'll drive down in time for lunch. I'll take you out this time. Where shall I meet you?"

They agreed on Lahiere's at noon. Nothing but the best for Oliver Hunt.

MCLEOD WAS VERY glad to see tall, good-looking Oliver Hunt, with his confident air. He fussed over her kindly and made sure they had a good quiet table where they could talk undisturbed.

"Tell me what's going on," Oliver said as he sipped a martini. McLeod drank soda water and began her story.

He was astonished that she had been with Cliff when he found the body. "Talk about being in the right place at the right time," he said. "Give me some background. Did you know him?"

"Yes, I did," said McLeod. "He was at my house for Sunday brunch just a few weeks ago. He was brash and outspoken, but a nice young man and, as I understand it, an excellent teacher." She went on to describe Bob Dewey's situation.

"A Marxist, was he? At Princeton?" Oliver was surprised.

"He was a Marxist critic," said McLeod. "I don't think that means he was necessarily an actual Marxist. In fact, he might have been aghast if there were a revolution. But he looked at literature from the point of view that a revolution of the proletariat was inevitable. He would read *Silas Marner* as part of the class struggle."

Oliver digested this in silence.

"He was such a nice young man," McLeod went on. "He tended bar for me at my house."

"Was he married?"

"No," said McLeod.

"Was he gay?"

"I don't think so," said McLeod. "He said his girl friend was in Rome."

"Why do you think he was killed?" asked Oliver.

"If I tell you what I really think, you're going to say I'm crazy," said McLeod, remembering Ginger's skepticism that morning.

"Try me," said Oliver as their lunches arrived.

"You know, you got my students all excited when you talked to my class," she said. "They wanted to investigate the deaths of two professors, although nobody, but nobody, thought they were murders. You see, one of the professors was named Archie Alexander . . ."

McLeod told him the whole thing—all about Archie, Dexter, the cosmopolitans, including the one drunk by Archie, the one spilled by Dexter, and the one finally drunk by Dexter.

"The students—and I, too, I must say—thought somebody must have poisoned the cosmopolitans and it had to have been somebody at my party. Each of my students involved interviewed one of the people who had been at the brunch and then another student went around and asked more questions. They were picking up a lot of information. I don't think we realized the importance of all we had.

"Now who mixed that second drink?" she asked. "That's the crucial question. Bob Dewey could have told us. He tended bar, and he brought it to Dexter after Dexter spilled the first one. A student, Marcy Flowers, had an appointment with Bob on Thursday morning—yesterday. And Bob Dewey didn't keep it. He was already dead, killed sometime on Wednesday. And I think he was killed by the person who killed Archie and Dexter so he couldn't tell who had mixed that fatal cosmopolitan."

Oliver shook his head. "It's complicated. What did the police say about all this?"

"I didn't tell them about it," McLeod said. "If you think

it's complicated, what do you think the police would say about it? I just didn't go into it last night."

"It'll probably turn out that he was killed by his girl friend or a jealous lover or something," he said. "It nearly always does."

"We'll see," said McLeod. They had finished two elegant plates of veal by now. Neither wanted dessert, but they ordered coffee.

"You come along with me to see the police and we'll get you accredited, at least," said Oliver. "You can be our stringer or something. I'm sure our student stringer isn't up to a story like this. Anyway, we'll get you legitimized. Who's handling the investigation?"

"The Borough Police," said McLeod. "They have an office on campus in McCosh, where the murder happened, but I suppose we should go by Borough Hall first."

"Let's go," said Oliver, signing the check with a flourish.

They walked down Nassau Street to Borough Hall and learned at police headquarters that there would be a press conference on campus at three o'clock.

"Where on campus?" McLeod asked.

"In Nassau Hall," said the clerk. "The faculty room, I think they call it." She said the chief of police and the chief of detectives would be there, as well as the Mercer County medical examiner. No, the press was not being admitted to McCosh yet. "We're still too busy there—scene-of-the-crime stuff, you know," she said.

Oliver cut a wide swath at police headquarters, McLeod noted. Not only did the police appear to be in some awe of the *New York Times*, but other newspaper people deferred to him. With his backing, McLeod had no trouble getting equipped with a press card.

"We have a while to wait until three o'clock," Oliver said. "Let's walk back and you can show me McCosh."

They walked back to campus and McLeod pointed out McCosh, most of which was still taped off, with police

cars still parked in front of it. McLeod casually pointed out
Stanhope Hall, where the campus security people had their
offices. "Let's go in," said Oliver. "Might as well meet
them. They're probably feeling left out."

Oliver introduced McLeod and himself to the recep-
tionist and asked to speak to Sean O'Malley, the director.
O'Malley came out personally to greet the representative
of the *New York Times.*

"This is a terrible thing to happen on a college campus,"
O'Malley said. In answer to a question from Oliver, he
said that no, his department was not involved in the investigation. "We'll stay out of it, unless the Borough asks us
for some specific help," he told Oliver. "We're here if they
need us. When they called us from McCosh, we immediately called the Borough. Turned it over to them."

"I'll bet you guys end up helping them with information
and background and that kind of thing," Oliver said.
"Anyway, I'm glad I met you. Has there ever been a murder at Princeton before?"

"No," said O'Malley. "Not on the campus. Too bad it
had to happen on my watch."

"That was a public relations call," Oliver told McLeod
when they were outside. "You never know."

"I felt sorry for him," said McLeod. "He seemed to feel
to blame for the murder." Like me, she thought.

Thirty-three

❧

MCLEOD LED OLIVER through the main door of Nassau Hall, the eighteenth-century building where the Continental Congress had once met. In the foyer, she showed him the wall with the names of Princeton men who had been killed in the country's wars. As Oliver looked around him, McLeod pointed out that during the Civil War just as many alumni died for the Confederacy as died defending the Union.

"I'm not surprised," said Oliver, who had gone to Ole Miss. "Don't they say Princeton is the most Southern of the Northern universities and the most Northern of the Southern ones?"

The faculty room was stunning with its long rows of benches stretching down each side toward the huge Palladian window that overlooked Cannon Green. Reporters and cameramen were directed toward the left side of the room, while law enforcement officers and various university officials occupied the right side.

McLeod was impressed this time with ruddy-faced John Ives, the Borough chief of police, although he gave out very little new information in the statement that he read to the assembled reporters and television cameramen. He was pleasant, articulate, and literate, all big plusses in her view.

The star of the press conference was Dr. Luther Scott, the medical examiner, who read his statement with some effort. ("Dyslexic," McLeod whispered to Oliver.) The gist of his message was that Robert Matthew Dewey, hereafter known as the deceased, had been a Caucasian male about thirty years of age in good health. Deceased had apparently been dead some time when his body was found, seated at his desk in Room 001 McCosh at Princeton University, on Thursday afternoon. Dead at least twenty-four hours, he said. The cause of death was asphyxiation: "deprivation of oxygen resulting from blockage of the airways into the lungs by garroting, or strangulation, with a woman's rayon scarf held tight around the throat."

Chief Ives then announced that Dr. Scott and Captain Perry, the chief of detectives who was in charge of the investigation, would answer questions.

It would have taken no great physical strength to yank the scarf tight and strangle Mr. Dewey, once the murderer got it around his neck, Dr. Scott said in answer to a question from the press. Yes, that meant that it could conceivably have been done by a woman. The trick would have been to get behind deceased and get the scarf around deceased's neck before deceased knew what was happening.

"Didn't the scarf indicate that the murderer was a woman?" asked one reporter.

"Not necessarily," said bald Nick Perry. "A man could have borrowed it or stolen it from a woman—or simply bought it."

Perry said that they couldn't say for sure but it looked like a premeditated crime. He said they had no suspects at this point. No, they had no plans to call in the State Police;

he thought the Borough Police could handle it. Yes, they were in touch with the prosecutor's office, and yes, they might call on the prosecutor's investigators. Yes, there were fingerprints in Mr. Dewey's office, lots of them. They hoped to identify them all. No, they did not know when Professor Dewey was seen last. They were trying to find out. No, they did not know who the scarf belonged to. They hoped to find out. Perry said he had no idea why no one had gotten worried about Mr. Dewey before Thursday afternoon. They were looking into that. They had already begun questioning Professor Dewey's colleagues in the English Department and would continue. They also planned to question his students and his friends. No, he didn't know whether Professor Dewey was a communist or not. (Chuckles from the more sophisticated reporters.) No, there was no intimation that this was terrorism.

There was a lot of work to be done and he had better get back to work at McCosh, Perry said. Yes, he said, they had set up a temporary field office there, and he had to get back to it. With a quick wave to Chief Ives, he left.

Chief Ives and Dr. Scott continued patiently to answer the repetitive questions that news people threw out. At one point Ives introduced a man from the Mercer County Prosecutor's Office, who stood up and bowed, but said nothing.

Then Chief Ives said he would call on Jim Macy, the university's director of public relations, and the vice president for public affairs. He thought they had something to say.

The vice president said that this was a terrible thing that had happened and he just wanted to make it clear that the university would cooperate with law enforcement officials in every possible way at every level of the investigation until the crime was solved.

The director of public relations said the university would cooperate with the media in every possible way but had nothing to add to what Dr. Scott and Chief Ives had said.

Noise erupted from the media's side of the room. Hands shot up.

"Are parents of students frightened for the safety of their children?" asked one reporter.

The vice president took that one and said smoothly that parents, while always concerned about their children's safety, had not raised an outcry.

"What about the faculty—are they scared?" asked another reporter. "Is the campus safe for anyone?"

Sean O'Malley took that one at a nod from the vice president. "The campus is as safe as we can make it," he said. "We've increased our patrols both day and night. We can't watch every room every minute, but we believe this murder was an isolated incident, not the work of a serial murderer who is going to keep on killing. Don't you agree, Chief?" he asked Ives.

Ives nodded as the questions went on. Why weren't classes canceled that day? Would any classes be canceled?

Princeton just didn't cancel classes, Jim Macy said, swallowing hard. (As a matter of fact, he had argued for canceling classes in a meeting last night, but had been overruled by his superiors, who said, in effect, that idle students were the devil's workshop and they were better off if classes and assignments went on.) Besides, Macy added for the press, there weren't very many classes on Friday anyway.

"Is the university considering hiring private investigators to get to the bottom of this thing?" asked another reporter.

"Not at all," said the vice president smoothly. "We have complete confidence in the Borough Police. And our own Public Safety Department, of course."

The questions went on. When would a memorial service be held? Where could they get some biographical information on the murder victim?

"I have Professor Dewey's biography right here," said Jim Macy. "For any of you who want it." He held up a stack of papers. When Macy passed them around, Oliver and McLeod each took one.

McLeod saw that Bob Dewey was growing in stature since his death. They'll probably grant him tenure post-mortem, she thought.

Who were his friends? the press was asking. Did he have a girl friend? As the questions ranged further afield, McLeod's attention wandered. She read Dewey's bio.

Finally, the press conference was over, and Oliver said he'd be leaving. He'd go back to New York to write his story. "Stay on top of it for us," he said. "I'll be in touch."

McLeod walked over to her office, where, checking her e-mail, she found several messages from students—it seemed that everybody in the class wanted to talk to her. Well, it was Friday night, she told herself. She deserved a break. But she put her campus telephone directory in her book bag—she'd call the students when she got home. I'm sick of this campus, she allowed herself to think.

Thirty-four

❧

AS MCLEOD STARTED home, she wondered if she had anything to eat in the apartment. Should she pick up something at Olive's? It seemed to her that she had a decent meal these days only when she ate out or at the Kingsleys' house. She really ought to cook more. How could she cook, though, when her friends were getting killed right and left?

She went to Olive's to buy some soup to take home, and ran into Stephanie King, well dressed as usual.

"Getting takeout?" asked Stephanie. "So am I."

"We're a pair of lonely old women, aren't we?" said McLeod. "Why don't we forget takeout and go to the Annex? Have a hot meal and sit down."

"That would be wonderful," said Stephanie.

Off to the Annex they went, got a table, and ordered— Stephanie asked for a glass of chianti with her ravioli and McLeod decided to do the same. She looked at Stephanie and decided she was competent enough to run the world.

"This is wonderful," said McLeod. "I'm ashamed that I never cook anymore."

"It's good to take a break."

"And sit down and forget about work," said McLeod.

"It's hard to forget about work," said Stephanie, "if there's been a murder in the office."

"You're right, of course. I wasn't thinking," said McLeod.

"Murder puts the mind on work, so to speak," said Stephanie.

Puzzled, McLeod frowned, then grinned as she realized Stephanie's turn of phrase, "puts the mind on" was simply the opposite of "takes the mind off."

"Speaking of the murder, I liked Bob Dewey," she said. "And he was so young."

"I know," said Stephanie. "I liked him, too. He was brash but he was okay. His parents drove down from Massachusetts today," said Stephanie. "It was horrible. They came to the department. They wanted to see Bob's office, and of course the police had it taped off. Did you know Bob's father went to Princeton? He was class of 1948, I think."

"That's amazing," said McLeod. "I thought Bob came from a proletariat background, since he was a labor organizer and a Marxist."

"No, his father is the CEO of a factory in Lowell," said Stephanie.

"Where are his parents staying?" asked McLeod.

"The Nassau Inn," said Stephanie. "Cliff and the president went over to call on them today. I tell you, it's just ghastly."

McLeod murmured sympathetically as the waitress brought their food.

"I can't figure out why anybody would kill Bob Dewey," said Stephanie, "unless a madman is loose in McCosh. And I don't like to even consider that possibility."

"It doesn't seem very likely," said McLeod.

"I don't like to think about the murder at all," said Stephanie. "Except I can't think about anything else."

"What line do the police seem to be taking?" asked McLeod.

"Today they were talking to nearly everybody in the department," said Stephanie. "As far as I know, they asked the usual questions: Did he have any enemies? Was anybody mad at him? But again, as far as I know, nobody told them anything helpful. How could they? And I don't know of any enemies he had."

"Unlike Dexter Kinkaid," said McLeod.

Stephanie looked at her sharply. "What do you mean?"

"Mystique Alcott got livid when she talked about Dexter. And Bob Dewey did, too, before he died. Dexter seems to have had the reputation for being a cold, rigid tightwad."

"That's one way to put it," said Stephanie. "He didn't gush, and he didn't waste departmental funds."

"But then you hear about his 'integrity,' " said McLeod. "His exemplary scholarship. His administrative skills."

"He was a good administrator. He never let things slide," said Stephanie. "We've had chairmen—I mean chairs—I don't want Gertrude Sergeant to hear me say chairmen—anyway, we've had chairs who didn't return phone calls, didn't answer mail, didn't do the basic work. But Dexter was efficient. He did his job. Of course, running things properly is always going to make some people mad," said Stephanie.

"Like who?" asked McLeod, her curiosity churning.

"Oh, where to start?" said Stephanie. "You know, like the Dewey tenure thing. Dexter made a point of telling Bob early that he wasn't going to get tenure. He told him early so Bob could begin to look for another job in earnest. I don't think Bob appreciated that."

He sure didn't, thought McLeod.

"And last year a graduate student wrote a dissertation for Archie on an astrological interpretation of *Romeo and Juliet* and Dexter just happened to see it," Stephanie went on. "Dexter wasn't even on the committee—but he said it was preposterous. Well, Archie thought the dissertation was odd, but okay. He said it was 'quirky.' Anyway, Dexter never wavered. He held his standards. That thesis wasn't acceptable and the guy never got his Ph.D."

"Who was he?" asked McLeod, thinking here was a man with grounds for murder if there ever was one. "Is he still around?"

"No, he went to Wall Street and he's already made a fortune," said Stephanie. She was drinking her second glass of chianti. "And Dexter never compromised his standards, not even for poor old Liz Finley, who's been his adoring sycophant all these years. He didn't think her new book was good enough, and he kept the Princeton University Press from publishing it."

"I heard about that," said McLeod. "I found it hard to believe."

"He dictated the letter to me," said Stephanie. "I'm telling you he was a stickler for what's right."

"His rock-like integrity?" mused McLeod, with some irony.

"Yes, Dexter was famous for it," said Stephanie innocently. "Everybody knew they could trust him."

"And I guess they should, because he didn't let a relationship stand in his way, did he?" said McLeod. "I heard he and Liz were lovers. They were, weren't they?"

"Oh, they were," said Stephanie. "Liz Finley really loved him, for sure. But that affair has been over for some time."

McLeod thought it odd that adultery did not diminish Dexter's "rock-like integrity" as far as Stephanie was concerned. "I should think Liz Finley would have wanted to murder him." She watched Stephanie as she said this.

"Not Liz," said Stephanie, and then stopped. She carefully buttered a slice of Italian bread. "She adored him. Even after he told her what he had done at the Press."

"He told her?" McLeod was incredulous.

"That was Dexter. He did what he thought was right and took the consequences."

McLeod was appalled but said nothing else.

The waitress took their plates, and they both ordered coffee.

"What about Gertrude Sergeant?" asked McLeod. "Did she get along with Dexter?"

"He tried to help her," said Stephanie. "He advised her over and over not to be such a militant feminist."

"That's like telling the wind to stop blowing, isn't it?" said McLeod.

Stephanie laughed. "I guess so," she said. "He put her on lots of committees because he thought that might keep her busy and make her stop agitating for all these new courses she wanted to teach."

"New courses?" asked McLeod.

"Dexter kept her from teaching two courses she really wanted to add—one on the suppression of American women novelists like Kate Chopin and another on the infantilization of women in the English domestic novel. He said there just wasn't a basis for her thesis in either case."

"Did that make her mad?" asked McLeod.

"She was furious," said Stephanie. "She went to the dean, but it didn't do any good. That was just last spring."

Stephanie might not think Dexter had any enemies, but it seemed to McLeod that he had had plenty. I'm surprised he lived as long as he did, she thought.

Thirty-five

❧

WHEN SHE GOT home, McLeod picked up that morning's Trenton *Times* to read the comics, which she had skipped earlier. She turned, as she always did, to the next page to read Dr. Peter H. Gott's column, called "Family Doctor."

After she read it, she knew how Archie and Dexter were killed.

Over the course of the year, Dr. Gott gave advice in his column about everything from prostate cancer to postpartum depression, answered questions about whether cooking in aluminum pots caused Alzheimer's or cooking with wine could make an alcoholic take up drinking again. McLeod had read him on high blood pressure, weight reduction diets (he said he personally kept his weight down by never eating sugar or flour), and rare diseases like scleroderma. Today he was warning about the dangers of taking too much acetaminophen, or Tylenol. It could cause liver damage, he wrote. Ten grams would kill you, he said, and a smaller dose than that was fatal if taken with alcohol.

McLeod went into the bedroom, sat down on the bed, and called her friend Phyllis Meriwether in Tallahassee. Phil was her doctor, a beautiful woman, who also knew everything there was to know about medicine, cooking, and fishing.

By a miracle, she caught Phil at home and asked her if it was possible to murder someone with Tylenol.

"Of course, it is," said Phil. "I've always thought it was the perfect way to do a murder. All you'd have to do is take about a handful of those caplets and empty them into a glass. Dissolve the powder in a nice strong cocktail, feed it to somebody you don't like, and he's dead."

"Immediately?" asked McLeod

"No, that's the beauty of it," said Phil. "You feed it to them. They drink it and they get sick—they get diarrhea—they get weak—and they die. Tests don't reveal what caused it, unless the doctor knows what to look for when the victim first gets sick. What's going on? How's your health? Did somebody feed you Tylenol?"

"No, no, I'm fine," said McLeod. "It's just that two people up here have died from mysterious liver ailments . . ."

"And you're curious!" said Phil. "I know you. I'll send you the literature. I can fax it to you. Do they have anything as modern as fax machines in Princeton? I always think they must still be using quill pens. Didn't Madison go to Princeton? He used a quill pen to write his share of the Federalist papers, you know."

"I do have a fax," said McLeod. "I'll be very grateful. What's happening at home?"

"Not much," said Phil. "Charlie Campbell came to see me with boils on his neck. That means he can't go out in the sun; he can't fish until they get well. Poor Charlie. And the redfish are biting like crazy off Dog Island."

Charlie was McLeod's boss, the editor and publisher of the *Star of Florida*, and he was as big a fisherman as Phil was. "Poor Charlie," she said, "I'll send him a get well card. Or a sympathy card for not being able to go fishing. What else is happening?"

"It's still warm down here," said Phil. "But the hay fever season seems to be over." She added that Prudence Campbell, Charlie's wife, had at last revealed her aunt's recipe for bouillabaisse. "I tried it. It took eight hours to make, but it sure was good. Prudence said she only cooked it once—down at the coast last summer when that old man got killed. Said she'd never cook it again."

"She doesn't cook much of anything anyway," said McLeod. "Phil, I won't keep you. Thanks a million. You always know everything and it's wonderful. Thanks."

MCLEOD E-MAILED LYLE. "I know how Archie and Dexter were killed," she wrote. She keyboarded the brief item from Dr. Gott's column and told him what Phyllis Meriwether had said.

"You rock!" Lyle replied tersely. "You cracked it."

"Not at all. We know HOW—Tylenol in those drinks— but we don't know WHO."

The exchange continued. McLeod got ready for bed, but checked the laptop every few minutes.

"Project members should meet tonight or tomorrow," Lyle wrote.

"Not tonight. I know students stay up till two o'clock in the morning, but I don't. Tomorrow is okay. Why don't all of you come here for brunch tomorrow. Noon."

"Great! I'll let the others know."

McLeod turned off her computer and went to bed with a Trollope novel, but let it slide from her hand while she thought. Something was bothering her; something she'd forgotten was clawing gently at her consciousness, something important. She had to remember . . .

Thirty-six

❧

ON SATURDAY MORNING, McLeod rushed around,
cleaned up the apartment, and went to the grocery store for
bacon, sausage, eggs, and other staples. She mixed waffle
batter, cooked the sausage and bacon, poured the orange
juice, made coffee, and waited. Then she reminded herself
that students were never on time except for class, and
reread the day's newspapers.

Everybody arrived at once, having come in Ben's car.
McLeod looked at them as they came in and thought what
a good-looking bunch of students they were. Ben True,
looking scrubbed and blond and a little older than the
rest, brought a bottle of wine. Lyle, skinny, with his
glasses smeared, carried a bunch of chrysanthemums.
Daisy Wood, red hair standing on end, stud still in her
lip, and Tina Martinez, black hair pulled back in a pony-
tail, presented her jointly with a box of chocolates.
Marcy, green eyes sparkling, had a bag of shelled pecans.
"My father shells them and sends them to me," she ex-

plained. "If I eat any more, I won't be able to get into my clothes."

"Nuts are good for you," said McLeod. "Everybody, even Dr. Gott, says so."

"And praise be to Dr. Gott," said Lyle.

"Who is Dr. Gott?" asked Daisy.

"You explain, Lyle," said McLeod, "and I'll make waffles."

It took forever to get everybody fed, and at one point McLeod wished she had borrowed a waffle iron from Ginger so she could cook on two at once. But eventually everyone did get enough to eat, and they were all so delighted with her homemade waffles that McLeod decided they were worth the trouble.

Meanwhile, Lyle told them about Dr. Gott. They all looked at his Friday column, and McLeod passed around the fax about acetaminophen poisoning that Phyllis Meriwether had sent.

" 'Clinical manifestations are nonspecific,' " Tina read out loud. " 'Symptoms are lethargy, pallor, nausea, vomiting, and diaphoresis . . .' "

"What's diaphoresis?" asked Marcy.

"Sweating," said Ben.

" 'There are no acid-base derangements like those which may accompany aspirin overdoses,' " Tina continued. " 'So the bloodwork will come back normal or close to normal at the outset. Hepatic—'."

"That's liver," said Ben.

" 'Hepatic damage,' " Tina went on, " 'the most important manifestation of acetaminophen toxicity, becomes evident one to two days after ingestion. While some patients show only elevation of serum transaminase'—somebody's penciled in 'a liver enzyme' here—'and others show tender hepatomegaly'—another note, 'liver enlargement'—and jaundice.' "

Tina read on and they learned that severe damage could

include hyperammonemia, asterixis, coma, bleeding, and death from acute liver failure.

"It all matches Archie Alexander's symptoms," McLeod said. "And I think Dexter Kinkaid was exactly the same way. I didn't know him as well, but from what I hear, his symptoms were the same."

That clinched it, they all agreed, as far as the murder method was concerned. "And acetaminophen is so easy to get hold of," said Lyle. "Everybody's got some Tylenol in the medicine cabinet."

"Everybody has Tylenol, and mixing a drink for some-body at a party is not too hard," said Tina. "But could somebody have put all that Tylenol in that drink without being noticed?"

"That's a good point," said Ben, causing Tina to smile blissfully. She looked, thought McLeod, as though she heard angels singing.

"If everybody was focusing on Kinkaid, the murderer could have acted swiftly," said Lyle. "He would have had the powder ready, dumped it in, and stirred it. Couldn't he?"

"Let's try it and find out how long it takes to dissolve in cranberry juice."

McLeod was able, miraculously, to produce a can of cranberry juice from her cupboard. She had bought two be-fore the Halloween brunch.

It took the powder forever to disappear. They agreed the murderer must have carried it already dissolved in a small vial, a medicine bottle maybe, and then put it in the drinks.

"That's *how*, but we still don't know *who*," Lyle said, quoting McLeod's e-mail.

"We have more suspects, more motives," said McLeod. "I had supper last night with Stephanie West, the adminis-trator who runs the English Department. She told me Kinkaid stopped Gertrude Sergeant from teaching some courses she wanted to offer—one was on the infantiliza-tion of women in English literature."

"What a great course!" said Daisy Wood.

"And there's another thing that bothers me," McLeod went on. "Can we be sure Bob Dewey's murder is a result of the two other murders?"

"He worked as a union organizer in Detroit," said Lyle. "Do you think one of the big automobile companies came and killed him?"

"He grew up in Lowell—that's a mill town—and he got into Harvard," said Ben. "His blue-collar background must have made him do the union work. Even when he went back to graduate school, he was a Marxist critic, still trying to be loyal to the proletariat."

"I'm sorry to disillusion you," said McLeod, "but he didn't spring from the working classes. His father is Michael Dewey, Princeton Class of 1948, and he's the CEO at a big factory in Lowell. This makes me curious about Dewey. People are never just the cardboard figures they seem. Was he really murdered to keep him from telling who mixed that cosmopolitan? Or was there some other reason? I'm curious, I tell you."

The students dismissed it. Nothing was ever tidy and neat, they said. There were always odd things about people. The thing they had to do was to sit down and figure out who had mixed the cosmopolitan that Dewey brought over to Kinkaid.

Lyle made a list of their suspects on a legal pad that McLeod brought from her study.

"Write down Mrs. Kinkaid," Ben said, "because the wife is always a suspect."

"And we have Mystique Alcott—a suspect if there ever was one—she could easily have done the drink at her house," said Lyle, writing busily.

"Elizabeth Finley, onetime lover of Dexter Kinkaid, but then betrayed," said Daisy dramatically.

"I feel sorry for her," said Marcy.

"But she has a motive—her book," said Lyle, adding her name.

"Gertrude Sergeant, the ardent feminist who didn't get to teach a course she wanted to," said Ben.

"That's not much of a motive," scoffed Daisy.

"But she's got muscles," said Tina, supporting Ben.

"And Grady Schuyler, the Queer Theorist," said McLeod. "Though he seems so insouciant, I can't believe he'd kill somebody because of a bad job recommendation."

Lyle wrote Schuyler's name down, and said, "What about Cliff and Ginger Kingsley?" he asked. "They were at both parties."

"They're both so sweet," said McLeod. "More important, they don't have a motive."

"All these people had the opportunity, in the sense that they were at both parties," said Lyle. "Surely somebody saw something suspicious. Daisy, did you ask Mrs. Kinkaid if she saw who mixed the drink that Kinkaid drank?" asked Lyle.

"How could I?" said Daisy. "She left."

"I asked Mystique Alcott and she said she didn't see who did it and she had no idea who had made the cosmopolitan at her house. She was outraged," said Ben True. "Why does everybody get so mad when you suggest Dexter was murdered?"

"They feel threatened," said McLeod.

"Tina, what about Elizabeth Finley? Did you ask her?" Lyle inquired.

"She didn't say she saw who did it, but she said it must have been Mrs. Kinkaid," said Tina.

"Awesome," said Lyle.

"I didn't ask Grady Schuyler," Ben said. "Actually, nobody went to him for the second round of questions. He might have seen something."

"Sergeant said Bob Dewey fixed the one at McLeod's house and she thought he had a good motive for murder," said Lyle. "The trouble is that Bob Dewey may have had a good motive for killing Kinkaid, but he's been killed himself." He was gloomily silent and then went on. "The fact remains that we haven't asked Mrs. Kinkaid or Elizabeth Finley or Grady Schuyler."

"It's hard to believe we left out such a crucial question," said McLeod. "I did ask the Kingsleys and they both swore they didn't notice. Ginger was in the bathroom and Cliff, of course, was in the kitchen checking out the food I was cooking."

"Cliff Kingsley has been named chair of the department," said Lyle. "Maybe he killed Kinkaid so he could be chair. Isn't ambition a prime motive for murder, like sex and money?"

"Nobody could be less ambitious than Cliff Kingsley," said McLeod. "And nobody was more surprised than Cliff when he was named chair. I don't think he even likes being chair. I mean, even if there weren't all the hullabaloo about the murder. Cliff likes to read and cook and teach a little—that's about it."

"I talked to both the Kingsleys, remember," said Tina. "And I think we can eliminate them."

"Of course these people that told us they didn't see anybody mix a cosmopolitan might well be lying," said Lyle.

"Think about it," said Daisy. "Mrs. Kinkaid said it was Finley who mixed the drink and Finley says it was Mrs. Kinkaid. *Nobody* is telling the truth."

They all agreed Liz Finley was a great suspect because of the rejection of her book.

"Actually, you know, it was probably a sexist thing anyway," said Daisy. "Kinkaid was probably jealous of her work."

"Would he have been jealous of the work of a woman he'd once had an affair with?" asked Ben.

"Of course, he would have been," said Daisy." Even more. Husbands are jealous of their *wives'* work, for heaven's sake. Kinkaid could maybe stand all those other, earlier books, because they were dull old scholarly things.

But this one, wasn't it supposed to be a breakthrough or something?"

But then there was Mystique Alcott. And Professor Kinkaid's wife. And to some extent Gertrude Sergeant. And the Kingsleys.

"We need to talk to Mrs. Kinkaid and Schuyler, and we need to ask Finley to be more specific," said Lyle. "That's three possible eyewitnesses. Should we go back to Sergeant?"

"Wait a minute," said McLeod. "I think you'd better stop right here. No more interviews. What if our questions drove the murderer to act against Bob Dewey? Who knows what might happen next?"

They all protested mightily, but McLeod was adamant.

"We can all use our heads and think about it, at least," said Lyle.

"I think we ought to go to the police," said McLeod.

"You mean you're going to go talk to them?" asked Lyle.

"Let's all go," said McLeod. "In a group. Now."

"Now?" They were clearly startled.

"Now," she said. "Let's go. I ought to check up for the *Times* anyway. I'm being a very poor stringer."

They pulled on their coats and divided up, half in Ben's car, half in McLeod's, and drove to Borough Hall.

Thirty-seven

❧

THE UNIFORMED OFFICER behind the window at Borough Hall must have recognized McLeod from the press conference. Before she could say a word, he told her there were no developments and handed her a press release: The Borough Police "were working twenty-four hours a day on the case and would not stop until they had apprehended the murderer."

"What line is the investigation taking?" she asked.

"We're not releasing any details," said the officer.

"Do they expect an arrest soon?" asked McLeod.

"We're not talking about it," he said.

"Do they think it was an inside job?" asked McLeod.

"We're not talking about it," he said.

McLeod gave up and thanked him.

"We'd like to see Captain Perry," she said.

"What did you want to see Captain Perry about?" asked the officer.

"We have information for him about the murder at the university," McLeod said.

"Captain Perry is really very busy. Can you talk to someone else?"

"No," said McLeod. "I think not."

"Tell me what kind of information you have," said the officer.

"It sounds too crazy and it's too complicated," said McLeod.

Lyle interceded. "Ms. Dulaney is a member of the faculty at the university," he said. "We're her students. We're not cranks."

"Just a minute," said the officer, and left. In Princeton, a teacher at the university was to be treated with respect.

While they waited, McLeod turned to three people, obviously journalists, who were sitting in the anteroom and introduced herself. "I'm stringing for the *New York Times*," she said. "Are you with the local papers?"

They were with the Trenton *Times*, the *Princeton Packet*, a twice-a-week local paper, and the *Newark Star-Ledger*. McLeod asked them what they thought was going on and they said they had no idea. "No press conference today," said one. "Not a crumb."

"I don't know why I'm sitting down here," said the man from the *Star-Ledger*. "They're not going to tell us anything. I guess I'm sticking around just because if I go home I'll have to rake leaves."

"Can't you see who comes in for interviewing?" asked McLeod.

"They bring them in the back door," said the *Packet* reporter. "And they won't let us back there where the cars park. I think they're still interviewing people at McCosh, but the university people can slip in and out without our being able to tell if they're being interviewed or not."

McLeod offered them her sympathy and said she was sure she'd see them again. "They'll break this case someday," she said. Or we will, she thought.

When the officer came back, Captain Perry was with him. "You wanted to see me?" he said. "Let's go in here."

He opened the door of a small room with a table and several chairs.

"An interrogation room! Wow!" said Lyle.

Perry smiled. "Sit down," he said. "What's this all about?"

"It's about the murder of Bob Dewey," said McLeod.

"What about it?" asked Perry.

"We think we should tell you that we're sure Bob Dewey knew too much about two murders that had already been committed," McLeod said.

Perry stared at her and, without diverting his gaze, got up and went to the door. Then he had to look away as he called out to the officer on duty, "Ask Phil to come in— and bring his machine."

Perry sat down again and said, "I hope you don't mind if I record this talk. I want to be sure I have your names and addresses straight, and I want to have a record of what you say. Ah, Phil, is there room for you in here? Ladies and gentlemen, this is Officer Phil Vaccarella. And he has a tape recorder. I want each of you to tell Phil your name and telephone number, and your campus address. Go ahead." He nodded at McLeod.

"I'm McLeod Dulaney," she said, spelling each of her names in turn, and then giving her address and phone number.

"And you are a professor?" asked Perry.

"I'm a visiting professor," said McLeod. "I'm a journalist by trade and I'm teaching the nonfiction writing course this semester. These are some of my students."

"I'm Lyle Cramer. I live in Spelman Hall." He gave his phone number, and the other students followed him.

"Now what is it you have to tell me?" said Perry.

McLeod looked at the others and they all nodded at her. She began. "We believe that two members of the English Department were murdered this fall, one by accident, one on purpose," she said. "We think Bob Dewey was killed because he knew who committed the murders . . ." and she began the story that she had told so often, from Mystique's party to Archie's death, her own brunch, and Dexter's death.

"My class got interested in these deaths. One of the students in particular was sure they were murders. I was intrigued. The students wanted to emulate the Northwestern class that investigated a crime and got a man off death row. So we began asking questions."

McLeod faltered. "As I tell you this, I feel that we may have been to blame for Bob's death. If we hadn't been asking questions, the murderer might not have gotten scared and killed Bob." She paused; the room was silent. "But you *have* to ask questions—about everything, and especially about murder, don't you?"

Perry was not smiling now. "It's always dangerous for civilians to investigate crimes," he said sternly. "I can't believe a responsible citizen, a teacher at Princeton University, would undertake an investigation—"

Lyle interrupted. "Look, Captain," he said. "As far as the police were concerned, as far as *anybody* was concerned, there were no crimes. Nobody believed us."

"I called the prosecutor's office and they said they had no plans to investigate the first deaths," said McLeod. "No one thought it was murder. My own friends thought I was nuts. The students, however, are bright and have open minds, and they, especially Lyle, leaped at it."

"What did you do and how did you do it?" asked Perry.

"I think we began in an amateurish way," said Lyle. "Each of us went to see one of the suspects, as we called them, and asked questions about their relationship to Dexter Kinkaid. We thought the real objective of the murderer was to kill Kinkaid, not Archie Alexander."

"You should have come to us," said Perry sternly.

"I wonder how much attention you would have paid to us before Bob Dewey was killed," said McLeod.

"Why didn't you tell us this Thursday night?" Perry asked McLeod.

"I honestly don't know," she said. "I wondered about that myself yesterday. Anyway, here we are now."

"Let's go over this again," said Perry. "You saw this cosmopolitan sitting on the bar at this party. Whose house was it?"

McLeod again went through the story of the cosmopolitans, Archie's death, her brunch, and Dexter's death.

"All right, let's get the names of everybody who was at this brunch," said Perry. "They were all at the first party, right?"

When McLeod and the project members had identified the people and spelled the names, Perry said, "We talked to Elizabeth Finley, Cliff Kingsley, Grady Schuyler, and Gertrude Sergeant, because they're in the English Department. We have not talked to Margie Kinkaid, Mystique Alcott, or Mrs. Kingsley. We'll take it from here, Ms. Dulaney."

"But you didn't ask Finley, Kingsley, Schuyler, and Sergeant about the deaths of Archie Alexander and Dexter Kinkaid," McLeod said. "You just asked them about Bob Dewey. You have to ask everybody about the first two deaths."

"The investigation is following several lines of inquiry," Perry said.

"Thank you," McLeod said with as much dignity as she could muster. The six of them filed out.

Outside, they stood in front of Borough Hall, undecided.

"Do you think they'll do anything about what we told them?" Lyle asked. "Really?"

"I think he'll do just what he said he'd do," said McLeod. "He'll get the autopsy reports, and maybe no more. But I do feel better now that we've told the police what we know. If we do know anything. When I tell somebody about this, it seems to evaporate right before my eyes."

"What do we do now?" asked Lyle.

"Drop it," said McLeod. "Leave it to the professionals."

"Oh, come on," said Lyle.

"We shouldn't be muddying the water," McLeod said. "And besides, it may not be safe to ask any more questions."

They stood around the Borough Hall parking lot. It was getting dark and the world seemed very gloomy to McLeod. The students apparently felt the same, for they looked at each other silently.

"Look, everybody come over to my place," said Ben. "We need to talk this over. Even if we don't do any more work on the project"—here he shot a look at McLeod—"we need to get closure. You too, McLeod. We can order in a pizza and talk it out."

"I can't come," said McLeod. "I have to go to Gertrude Sergeant's for dinner."

"Will you be safe?" Lyle asked her. "Shouldn't we come along?"

"There will be other guests, I'm sure," McLeod said. "And I'll be very careful."

"How about the rest of you?" Ben asked.

Everyone else agreed, and Ben appealed to McLeod again. "Can't you come by for a little while after dinner? You can have some coffee with us."

"Sure," said McLeod. "I don't think this dinner will last long."

She got directions to Ben's apartment on Park Place, a one-block-long street just off Nassau Street. "You can park in that metered lot across the street from my place," Ben said.

Driving home, McLeod wondered what other lines Perry could take on Bob Dewey's murder. What on earth could he have been talking about?

Thirty-eight

✿

MCLEOD WEARILY DRESSED for dinner at Gertrude Sergeant's in black velvet pants—she wore pants in Princeton a lot more than she had in Tallahassee—with a sweater, and drove to Sergeant's house on Markham Road.

She parked on the street, in front of Trudy's arts and crafts–era house. Walking toward the door, she noticed Sergeant's car in the driveway. She stared at it. It had a long, deep scratch on the left front fender.

She rang the doorbell and was astonished at the interior of Sergeant's house. She had been there only once before for a cocktail party when the house had been so crowded she had scarcely noticed the huge modern paintings, bold shapes in brilliant colors, that hung on the walls. Tonight McLeod stared in amazement.

"I'm stunned by the paintings," she said to Trudy Sergeant.

Trudy smiled. "I know," she said. "Nobody expects it in this bungalow. They belonged to my mother. She was a psychiatrist, and she collected modern art. After she died, my brother and I split her collection. He took the men and I got the women. That means he has Jackson Pollock, but I have Georgia O'Keeffe and Helen Frankenthaler."

"I see you do," McLeod said. "You made the right choice, I think."

"I made the *only* choice," Sergeant said. She took Mcleod's coat and the doorbell rang. "I'm just having four people," she said. "I'm not as brave as you are."

To McLeod's delight, the other two guests turned out to be the Kingsleys. Cliff offered to tend bar, and Sergeant refused, saying she didn't want to go along with the stereotypes of gender roles.

"Well, do you want me to cook?" asked Cliff.

"Oh, if only I had the nerve to accept that offer," Sergeant said. "I'm not a cook. Not like you, McLeod, and certainly not like Cliff."

"Cliff's in a class by himself," McLeod said.

"Let me make some drinks and then I'll finish up in the kitchen. What will you have?"

The Kingsleys asked for martinis, and McLeod reverted to her club soda persona. Trudy Sergeant vanished into the kitchen.

Ginger, who was wearing a caftan with big flowers on it, twirled around. "I know I look like Mystique in this," she said, "but it is so comfortable."

"I agree," said McLeod. "Caftans are much more comfortable than pants. Nothing around the waist."

"But you look so skinny in those pants, McLeod," said Ginger. "I don't see how you do it."

"You mean how do I eat so much and not get as fat as Mystique?"

"Or me," said Ginger gloomily.

"You're not nearly as fat as Mystique," McLeod reassured her.

"Maybe not quite," said Ginger, but she looked more cheerful.

"What's going on in the English Department, Cliff?" asked McLeod, to change the subject.

"I had to go into the office this morning," Cliff said. "Bob Dewey's parents are here. That was one of the unpleasant things I had to do today. The president went, too. I must say they're very nice. But what a visit!"

"Was Bob an only child?" asked McLeod.

"No," said Cliff. "He had at least one brother—he was supposed to get here today." He sipped his martini and then continued, "The police are still ensconced in McCosh. They're using Dexter's office."

"How are the police getting along?" asked McLeod.

"Let's see, Thursday night they talked to me and Stephanie," said Cliff. "Yesterday they interviewed the rest of the secretarial staff and began on the faculty. Today I think they finished interviewing the English faculty and started on Bob's students."

"How on earth did they do that?" asked McLeod.

"They got the Registrar to open up this morning and give them the list of students in his classes," said Cliff. "Then they got the addresses and telephone numbers of the students and called them in. They were lined up in the entryway when I left."

"Do you have any idea what the police have learned?" asked McLeod.

"Not really," said Cliff.

"Do they seem encouraged? Do they have any idea who the murderer is?" asked McLeod.

"They don't confide in me," said Cliff.

"You know, McLeod," said Ginger, "you have a lot of curiosity, and I can see where that's great for a reporter. And you're teaching your students to be curious, too. That's wonderful, in a way. You're doing such a good job with your class that I hate to say anything, but to be honest, I think you're encouraging them to be *too* curious. I'm getting complaints about your students and their 'project,' as they call it."

"Oh, Ginger, I'm sorry," said McLeod.

"They're not really formal complaints, but I saw poor Margie Kinkaid at one point and she said she did wonder what was going on. Liz Finley said something, too. And Mystique Alcott didn't complain to me, but she called the chair of the Humanities Council."

"Oh, dear," said McLeod. "Oh, dear. And he called you?"

The chair of the Council of the Humanities was a world-famous scholar with a towering reputation in his field, who seldom communicated with the people under him—or with anyone else at all, except the obligatory class of undergraduates that he had to teach from time to time in order to remain on Princeton's payroll. Most of the time he was on leave. Ginger, as executive director, did all the work, but clearly held the chairman in awe. He must be the only person on earth who awed her, McLeod thought, feeling guilty.

"I told the chairman that it was an investigative journalism project that some members of the class had taken on—quite voluntarily—but I told him I'd speak to you about it."

"I'm sorry, Ginger, I really am. I've actually told them to stop," she said. "This afternoon."

"Good," said Ginger.

"It's all very well for a class to do an investigative project," said Cliff, "as long as they don't investigate anybody on the faculty. If they were out interviewing ex-cons about some criminal case from several years ago in the slums of New York, it would be okay. But if they're investigating a situation here on campus, it's going to cause Holy Hell."

Trudy came in and announced that dinner was ready, and they went into the dining room, where the walls also held big splashy paintings. The table was set with very modern china, and the soup bowls steamed. It was a winter squash soup, and when McLeod complimented it, Sergeant smiled.

"I have to confess," she said. "It came from Nassau Street Seafood. In fact, the whole dinner did. I simply cannot cook."

Both Ginger and McLeod assured Trudy that food from Nassau Street Seafood was fine, while Cliff sadly shook his head.

"Did I hear you talking about the murder while I was putting the soup on the table?" Trudy asked when they had all sat down.

"Cliff was just saying that he didn't know what the police were up to," McLeod said.

"How's your class's Murder Project going?" Sergeant asked McLeod.

"I was just telling Ginger that I told them to stop it," McLeod said. "We told the police everything we found out. I'm seeing them all on my way home tonight—I've been invited to join them at Ben True's apartment—and I'll emphasize again that they must drop it."

"It's probably just as well," said Sergeant. "I was intrigued that students were taking the initiative. That impressed me. I like to see students—especially women—with initiative. Daisy Wood was involved and she's one of my favorites. But as I warned Daisy, asking questions about murder could be dangerous."

She got up to take away the soup plates. Cliff rose to help and the two of them brought in plates with the main course: sole stuffed with crabmeat and creamed spinach, all from Nassau Street Seafood.

"Did you and the students find out anything substantial?" Sergeant asked when she sat back down.

"We think we know how the murder was done," McLeod said.

"It was strangulation," said Sergeant.

"Bob Dewey was strangled, that's right," said McLeod. "But you know, we thought Dexter Kinkaid and Archie Alexander were murdered, too. You told Lyle that Bob Dewey made that cosmopolitan for Professor Kinkaid at my house. But it doesn't make sense—since he got killed himself. We're sure the same person killed all three men. Are you sure you saw Bob Dewey make that second drink?"

Sergeant was quiet for a minute. "I thought I did, but if your theory's right, I was wrong, wasn't I?"

"I guess so," said McLeod. "Incidentally, is it true that Dexter wouldn't let you teach a course on the infantilization of women in English literature? It sounds like a hot course to me."

"It was annoying," said Trudy Sergeant, "but let me make it clear that I didn't get mad enough to kill anybody. I'm writing a book about the subject and the Yale University Press is very interested. Teaching a course on it would have been fun, but it wasn't a matter of life and death. And hey, maybe now I can teach it after all. What do you think, Cliff?"

"Trudy, it's okay by me, if you can get it through the curriculum committee," said Cliff. "I'm easy."

"Not only did I not kill Dexter Kinkaid, but I didn't kill Bob Dewey. And I bet you no woman did. Men are responsible for the violence of this world. You can be sure of that."

"I certainly wasn't accusing you of killing anybody," said McLeod. "I'm just always curious and I always ask too many questions. I hope the book goes well, and I hope you get to teach the course. But I have one other question. How did you get that big scratch on your left front fender?"

Sergeant looked at her, apparently puzzled. "Why do you ask?"

"I'm always getting dings on my car, and I just wondered about yours," McLeod said.

"I got it in the parking lot at Wild Oats. I went over to Nassau Street Seafood, and when I came back, the scratch was there."

McLeod did not believe her.

Thirty-nine

❦

THE KINGSLEYS AND McLeod left Sergeant's house fairly early. McLeod wondered if dinner parties tended to be shorter if the food was takeout, even upscale takeout. There was just less to talk about.

She drove to Park Place and found the old frame house where Ben's apartment was located. She buzzed him and he came down to let her in.

"I'm on the third floor. Follow me," he said, leading the way up the steep, dark stairs.

His apartment was typical of graduate student housing: beat-up old sofa, two worn upholstered chairs, a threadbare rug on the living room floor. Ben took her coat and showed her his bedroom and study. McLeod was impressed with the neatness of it all. Ben was truly disciplined.

The living room was somewhat cluttered, but only because Lyle, Daisy, Marcy, and Tina were all sprawled about. Nobody had eaten supper.

"When we finally got around to ordering pizza, Papa John's was backed up with orders," Ben said. "That was hours ago. It should be here any minute."

"We've eaten a ton of potato chips and pretzels," said Tina.

"Some of us have had some beer and some of us have had some root beer, and some of us have had both," said Lyle.

"I promised you coffee," said Ben. "Would you like some?"

"If you haven't eaten, nobody wants coffee," said McLeod. "And I had some at Trudy Sergeant's. No, thanks, Ben."

"Listen, McLeod, we want to go on with the project," Lyle said.

"No, no, no," said McLeod. "It's over. The police are investigating. It's not safe."

"We've been talking," said Lyle, "and we decided one thing we could do is make a systematic survey of everybody who has an office in the basement of McCosh and ask them who they saw on that Wednesday afternoon. Then we'd have a list of possibilities and we could maybe begin to eliminate them."

"No," said McLeod. "No. Don't do anything. Leave it to the police. Somebody is bound to be annoyed by your questions and call Ginger or the chairman of the Humanities Council. I could lose my job. Or at least be in terrible disgrace."

They looked at her, surprised.

"We can still talk about it," McLeod said. "Just don't do anything else."

"You know what you need?" said Ben. "I actually have some brandy. My grandfather bought it for me when I moved into my own apartment. He said every bachelor should keep brandy on hand in case a young lady fainted in his house. I've never had occasion to use it, but I think this is a good time to break it out. It's supposed to be good stuff. Let me get you a glass."

"Thanks," she said.

Marcy slipped off the sofa onto the floor to give McLeod a seat, which she accepted gratefully. Ben showed her the bottle—it was Armangac—and she nodded. She never drank after dinner, but it somehow seemed like a good idea tonight. She sipped the brandy, and it was like swallowing a burning coal. It wasn't destructive, it was stomach-warming, heart-warming, and wonderful.

They all talked about the murder. Everybody had a favorite suspect, but the students seemed able to switch favorites from minute to minute.

"I really think," said Lyle, "we ought to talk to those people in McCosh basement."

"No," said McLeod.

Just then the buzzer sounded.

"Pizza!" everyone shouted.

"I'll go get it," said Ben. He patted the hip pocket in his jeans to make sure he had his billfold, and opened the door.

"I'll come down with you," said McLeod. "The brandy was wonderful and I've enjoyed talking to you all, but I've got to go home. This is very late for me." It was one o'clock in the morning.

She followed Ben down the dark stairs, holding on to the heavy banister for safety's sake. After they left the second floor, as they went down toward the first floor, McLeod could smell smoke. Ben was rushing to the front door. He opened it and took the big white boxes.

"Hey, man," said the delivery boy. "You got a fire there."

Ben looked behind him. He and McLeod, who was not all the way down the stairs, could see the fire. Under the row of mailboxes set in the wall of the little vestibule, a cardboard carton with newspapers and kindling in it was on fire. So that was the smoke she had smelled, McLeod thought, stunned. The burning box sat right against the old wood wall, and as McLeod stared at it, the flames took hold and leapt higher. Ben pushed past her on his way back upstairs.

"The others!" he said.

"Call 911," McLeod said, turning to follow him up the stairs.

"Get out!" Ben cried as he reached his door. "Go! There's a fire."

He picked up the phone and called 911, while McLeod waved Tina, Daisy, Marcy, and finally, Lyle out the door and down the stairs. Ben went into his office, and McLeod followed him.

"Come on, Ben, come on."

She saw what he was doing, taking the zip drive out of his computer and putting it in his pocket. "Everything I know is on here," he said apologetically.

"You go on down," Ben said. "Let me knock on the doors of the other apartments up here."

"I'll do the second floor," said McLeod, although she wanted more than anything else to get out of the house.

It didn't take long, but it seemed forever before McLeod and Ben had knocked on every door in the house and could hurry past the now blazing fire in the front hall and out the front door and across the porch. Soon afterward the first fire truck came roaring up and firemen took over. In full battle gear, they charged into the house with hoses spraying powerfully.

By the time other engines came careening into little Park Place, the fire was out.

All the occupants stood across the street, most of them in their nightclothes looking like refugees. The Murder Project members showed remarkable aplomb, McLeod thought. They sat on the curb and ate pizza.

"It's a good thing we got here when we did," McLeod heard one of the firemen say. "That old frame house would have gone up like a box of matches."

The captain came over to talk to the residents. "Who set that fire?" he asked.

"It wasn't one of us," said a man who lived on the second floor. "We wouldn't commit suicide that way."

"There are lots of crazies around nowadays," the captain said. "Know one that would like to set fire to your house?"

Nobody answered. McLeod wondered if wiping out the Murder Project had been the object of the enterprise. She tried to imagine each of the suspects putting newspaper and kindling in a cardboard box, setting it in the hallway of a wooden apartment building, and lighting it. Mystique? Grady Schuyler? Margie Kinkaid? And suddenly she thought, Gertrude Sergeant! Gertrude Sergeant whose automobile had a long scratch on the left front fender that she could certainly have gotten when she swerved into the woods from Faculty Road. Gertrude Sergeant, who knew I was coming here to meet the project members. Gertrude Sergeant, who has muscles like iron and whom everybody calls "tough."

"Anybody could have set it," Ben was saying. "Nobody ever locks the outside front door." The captain left them and moved to another group of refugees. McLeod shivered. Gone was the warmth of the brandy. And arson was a crime that chilled.

"Anybody who would try to burn down a house full of apartments with people in it is crazy," Daisy said.

"And to put it right there by the front door," said Marcy. "We all would have been trapped."

"It was lucky for us that the pizza man came when he did," Lyle said. "If we had ordered pizza at a decent hour and eaten it earlier, we would never have seen the fire in time."

"You can go back in now," the captain said. "There's just a little water damage in the front hall."

"I bet it's awash in there," Ben said. "Coming back, anyone?" he asked.

"What an adventure," said Marcy. "I think I'd better get back to my room and recover."

"I'll walk them back to their dorms," Lyle said to Ben.

McLeod offered a ride to anyone who wanted one, but the young people all wanted to walk.

Forty

✢

MCLEOD WAITED UNTIL nine o'clock on Sunday morning to call Bob Dewey's parents at the Nassau Inn and ask if she might come over. "I was a friend of your son's," she explained, "and I'm so sorry about what has happened."

Mrs. Dewey suggested she come that afternoon, since they were going to church. McLeod agreed, then decided to go to church herself. She had gone every Sunday when the children were growing up, and still went often at home. But not here.

She dressed for church in her best suit, took her topcoat—it was definitely cold now—and set out. Preaching that morning was a young woman who looked to McLeod about as old as the students in her writing class. From the bulletin, McLeod learned she was a seminary student, doing her internship at Nassau Presbyterian Church. This was obviously her first real sermon, but it was very good, McLeod thought. Taking as her text the twenty-second Psalm, which begins, "My God, my God, why hast thou

forsaken me? And art so far . . . From heeding my
groans . . . I am a worm, not a man . . . my mouth is as dry
as a potsherd, and my tongue sticks to my jaw . . . My
strength drains away like water and all my bones are
loose . . ."

The young woman spoke earnestly and movingly about
calling on God in time of despair, promising He would be
there.

McLeod decided she would never think of the familiar
old twenty-third Psalm again without remembering the
powerful lament in the one before it.

After the service, she congratulated the young woman
on her first sermon and ran into Margie Kinkaid outside
the church. They greeted each other and decided to eat
lunch together at the Nassau Inn, since Lahiere's and the
Annex were closed on Sunday.

"That sermon was good for someone like me, who really is in despair," said Margie when they were settled in
the Inn's taproom. The tables were carved with the initials
of bygone Princeton men who had drunk gallons of beer
here. Nowadays the students drank on campus and the Tap
Room was no longer a preserve for undergraduates, but the
photographs of long-ago athletic teams—all male—still
crowded the walls. "Somehow quite comforting," Margie
was going on about the sermon.

"I'm glad," said McLeod.

They ordered salads and made small talk.

"Look," said McLeod, "before the food comes, I want
to ask you something. Think back to that party at my house
on Halloween. Before spring break."

"Oh, yes, that's the last happy time we had, Dexter and
I," said Margie, "and it was at your apartment, McLeod.
I'll always remember that. Dexter got sick that night."

"I know he did, Margie, and I want to find out why,"
McLeod said. "I know you don't think he was murdered—"

"I don't want to talk about it!" Margie interrupted.

"Even the students are persecuting me with this idea. No, McLeod."

"Margie, bear with me a minute," said McLeod, suddenly inspired and not above uttering a small untruth, or a twisting of the truth, really. "What I'm trying to do will show us if he was not murdered. Just help me find out one thing, or two things. First, who fixed that second cosmopolitan for Dexter after he spilled the first one? Did you?"

"Mystique knocked his elbow—I saw her—and made him spill it," said Margie, ignoring the question. "Dexter was never sloppy. He would never have spilled that drink if she hadn't been so clumsy."

McLeod felt a thrill of excitement run down her spine and move over and settle somewhere in her abdomen. This was the first intimation that Mystique had made Dexter spill his first cosmopolitan. Mystique, the perfect suspect.

"And second, Margie, who mixed that second drink for Dexter? And gave it to Bob to give to Dexter?" she repeated.

Margie's glance shifted from McLeod to the photographs of former Princeton football players on the wall above the booths. "It was probably Liz Finley," she said, took a sip of water, and looked at McLeod as though in appeal.

"Not Mystique?" asked McLeod. It seemed to her that the murderer would be the one who made Dexter spill the harmless drink, making way for the drink laced with Tylenol.

"Not Mystique?" she repeated.

"I'm sure it was Liz Finley," repeated Margie. "She always pretended to be closer to Dexter than she was. If I had had a jealous nature, I would have been quite cross with her at times."

It didn't make sense—for Mystique to jar Dexter's elbow and Finley to mix the new drink. Unless they collaborated . . . Oh, Lord, oh, Lord . . . she thought.

Their salads arrived.

"I don't see how that helps you prove it wasn't murder," said Margie. "But I certainly hope that rumor can be laid to rest?"

"It helps," said McLeod obscurely. Why on earth was Margie in such denial? McLeod wondered. Why was she so eager to prove it wasn't murder? Was it because she herself was the murderer?

They talked of Margie's present chores. "I had to stop clearing out Dexter's office," said Margie, "because the police wanted to use it for a command post. When they get through, I'll have to finish the clearing out. They just pushed everything over against the wall, but they wouldn't let me take anything away. They said they wouldn't bother anything but just to leave them alone. So I did."

When they had finished their lunch, they walked outside into Palmer Square. "The wind is cold," said McLeod.

"Ah, yes," said Mrs. Kinkaid. "You're from the South. You feel the cold, don't you?" She seemed almost pleased, McLeod thought, as they parted on Nassau Street.

McLeod, unwilling to let Margie know she was going to see the Deweys, waited until she left and then headed back to the Inn and the house phone in the lobby.

Forty-one

❧

THE DEWEYS, A very attractive couple in their late fifties or early sixties, greeted McLeod in the sitting room of their suite. They were obviously well off, obviously congenial, obviously shaken. But who wouldn't be? McLeod wondered. If something happened to Harry, what would I do?

"It's so nice of you to come to see us," Mrs. Dewey said. "Bob told us he went to a party at your house. I think it was on Halloween Day."

"That's right," said McLeod. "He tended bar for me. He was very helpful. He was so nice."

"We're glad to hear that," said Mr. Dewey. "He could be cranky when he put his mind to it."

Mrs. Dewey flicked a sharp glance at him, and he shook his head, as though to clear it. "He could be quirky. I think that's a better word." McLeod noticed that he had on a good tweed jacket and a cashmere sweater. Mrs. Dewey was also nicely dressed. Her gray hair was beautifully cut and her face was the well-cared-for face of a rich lady. These were not blue-collar folks, she thought. No way.

"He was unfailingly nice to me," McLeod said. "And to everyone else, as far as I know. I'm glad I got to know him."

Mrs. Dewey reached for a box of Kleenex, took one, and wiped her eyes. "I can't believe this," she said. "I can't believe this has happened. I just can't. I keep thinking Bob will walk in the door and say, 'Hey, guys, I'm sorry I'm late. Hope you weren't worried about me.' And then he will say he was out talking to workmen somewhere, or something crazy."

Mr. Dewey stared out the window. "I can't help but wonder myself if his politics had something to do with his murder."

He sounded bleak, but who wouldn't? McLeod asked herself. She also wondered if they'd gone to the Presbyterian Church that morning, and if they had, was the Scripture an echo of their own thoughts? "My God, my God, why hast thou forsaken me? And art so far . . . From heeding my groans . . ."

"It must be very hard," was all she could think of to say.

"He picked up these radical politics as a form of rebellion when he was in high school," Mr. Dewey was saying. "He said capitalism was oppressing the worker. He said it to bait me, I think, but I'd just laugh. Then for a while, I think he really liked blue-collar workers; he spent all his time with them and wanted to transfer from private school to public school."

"Did you let him?" asked McLeod, curious as always.

"What else could we do?" asked Mr. Dewey. "He would have gotten himself thrown out. So we let him go to public school. He still got into Harvard, though. I was afraid he'd turn it down and go to a state university, but he went. After he graduated, he went off to work for a union in Detroit, organizing. My friends said he was a traitor to us all, but I didn't see it that way. I thought he was just making his own way."

"It's so funny that we all thought Bob came from a working-class background," said McLeod. "He was so determinedly antiestablishment."

Mr. Dewey actually managed to smile. "Well, he went back to Yale for graduate school," he said. "I think he got kind of tired of the proletariat. Somehow he stumbled onto Marxist literary criticism and that was perfect. He could be radical, and still enjoy the life of the mind."

"Harvard. Yale. Princeton," mused McLeod. "He was certainly an Ivy League man."

"He was," said Mr. Dewey. "He wouldn't consider Princeton for undergraduate work, even though I went here and so did my father, or maybe *because* I went here and so did my father. I was surprised when he came here to teach."

"He seemed to like it," said McLeod.

"He sure did," said Mr. Dewey.

"What's not to like?" asked Mrs. Dewey.

"Oh, sweetheart, you know Bob. He was a rebel," said Mr. Dewey. "Anyway, I was glad he came here. I'm rather fond of Old Nassau myself, and I was proud to have a son teaching here."

"No more," said Mrs. Dewey.

An unbearable silence followed—McLeod tried to think of something to break it, but it was Mrs. Dewey who spoke. "The police keep asking us who would have wanted to kill him," said Mrs. Dewey, "and I think Michael's right. It must have been some crazy radical." She paused. "But you know, the police don't seem to think that makes sense. I guess it doesn't."

"Nothing makes sense right now," said Mr. Dewey sadly.

McLeod reflected on their theory of murder by a radical worker. "There aren't any labor unions in Princeton," she said, "or even any radicals. I don't see how any of them could have been involved."

"I suppose you're right," said Mr. Dewey. He sighed heavily. "Of course, we tried to stay in touch, but we don't know a lot about his life here. We have no idea who could have killed him."

"It must be very hard," said McLeod for the second time, feeling helpless, but wondering if she could tell them about the Murder Project and its theory. "Did he ever say anything to you about the drinks at my Halloween party?" she asked, feeling that this was probably as far as her curiosity should go, to ask the bereaved parents of a young murder victim if he had told them who fixed a poisoned drink.

The Deweys looked at her as if she had gone mad.

"I mean, did he—well, you said he mentioned that he came to my house for the party and I just wondered if he happened to talk about the professor who spilled his drink—" McLeod decided she was gabbling and stopped. "I'm sorry. Tell me about his girl friend. Bob said she was in Rome for the academic year."

"That's Mimi," said Mrs. Dewey. "We think they were quite serious. We had a hard time reaching her in Rome. But she finally called us back. She's flying home. I guess she's in this country by now and she's coming down to Princeton."

"Did he meet her at Yale?" asked McLeod.

"Yes, she was in graduate school in art history," said Mrs. Dewey. "She was a couple of years behind him and she had the chance to go to Rome for a year and finish her dissertation there. It's hard for them. It *was* hard, I should say." She reached for another Kleenex. "It was hard enough when she was still in New Haven and he was in Princeton, but this has been really hard. He went over there for fall break."

"Is she at the American Academy?" asked McLeod.

"I'm not sure," said Mrs. Dewey.

"You see, I have a son who's a graduate student in art history at Yale," said McLeod. "And her name's Mimi?"

"Mimi Howell," said Mrs. Dewey.

McLeod decided she had asked as many questions as she could get away with. "Look, is there anything I can do for you while you're here? Would you like to go anywhere? Meet any of Bob's friends? Is there *anything*—"

"You're very kind," Mrs. Dewey said. "We appreciate it. I can't think of a thing. We're just waiting for them to release—let us have Bob's body—to take him back home. We feel we should stay here until then."

"I see," said McLeod. "You must be bored with the Nassau Inn. Would you like to come to my house for dinner tonight, or maybe tomorrow? I'd love to have you. If you think it would divert you in any way." She hesitated.

"You're very kind," Mrs. Dewey said again. She looked hesitantly at her husband. He looked at her. They seemed to come to some agreement. "We won't come tonight, I don't think," said Mrs. Dewey. "Can we let you know later about tomorrow?"

"Certainly," said McLeod. "Whatever you feel like." She stood up to leave. "I'll leave my telephone number with you. I hope you will come." She took one of her cards out of her purse and laid it on the table.

They stood up to see her out, and thanked her for coming. When she left, she thought they still looked just as they had when she came in, shocked and grieving, "My God, my God, why hast thou forsaken me? And art so far . . ." Poor Deweys.

Forty-two

❧

WHAT A DAY! McLeod thought when she finally got back to her apartment. She made herself a cup of hot chocolate and thought about what she had learned. Margie Kinkaid said that Mystique Alcott made Dexter spill his first cosmopolitan, and that Liz Finley mixed the second one. She didn't say she saw Finley fix the drink, but just that Finley always pretended to be closer to Dexter than she really was. Unless Mystique and Finley were accomplices, it didn't make sense. Margie Kinkaid was not a reliable witness.

And there was something about Bob Dewey that didn't make sense either. We all thought he was such a viable suspect, and then he got killed himself. I can't help but wonder, is there someone else out there who wanted to kill Bob Dewey for some reason? What about this girl friend? Did he have a secret life? It sounded far-fetched. His family didn't know he wasn't going to get tenure, didn't know he would have to leave Princeton. Maybe he killed himself, McLeod thought, and then she realized you can't strangle yourself with a silk scarf. Bob's life is what the police must be looking into.

BEN TRUE HAD sent a message to tell her that he had seen Grady Schuyler, who had said that he hadn't even gone on the job market yet. He had rebuffed a feeler from Tufts because he thought he could do better and he hoped to get tenure here. Queer Theorists were salable commodities. "Even a stuffed shirt like Kinkaid wasn't going to penalize him because he was gay," Ben wrote. "He couldn't. The political price would have been too much. And Dexter was political. So there goes Schuyler's motive."

Another message was from Lyle. "I just want to know if you have any idea who the murderer is. We all talked so much Saturday night that I didn't hear what you really thought."

"It's one of four women, I think," she wrote to Lyle.

Lyle replied almost immediately: "I know which ones you mean. Okay. You may be right. We really ought to nose around. See what we can see."

"NO," flamed McLeod. "NO. Stay out of it. Stay out of it."

MCLEOD WAS TIRED, but she had one more thing to do before she went to bed. She wanted to call Harry and it was better to call him late at night than early on Monday morning. Like all students—graduate and undergraduate—he stayed up late and slept late.

Harry was in great form when he answered, and they chatted amiably for a few minutes. Finally, she got around to the reason for her call. "Do you happen to know a graduate student in art history named Mimi Howell?"

"Sure," said Harry. "I had lunch with her one day this week. She has a boy friend at Princeton."

"She *had* a boy friend in Princeton," said McLeod.

"Did they break up?" asked Harry.

"No, he got murdered," said McLeod.

"Wait a minute, you mean there's been another murder, besides your pal, Archie?"

"Two more," said McLeod. "Three murders in all."

"And Mimi's boy friend is the third? Is it safe for you to be there?"

"I hope so," said McLeod. "But it's very odd you saw Mimi Howell this week. She was supposed to be in Rome."

"She came back to see her advisor about something," said Harry. "I understand he was pretty pissed. If he'd gone to see her in Rome, the school would have paid his way. But she flew back here. Anyway, she was going to Princeton from here, she told me. Did you meet her—is that why you're asking?"

"No, I didn't meet her," said McLeod. "I don't think she's here yet. Her boy friend was Bob Dewey. I knew him slightly, and I went to see his parents. They told me about Mimi. They'd been trying to reach her in Rome and she had called them back and said she was flying home. Today, I think they said. It's very odd that she was in New Haven. Are you sure you saw her this week?"

"Of course, I'm sure it was this week," said Harry.

"What a curious situation," said McLeod. "There are several very odd things about Bob Dewey and his life—and death."

So that's why the Deweys had trouble reaching Mimi in Rome to tell her about Bob's death, McLeod thought after she had hung up. Mimi wasn't in Rome; she was in America. In New Haven, which was only a hundred and twenty-five miles from Princeton, where Bob was killed.

Did she go back to Rome, get the message from the Deweys, and return to America immediately?

She might very well have called Rome, gotten her messages, and called the Deweys back from New Haven, or wherever she was. And neglected to mention she wasn't in

Rome. And what then had she been doing all that time in this country? Had she come down to Princeton to see Bob? Had she come down to Princeton to kill Bob? Was the Murder Project barking up the wrong tree? Was this one of the lines of inquiry that the police were following?

Forty-three

❧

MCLEOD WOKE UP on Monday to a cold gray sky, against which bare black trees stood like ghouls. A grounds crew from the university was sucking up dead leaves into a machine that roared like a monster along the lake front.

It was, she realized, the Monday before Thanksgiving, and Harry and Rosie were coming in two days. She had better bestir herself and get started with some preparations.

But first, she wanted to meet Miss Mimi Howell. Well, why not call the Deweys? She should follow up on her invitation to dinner anyway.

Mrs. Dewey could not have been nicer when McLeod called her. Of course she remembered McLeod, she said.

Would she and her husband like to come to dinner? McLeod asked.

She was afraid not, Mrs. Dewey said. It was awfully kind of McLeod to invite them, but they didn't feel up to going out just yet. "We really do appreciate your asking us," Mrs. Dewey said. "It's so very sweet. I'm sure you understand how we feel."

"Of course, I understand," said McLeod. "Has Mimi Howell arrived yet?"

"Yes, she got in yesterday," said Mrs. Dewey. "She's staying here at the Nassau Inn. She wanted to stay in Bob's apartment, but the police said they weren't through with it. So she's staying here."

So she was here, thought McLeod. "Can I ask to speak to her? I'd love to meet her. My son knows her—you know I told you he was an art history graduate student at Yale."

"I remember," said Mrs. Dewey. "She's not here. She has her own room. I think she's there now, but she's very tired."

"I'll call her later," said McLeod. "Please let me know if I can help you in any way. You have my phone number—at the office and at home."

McLeod called the Nassau Inn again later, as promised, but not much later, and asked to speak to Mimi Howell, who agreed to meet her downstairs.

McLeod wrapped up in her warmest coat. It was a good thing, she thought, that she was teaching at Princeton in the fall, not the spring semester. If this was what November was like, how cold could January and February get?

She felt a little guilty as she and Mimi went in the Tap Room. She had insisted that the students stop their detective efforts and here she was, plunging ahead. It's just my curiosity, she told herself.

"Thanks for coming down," said McLeod after they'd both ordered hot tea. "I know you're tired and upset."

"I *am* tired and upset," Mimi said. And then she shrugged. She was a thin, pretty young woman, with brown curly hair and tiny round spectacles. She was tense now, and McLeod thought she must always be intense, if not tense.

"You said you were a friend of Bob's," she said.

"I knew Bob and liked him," said McLeod. "And my son knows you. He's Harry Dulaney."

Mimi's face lit up, as she smiled. "Is Harry Dulaney your son?" she said. "He's adorable."

"That's music to a mother's ears," said McLeod.

"I had lunch with him in New Haven," said Mimi. "It was just last week, but it seems like ages ago."

"When did you get to Princeton?" asked McLeod.

"I came yesterday," said Mimi.

"Were you in New Haven all that time?"

"No, I went back to Rome on Thursday," said Mimi.

"You didn't come to Princeton from New Haven?"

"Well, no, I didn't," said Mimi.

"Harry said you told him you were coming . . ." said McLeod. "I don't mean to pry . . ."

"This is mild, compared to what I had from the police," said Mimi.

"The police?" said McLeod.

"Yes, the police. They seem to think I murdered Bob."

"Good heavens! But you didn't, did you?"

"Of course not," said Mimi.

"Why do the police think you murdered him?"

"I was coming down here on Wednesday or Thursday, but then I was talking to Bob and we had another quarrel."

"Another?" asked McLeod.

"Yes, another," said Mimi. "The first was in Rome when he was there for fall break. I thought we'd broken up, but he didn't think so. He kept calling me, and when I decided to come back for this quick trip to see my advisor, he insisted that I come down to Princeton. 'Give it one more chance,' he said. So I said I would. But then I decided not to."

McLeod looked inquiringly at her.

"I can tell you're a kind soul," said Mimi. "I'll tell you all about it."

It was her white hair, McLeod knew, that made people

confide in her. Prematurely white hair could be a great advantage.

"I'm so stupid," said Mimi. "I lied. I did come down here on Wednesday, right after I had lunch with Harry. I came down on the train and took a taxi from Princeton Junction to Bob's apartment, but he wasn't there. I thought I'd just wait for him there. I was determined to break up with him once and for all. I had a key and I waited and waited and he didn't come home, so I just spent the night and went back to New Haven on Thursday. I was furious."

"Had you told him when you were coming?"

"Yes, and he said he had a preceptorial Wednesday afternoon but he'd be home right after that. Well, he never came. I left him a note that said, 'It's over, forever,' or something like that and signed it Mimi.

"My roommate in Rome called me on Friday and told me Bob's parents were trying to reach me and told me why. So I called them—I didn't say I was calling from New Haven, and they just assumed I was in Rome. I told them I'd fly home right away and come to Princeton on Sunday. I mean, I had broken up with Bob and I thought, 'It's over.' But I was terribly upset that he'd been murdered. So I did come down.

"I know it was silly," Mimi went on, "but I just let Bob's folks think I hadn't been in this country. But the police were a different story. They had found the note in Bob's apartment and they wanted to see my airplane ticket and I showed it to them and they said, 'But you were in this country . . .' And I told them I had been in New Haven. They asked me where I was on Wednesday afternoon and I realized I had to tell them I'd been in Princeton, and I did. But it was awful. They think I killed him, I know. I kept telling them that I was coming down to break up with Bob once and for all and that the person who kills somebody is the person who is broken up with, not the person who is breaking off the relationship. Do you know what I mean?"

"Certainly," said McLeod.

"I mean if anybody killed anybody," said Mimi, "it would have been Bob killing me. But the police don't see it that way."

"That's awful," said McLeod.

"What am I going to do?" asked Mimi.

"What about Bob's parents?" asked McLeod.

"They don't know what to think," said Mimi. "I could kick myself for not telling them when I called them back that I was in this country. They think I was deceiving them. And of course I was, in a way. I didn't want to tell them I came down to break up with their son, who has been murdered!"

"Of course not," said McLeod sympathetically. "I don't know what to tell you, but I don't think you killed Bob Dewey."

"Thank you," said Mimi.

"My opinion, unfortunately, is worth nothing," said McLeod. "I believe perhaps I'd get a lawyer if I were you."

"That's what my parents say," said Mimi.

"Where are they?" asked McLeod.

"In Berkeley," said Mimi.

"That's kind of far away," said McLeod.

"I know," said Mimi. "I think my mom's coming out here, though. She's about to have a fit."

"I should think so," said McLeod. "Shall I get some recommendations about lawyers for you?"

"Oh, would you?" said Mimi. "I'd be so grateful."

"I will, and I want to tell you why I don't think you killed Bob," and she told Mimi the whole story of the cosmopolitans and Archie and Dexter and the drink Bob had handed Dexter at her house. She told her, too, about her class.

"Oh, the whole thing makes sense now," said Mimi. "It was bewildering why anybody would kill Bob. I wanted to break up with him, but I didn't want to kill him—I couldn't imagine anybody wanting to kill him."

"Well, somebody did," said McLeod.

"But it wasn't because of anything Bob *did*," said Mimi, "or anything he *was*. It was just because of something he *saw*."

"That's right," said McLeod. "Let me get to my office, and I'll call you with the names of lawyers. Here, take my card so you'll have my name and telephone numbers."

BACK IN HER office, McLeod set about finding a lawyer for Mimi Howell. Once again she mourned Archie Alexander—he would have known exactly who to call. Ginger, her usual advisor on everything, could only recommend the lawyer she and Cliff had used to draw their wills, William Staples, who was with an old-time Princeton firm.

"I'm not sure they do criminal law, though," she said.

McLeod called Stephanie West and asked her about lawyers, explaining a little of the circumstances.

"No, I wouldn't get William Staples," said Stephanie. "Too stuffy. She needs Cowboy Tarleton. He's always suing the university. He loves offbeat cases. And he's smart."

McLeod thanked her and then asked her how things were going in the department.

"Cliff is turning out to be wonderful, always cheerful, always able to come up with a solution," said Stephanie. "For instance, this morning he hired Fanny Trimble to teach Bob Dewey's classes. She taught here for years and didn't get tenure, but she's living in town—her husband teaches at Rutgers—and she agreed to come in for the rest of the semester and next semester, too. So that's a load off Cliff's mind. For next semester, he's already thought of calling in some retirees in town to plug the gaps that Archie and Dexter left until they can hire new people permanently. The old guys are thrilled to be coming back."

"I'm glad Cliff is doing so well," said McLeod. "I do love the Kingsleys."

"I wish Professor Kinkaid was still alive to see how

well Cliff is doing. He didn't think much of him, really. He told Cliff he was tenured, and his teaching was fine, but that he had better boost his output of published material."

McLeod wondered if Dexter Kinkaid had admired anyone at all. "I'd love to know who was the last person to see Bob Dewey before he was killed," she said. "Do you know if the police have found out?"

"No, I don't," Stephanie said. "Of course, Bob taught his precept Wednesday afternoon," said Stephanie. "We knew that. Then it gets murkier."

"Who else has offices downstairs?" McLeod asked.

"Assistant professors," said Stephanie. "Guadalupe Hutchinson, John Pope, Ursula Barnes, Grady Schuyler. You know."

"How about Mystique Alcott?"

"She has a joint appointment in English and creative writing," said Stephanie. "So she technically has an office in McCosh. But she never uses it. Hmmm." She was distracted for a minute. "Maybe we could use her office for one of the pinch hitters. Anyway, she comes over occasionally. In fact, I saw her over there one day last week. I don't know when it was."

"Did you see Margie Kinkaid over there last week?"

"She was there every day, I'd say," said Stephanie.

"You wouldn't know if she went downstairs, would you?" asked McLeod.

"I wouldn't know unless I had gone down there for something. McCosh is such a warren, you know. On the first and second floors it has entryways, and each entry opens into a couple of classrooms and a few offices, the big offices for senior members of the department. And upstairs on the second floor, there are more offices in each entryway and those huge lecture rooms. On the first floor you can't get from one entryway to another very easily without going through offices. On the second floor, you can go through the lecture rooms. The basement is the only one with a long corridor. And all those little offices open off it."

What a layout for murder, McLeod thought.

MCLEOD CALLED MIMI Howell, gave her the two names, and told her what Stephanie had said about each man.

"I'll call Cowboy," said Mimi, giggling. "He sounds like what I need."

"I think so, too. Let me know how it goes," said McLeod.

Forty-four

❧

MCLEOD HUNG UP the phone after talking to Mimi and decided to do something not related to the Deweys or the Murder Project. She would go to Firestone Library and see what had already been written about the Bartrams, John and William, intrepid naturalists of Colonial times. Both of them had traveled all over the colonies. John had collected plants and sent them back to England, and William had been the artist who painted birds and animals and plants.

She searched the central electronic catalog and made her way downstairs to C-Floor, the lowest level of the library, far underground. The stacks in the section she wanted were the new movable kind, tall metal bookshelves on wheels in grooves in the floor. The user could shift each section by turning a crank on the end of the stack.

The system of movable stacks conserved space by packing more shelving into a smaller area. The arrangement could be a pain for the user, and McLeod had to move several stacks before she could open up enough space to gain access to the shelf she wanted.

A fat volume, *The Correspondence of John Bartram 1734–1777,* caught her eye, and she took it down and leafed through it, pausing here and there to read a passage. One, especially, fascinated her.

Written on November 26, 1769, it described a box of plants John Bartram had sent to John Fothergill, a London physician, that had also contained two snakes his son William had caught. "Ye biger [sic] one was swallowing ye lesser," Bartram wrote. He also had put in "two of our Bull frogs for ye King." They had come into his milk house spring to spend the winter.

A man who sent Pennsylvania bull frogs to the king of England was a man after McLeod's heart. Looking around, she saw nothing to sit on and she slid quietly down against the shelves at her back until she was sitting on the floor.

Riveted, she read Dr. Fothergill's reply that he had received the barrel of colocasia roots and live bull frogs and also a roll of William's drawings. The frogs were living in a shallow vessel of water until he could decide where to put them. "We have none of the kind in England. The King is acquainted with their arrival."

Entranced, McLeod read on. The library was very quiet this time of day—students tended to come later—but not empty. Out of the corner of her eye she saw someone walk down the aisle at the end of the stack where she sat. She felt oddly uneasy. She hated tunnels and basements, anything underground, and C-Floor was definitely underground.

Then she felt the stack behind her begin to move forward.

"Stop!" she called. "I'm in here."

McLeod looked toward first one aisle and then the other and waited for the expected flustered apology as the person turning the crank at the end of the stack stopped. But there was no sound except for the stack creaking as it moved inexorably against her back.

"I'm in here," she repeated, shouting. The shelves still crept forward.

Panicky, McLeod moved as fast as she could, dumping the books off her lap and scrambling to her feet. The space between the stacks was getting narrower, but in spite of her age and some stiffness, she was fast enough to slip out to the aisle before the heavy bookcase crushed her.

She heard rapid footsteps but saw no one, although she half expected to see Mystique Alcott or Liz Finley or Margie Kinkaid. Whoever had moved the stack had disappeared. McLeod hurried down the space between stacks and looked up and down the aisle at the other end. No one.

Had it been a mistake, or a serious attempt to hurt her?

She didn't know. She stood irresolutely in the aisle looking down the narrow space to where the *Correspondence of John Bartram*—all 810 pages of it—lay. Actually, she could have kept space for herself by dumping books on the floor, she realized now. But that was hindsight. It had been very scary five minutes ago.

The intrepid side of her nature triumphed over the fearful. She cranked wider the opening between the stacks, rushed down to pick up the thick volume, and took it upstairs to check it out. It was a relief to be at the circulation counter on the main floor, with light and space around her.

Forty-five

❧

MARGIE KINKAID CALLED the next morning and asked her to lunch that day.

"I'd love to," McLeod said automatically, wondering why on earth Margie wanted to have lunch with her again, the second time in three days. She had decided Margie was stark-raving crazy in her denial that Dexter had been murdered.

"Come to my house," said Margie. "We'll be ladies who lunch regularly."

McLeod was rather bored with Margie, and she was not delighted about being alone with her. Margie might be boring, but she also could be the murderer. As usual, curiosity overcame caution. She did, however, e-mail Lyle about her plans.

Margie offered her sherry, which McLeod refused, as she did further offers of wine or Bloody Marys or anything alcoholic.

"You don't drink?"

"Not at lunch," said McLeod.

"I think that's wonderful," said Margie. "So many women drink just as much as men do. I think it's awful."

"You don't drink?" asked McLeod.

"Well, I do," said Margie, "but that's different."

McLeod smiled, thinking Margie was joking, then realized she was perfectly serious, that she really set a different standard for herself than the one she had for other people.

"I'm so glad you could come," Margie said. "I've been meaning to have you over. But you know how it is. I've been so busy cleaning out Dexter's office, but now, as I told you, the police won't let me in there anymore."

For lunch at the mahogany table in the dim dining room, Margie served creamed chicken in little pastry shells. "Have another?" asked Margie. "You're so thin you can eat all you want."

McLeod refused seconds. Nobody ever seemed to realize that thin people were thin because they did not eat more. When Margie had polished off seconds, she got up. "Let me get dessert and coffee," she said.

McLeod quailed at the idea of dessert after the rich lunch. "Just a small serving for me," she called out to Margie in the kitchen. "Very small."

"All right," said Margie, arriving with two plates, each filled with a chocolate brownie topped with ice cream which in turn was topped with chocolate sauce. A puff of whipped cream finished off the whole thing.

"I can't eat all this," McLeod said. "I try not to eat desserts for lunch at all."

"You must eat this—it was Dexter's favorite," said Margie. "And it's good for you."

McLeod could not imagine how this dessert could be good for anybody. Was Margie trying to kill her with cholesterol? Death by calories—that would be a good title for a mystery, she thought. She had warned the students over and over about being alone with the people they were interviewing, and here she was alone with one of her four suspects, the wife of the prime victim. She shivered.

Come on, she said to herself. This is ridiculous. Pull yourself together. She may be a murderer, but she can't really kill with calories.

When Margie sat down, McLeod began to eat her dessert. It was good, she had to admit. She only hoped it wasn't poisoned—and ate away.

"I want to talk to you," Margie said. "I know I was always very negative whenever anyone mentioned that Dexter might have been murdered. It would be such an undignified end for the life of a great man like Dexter. I just simply could not accept the idea. But I've been thinking about some of the things you and that student said and I've come to the conclusion that perhaps he was indeed murdered."

McLeod waited, wondering why Margie had finally decided to stop denying what seemed obvious to everyone else.

Margie went on. "Now who could have fixed that drink? I asked myself. At first, I said Liz Finley. That was a little spiteful of me, I'm afraid." Margie smiled.

As though it were funny to accuse someone of murder, thought McLeod.

"You know," said Margie. "Of course, I knew all about Dexter and the ladies. But what could I do? Men will be men. I just pretended I didn't know. Liz Finley was one of the first, and lasted longer than some of the others. In a way, I'd like to think she is the murderer, but I have to say, in all honesty, I don't think she is."

Margie scraped her plate with her dessert spoon and fork and reached for McLeod's plate. "Oh, you hardly touched your dessert! How could you! You'll have to sit there until you eat it! Did your mother ever say that to you?"

"No," said McLeod. "She never did."

"One time I made my son sit at the table for hours until he ate his dinner. It was good pot roast and vegetables and I told him to eat it—or else."

"What happened?" asked McLeod.

"He never did eat it," said Margie. "It turned out Jamie was coming down with measles and didn't want *anything* to eat. He threw up that night, in fact. I felt bad about that, but I did think you had to be firm with children. They need boundaries."

"What happened to Jamie?" asked McLeod.

"He dropped out and became a carpenter," said Margie. "We never see him. He's living in a commune in Vermont, I think. It's such a waste of brainpower for him to be a carpenter."

"The world needs carpenters," said McLeod. "Smart carpenters."

Margie poured the coffee from a silver pot into their cups. It would be hard to poison one cup if they both came from the same pot, McLeod thought happily.

"To get back to what I was saying, I don't think it was Liz," said Margie. "I mean I don't think she's the murderer. I've thought and thought and I think I know who it is."

"Who?"

"It's Mystique," said Margie. "Mystique Alcott."

"What makes you think she's the one?" asked McLeod.

"When Mystique got turned down for a Guggenheim, she went around saying Dexter's letter had sabotaged her chances. She has resented Dexter ever since then. Dexter always leaned over backward to write positive letters for his graduate students and colleagues. Actually, I think Dexter called the Guggenheim office—he had a friend there—and learned that Mystique's application had gotten in late. And they are very strict about the cutoff date for applications."

McLeod hated to see Mystique's motive go down the drain. On the other hand, it didn't matter whether Dexter's letter had been bad or good; as long as Mystique thought the letter had been unfavorable, she would harbor a grudge against Dexter. And Mystique still thought it had been a negative letter, or she wouldn't have told a student about it. So it was still a motive.

But Margie was continuing. "But there's another reason Mystique—I hate that name, don't you? Her real name is Miriam."

"Really?" asked McLeod.

"Really," said Margie. "Would you like some more coffee? Would you like to move into the living room?"

"I'm fine, thank you, Margie," said McLeod. "How do you know about her name?"

"She had to bring in a birth certificate or a passport for something," said Margie. "She couldn't find her passport, which is in her new name. She legally changed it. So she had to use a birth certificate."

"It's an odd change," said McLeod. "I like Miriam better. But why do you think she may have murdered Dexter?" she asked.

Margie looked at her, and her eyes flashed.

"Because of the plagiarism," she said.

"Plagiarism?" asked McLeod.

"Yes, Dexter found plagiarism in her latest novel," said Margie proudly.

"He did? In *Illumination*?" asked McLeod.

"Yes, in *Illumination*, the book that's been nominated for a National Book Award," said Margie, still proud.

"What? I mean, how . . . ?" McLeod stuttered.

"You know it's a historical novel," said Margie. "It's about Keats and Fanny Brawne and Leigh Hunt, and of course this is Dexter's period. He is the world's authority on the Romantic poets. And he saw where Mystique had lifted great chunks of social history for her narrative. Dexter recognized passages from Bate and Gittings. He was really, really upset. He said he had never seen such a gross example of plagiarism in his life."

McLeod tried to remember what she knew about *Illumination*, but could only recall that she had never been able to finish it because of its density and shifting time structure. Reviews had been mixed. "What did Dexter do?"

"He hadn't done anything about it when he died," said Margie. "He spoke to Mystique—he wanted to give her a chance to explain. She couldn't explain it, of course, but he told me he was going to give her time to prepare a defense before he went public. He really did seem to be at a loss about what to do. He said it was the most shocking thing he'd seen in his academic career. I suggested he tip off a younger scholar, who would love to go public with the charge. He said he was not going to hide behind some young Turk."

"It gives Mystique a good motive for murder, doesn't it?"

"I thought so," said Margie smugly. "It's hard for me to think that anyone, no matter how evil, would murder Dexter, but I thought I ought to tell you about it."

"I'm glad you did," said McLeod. "And now I'm afraid I really must go. I have a student conference in five minutes. It's been a lovely lunch. Oh, by the way, think back to last Wednesday. Were you in McCosh that afternoon?"

"Let me look at my calendar." Margie went to the library next door and took a calendar off a desk and riffled through it. "Yes, I suppose I was," she said. "I was still cleaning out Dexter's office then."

"Did you go downstairs?"

"Let's see," said Margie. "Oh, that was the day before poor Bob Dewey's body was discovered, wasn't it? Yes, I did go downstairs."

"Did you see Mystique down there?" asked McLeod, "or anybody else who didn't belong?"

Margie wanted to say yes. McLeod could see it in her face.

"Is she ever over there?" asked Margie. "But you know, I believe I did see her down there, a flash of those flowing garments she wears . . ."

McLeod did not believe her for a minute. Margie, she thought, lacked credibility.

Forty-six

❧

WHEN MCLEOD GOT back to her office, she had several messages in her voice mail: Mystique, Trudy Sergeant, Elizabeth Finley, and one from Mimi Howell.

She called Mimi first, and was delighted to learn that she was on her way out the door, and about to go to California.

"The police said I could leave," said Mimi. "I'm not a suspect any longer, thanks to Cowboy Tarleton. I really appreciate your telling me about him. My mother's here, and I'm flying home with her for Thanksgiving. I'll come back for Bob's funeral wherever or whenever that is."

McLeod congratulated her on her freedom, and they exchanged expressions of warm regard and hopes of meeting again.

When she called Mystique, she was surprised to be invited to dinner that night at Acacia, a fancy restaurant in the neighboring village of Lawrenceville.

"My treat," said Mystique expansively.

"That's very generous of you," said McLeod. "Can I bring the wine?" Acacia's main fault was its lack of a liquor license. Archie had said it was the only four-star BYOB he had ever heard of.

"Oh, no, I've got something special," said Mystique. "See you at seven."

Trudy Sergeant, when reached, told her she was so interested in McLeod's class and its investigation—"even if you have stopped it"—that she'd like to visit her class.

"Fine, you're most welcome," said McLeod. "The only thing is we meet on Thursday and this Thursday is Thanksgiving, so the next class will be Thursday, December first. It's from one-thirty to four-thirty."

"I'm disappointed," said Trudy. "I was hoping it was today or tomorrow."

"Nope," said McLeod.

"Right," said Trudy. "I'll be there on December first, if you're sure it's all right."

"Why not?" said McLeod. Why not, indeed? Why on earth would Gertrude Sergeant want to visit her class? She had been very nice to McLeod lately, but was she part of the Politcal Correctness police, checking on gender bias in nonfiction writing?

She called Finley back and got another jolt.

"McLeod, I understand your children are coming for Thanksgiving," Finley said.

"That's right," said McLeod.

"I have worlds of dahlias in my yard," said Finley. "And I thought I'd like to bring masses of them by for you tomorrow. I remember that party you gave on Halloween and I never thanked you properly for that. But if it's all right, I'll drop these off tomorrow before I leave town."

"Oh, where are you going?" asked McLeod.

"I'm going to my brother's house," said Finley.

The phone rang as soon as she hung up. "McLeod, dear, we're going out of town for Thanksgiving, but our house will just be sitting here empty." It was Ginger. "And Cliff and I wondered if your kids would like to stay over there. You're welcome to it."

"Oh, Ginger, you are so sweet," said McLeod. "But we'll manage. Harry, I think, will only be here one night, and he can sleep in the living room—the sofa turns into a bed. Rosie can have the bed in my study."

"If you change your mind, the key's under the mat," said Ginger. "Feel free."

"Thanks, Ginger, you're wonderful."

"Oh, no, I'm not," said Ginger. "Can you come to dinner tonight? It will be a scramble, since we're actually going to get away tomorrow."

"Oh, I can't, Ginger. I'd love to see you and Cliff before the holiday. But Mystique Alcott has asked me out to dinner tonight. At Acacia."

"I'm sorry we won't be seeing you. Oh, are you going to cook Thanksgiving dinner yourself?"

"Yes, I am and I haven't even bought a turkey," said McLeod. "I thought I might take them out, but that's not very homey, is it?"

"Cliff would die," said Ginger.

"So would I," said McLeod. "I'll cook."

She really had to get started on this Thanksgiving dinner, she thought as she trudged home. Before she got ready for her dinner with Mystique, she made a grocery list. Its length paralyzed her. Should she buy some of this dinner already cooked? She had seen advertisements in *Town Topics* for prepared turkeys, stuffing, cranberry sauce, oyster bisque, sweet potatoes, green beans, pumpkin pie, and anything else you might desire in all the good takeout places—Main Street, Chez Alice, and Bon Appetit. Maybe that's what she should do. Otherwise, she'd be cooking all day tomorrow and all morning on Thursday and have no time to talk to Harry and Rosie.

She pulled last week's *Town Topics* out of the recycling bag and read the advertisements again. She would, she decided, do the turkey herself. The roasting turkey would make the apartment smell like home. She would make her famous hot rolls—the children loved them. And she'd buy the rest. So there. She made a phone call to Chez Alice to reserve what she needed.

"Just in time," said the brisk young woman who took her order. "When will you pick this up? Tomorrow or Thursday?"

"Thursday," said McLeod. That was done, and she felt immeasurably better. She hated pumpkin pie anyway, but felt that it was obligatory on Thanksgiving. Now she wouldn't have to make it, just eat it.

Forty-seven

❧

MYSTIQUE WAS ALREADY seated at a prime table by the window at Acacia when McLeod arrived. A champagne bottle was in the wine cooler next to the table.

A waiter appeared to pour the wine and McLeod saw it was Perrier-Jouët. "What a lavish hostess you are," she said to Mystique. "This is lovely."

Mystique looked pleased. "I thought you needed a little treat," she said. "Here's to you!" She lifted her glass.

"Why me?" asked McLeod.

"Well, you and that class are working so hard on this murder investigation," said Mystique. "The police aren't doing a thing."

"I think they've got their own line of inquiry. Everybody is suddenly interested in my class and the investigation," she said. She sipped her champagne, enjoying the wonderful taste and, the best part, the aftertaste. She felt a buzz immediately, realizing that getting a buzz from one sip of champagne was a side effect, a bonus, of drinking as little as she did.

"It's so interesting," said Mystique. "I hope you find the murderer. At first, I thought it was bizarre, impossible that Archie and that old fool Dexter had been murdered. Then the more I thought about it, the more your theory made sense. Think of all the people with a motive to knock off old Dex. I guess we'd better order—the waiter's hovering."

They ordered, Mystique a shrimp cocktail and a big steak, McLeod crab bisque and pompano. "I love pompano," she said. "I didn't know you could get it up here. It's such a Gulf Coast thing." She returned to the previous conversation. "Tell me everybody who has a motive for 'knocking off old Dex,'" she asked. "Whom were you talking about?"

"Well, nobody liked him, except whoever he was sleeping with at the moment, and Liz Finley," said Mystique. "And I understand he double-crossed her about her big book on all her boring old eighteenth-century 'boys,' as she calls them."

"That must have been hard for her," said McLeod, sipping champagne. "Who else?"

"Well, Bob Dewey," said Mystique, "but of course he's out of it now. And Stephanie West—God, that woman has taken his shit for years. The worm turns, you know."

"But she couldn't have doctored either cosmopolitan," McLeod pointed out. "She wasn't at your party or my party."

Mystique's face fell. "That's right," she said. "I don't suppose there's any way she could have done it. Then there's his adoring wife, his helpmeet." Mystique spread hot pepper–flavored butter lavishly on yet another piece of bread. "She lived for him, supposedly. She typed his manuscripts. She ironed his shirts. She raised his children. She waited on him hand and foot. Even that worm, the lowliest of worms, Margie Kinkaid, might have turned. Maybe she found out about the other women."

"She says she knew about them," said McLeod. "But as you say, the worm can turn. Still, then there's this problem with her at your house. She couldn't have come with Dexter and then had that doctored drink sitting out there before Dexter got there. Or could she have come early? Hmmm." She paused while the waiter brought their first courses.

"Don't be offended," McLeod said when the waiter had left, "but what about you, Mystique? You were mad at him about a recommendation for a Guggenheim."

"Yes, I was," said Mystique. "I was indeed."

"And didn't he bring up some plagiarism question?" asked McLeod.

Mystique eyed her with hostility. "How did you hear about that?" she said.

"Somebody told me," said McLeod. "I did not necessarily believe it."

"You better believe it," said Mystique, her small eyes flashing wildly. "He did bring it up, but it was a ridiculous case. Some of the background I had in there, he said, was lifted verbatim from biographies of Keats. That's ridiculous. I don't need to do that. I can write better than any biographer. I decided we must have gone to the same original sources, the biographers and I. And I decided Dexter was just trying to get back at me. He knew I didn't like him. Anyway, I'm braced for a public attack. I have all my defenses ready. I'll give anybody back as good as they've got." She sounded quite fierce.

"I was sure there was some explanation," said McLeod tactfully. She longed to ask Mystique why she'd changed her name, but didn't dare.

When the main courses came, Mystique revealed her real mission. "I want to know how your investigation is coming. Whom do you suspect?" she said.

"The investigation is—was fruitless," said McLeod. "I

just wish the police would pay more attention to our premise—that the murder of Bob Dewey rises out of the two previous murders. They have the resources to really go after all the people and get to the bottom of it. But they seem to be off on some other tack. The students and I could just ask polite questions. And actually we decided to stop even that."

"How has everybody reacted to all those questions?" asked Mystique.

McLeod took her life in her hands and replied quite frankly. "Several people have called Ginger Kingsley at the Humanities Council, but I think you're the only one who threatened to report a student to the Dean," she said.

"That was naughty of me," said Mystique, closing her eyes and lowering her head as she pretended to be a remorseful child. "Of course, I never did report him and never would. I was just tired that day. He caught me during office hours. I hate office hours. That other student that came to the house was kind of cute, though."

Poor Lyle, thought McLeod. Capturing the heart of an unlovely professor. "He's adorable," she said shamelessly. "Mystique, where were you last Wednesday afternoon? Did you by chance go to McCosh, down in the basement, and maybe see somebody who shouldn't be there?"

"I was in New York Wednesday," said Mystique. "And I can prove it. I caught the ten o'clock bus to the city that morning and didn't get home until late that night. I met my editor for lunch and my agent for dinner. We were talking about what I'm going to do next."

"Would you mind telling me who your editor and agent are?" said McLeod.

"Not at all," said Mystique. "I've ceased to be shocked by your inquiries." She gave McLeod the names and phone numbers and McLeod wrote them down.

"You realize that gives you an alibi for Bob Dewey's murder?" said McLeod.

"It does, doesn't it," said Mystique. "So you haven't solved our murders?"

"Not at all," said McLeod.

This seemed to cheer Mystique.

They chatted inconsequentially over dessert and coffee. I am going to be as big as she is, thought McLeod, if I keep on eating this way.

Forty-eight

❧

WHILE SHE DRANK her coffee the next morning, McLeod
made another grocery list. Although she did not have to cook
Thanksgiving dinner, she still had to lay in a good many pro-
visions, get things for a relish tray, buy soft drinks, liquor,
and food for them to eat at the other meals besides Thanksgiving dinner. And buy a turkey. She had heard about a
turkey farm in Hightstown that sold fresh, organic turkey.
Maybe she could go over there. I could, she thought, if only
Liz Finley would hurry up with those dahlias.

As if on cue, the doorbell rang. It was not Finley, however, but Ginger Kingsley, looking rosy underneath all her
freckles, her hair flying wildly around her head.

"Ginger! Come in. What a pleasant surprise!"

"I can't stay," said Ginger. "We're leaving any minute
now. But I wanted to bring you this turkey."

She carried a carton labeled, LEE'S TURKEY FARM. "You
didn't already buy one, did you? I hope you have room in
your refrigerator for this."

"I'll make room," promised McLeod. "Don't worry. How nice of you. You must have read my mind—I had heard of that turkey farm and I was wondering where it is. I thought I might drive over there, but you've saved me the trip. That's wonderful. Ginger, you're always so good to me."

"I just thought I'd bring it by," said Ginger. "I'm glad I caught you here." She stood uncertainly by the door.

"Can't you have a cup of coffee?" asked McLeod.

"I'm afraid I can't," said Ginger. "We really are about to leave."

"Where is it you all are going for Thanksgiving?"

"We're going to Cliff's brother's in Providence," said Ginger. "And Miranda is joining us there. But we'll be back Friday. Two nights is as long as Cliff can stand his brother's wife." She hesitated again. "Your students have dropped their investigation now, haven't they?"

"I hope so," McLeod said.

"Good," said Ginger. She seemed nervous, pulling at her gloves.

The doorbell rang and McLeod opened it to Elizabeth Finley. Ginger gathered herself together and left. "Have a good trip," McLeod called after her, as she turned to usher Finley in.

McLeod was overwhelmed at the quantity and variety of the dahlias. Some were purple, some red, others ranging from white to yellow to russet. They were dazzling and McLeod said so.

"Dahlias don't live through the winter here, do they?" she asked, rather proud of producing this tidbit of horticultural lore.

"No, you have to lift the tubers before a hard freeze," said Finley. "You replant them in the spring. You have to stake them, too. And when you cut them, you have to burn the end of each stem. They're trouble, but most worthwhile things are trouble. I love dahlias."

McLeod had always considered them rather gloomy and stiff, but she was still grateful.

"I've already burned the ends of the stems for you," Liz was saying, "so all you have to do is stick them in water."

While McLeod put the flowers in a big pitcher of water—"I'll arrange them later," she said—Liz was still talking.

"I like dahlias so much better than summer flowers," she said.

"Why?" asked McLeod, out of genuine curiosity.

"For one thing, they're at their best when everything else looks faded and leggy," said Liz. "They're late bloomers. Maybe I feel a kinship with them."

"Will you have some coffee? It's all made," said McLeod.

"I'd love some," said Liz.

They sat down in the living room with their cups and eyed one another. "Surely you've bloomed already?" said McLeod. "You're no 'late bloomer.'"

"Oh, yes, I am," said Liz. "I finally got my contract from the Harvard University Press this morning. When I sent them my manuscript, the editor-in-chief loved it and they sent it out to readers, and they all liked it. And the press wanted to publish it, but I didn't want to tell anybody about it until they had signed the contract. And now they have. It will be their big book next fall."

"That's stupendous," said McLeod. "I'm so glad." She suddenly knew that she really wanted to write the Bartram book. She wanted to undertake this huge project, as Liz had done, and carry it through. She'd really get on with it. Maybe she could get somebody to go down to the C-Level library stacks with her, though.

"Wasn't there some trouble about your book with Dexter Kinkaid?" asked McLeod.

Liz looked at her sharply. "How did you hear that?" she said.

"I honestly don't remember," said McLeod, hoping that lightning would not strike her dead for this lie.

"Oh, I guess everybody hears everything at Princeton," said Liz. "I know too well that there are no secrets here. Everything leaks—it's a great Gothic sieve. Yes, Dexter did have doubts about it, and he's on the board of the Princeton University Press, and they turned it down. I never quite understood what he objected to. The outside readers liked it. I just don't know what was going on with Dexter. I made some changes, not many, before I sent it off to Harvard, and they seem to think it's quite spectacular. I feel vindicated. Really vindicated." Liz smiled and sipped her coffee.

She looked like a different person, McLeod thought. Younger, pinker, and, well, *sexier*.

"That's glorious!" McLeod said. "Let's drink champagne. I don't have Perrier-Jouët. It's Chandon from California, but it's cold." She moved toward the refrigerator.

Liz looked at her watch. "It's only ten o'clock," she said. "But why not?"

McLeod opened the champagne and they drank to late bloomers.

After a glass or two, McLeod said, "So you're not glad Dexter's dead?"

Liz Finley looked at her sharply. "No, I'm not glad. I didn't kill him over my book, if that's what you've been thinking. I had enough faith in my own work to know it would be published somewhere. I found Dexter's attitude inexplicable, unless it was a deep, unconscious jealousy. I was his protégée. He brought me here. And we were lovers for a while. It's the only thing I can think of—that he begrudged me a big success. It was unworthy of him. And I have to say that I didn't like your students asking me questions about it.

"But I do hate it that he may have been murdered. That's why I've gotten interested in you and your class.

Everybody is talking about your investigation. What have you found out?"

"Nothing really," said McLeod. She did not tell Liz that it appeared as though she, Liz, had just put herself out of the picture as a suspect. "I'm just hoping the police will get on to it and use their superior resources to find out who did it. It's been a week now since Bob Dewey was murdered, and I think they're barking up the wrong tree on that one. Oh, well."

" 'Oh, well' is right, McLeod," said Liz, rising from the sofa. "Now that we've knocked back a bottle of champagne by ourselves, I think I'd better go. Have fun with your children."

"Thanks, Liz, and thanks for the dahlias," said McLeod. "Have fun at your brother's."

AS SOON AS Liz left, Lyle called to say that he wanted to see her. He had some information for her. Could he see her before he left to go home for Thanksgiving?

"What kind of information?" McLeod asked him.

"Information about the murder," Lyle said.

"I told you to drop it," McLeod said.

"I'll tell you about it when I see you," he said.

They agreed to meet at Small World.

Forty-nine

❧

"JUST EXPLAIN TO me why you didn't drop the Murder Project," McLeod said to Lyle as soon as they were settled at a table at Small World.

"I know you said not to do anything else, but Daisy and I decided to talk just to the people with offices in McCosh basement. We didn't think any of them was the murderer—you said that yourself. And we didn't think any of them would mind our asking them questions about other people they had seen. It wouldn't cause trouble for you or put your job at risk. It wasn't something they'd complain to the Humanities Council about."

"You make me sound so self-centered."

"No, no. We took your point, but we couldn't help ourselves."

McLeod remembered guiltily that she, too, had continued to ask questions.

"You taught us too well to be curious," Lyle said. "Anyway, it's absolutely awesome. Everybody in the university was seen by one or two people in McCosh basement last Wednesday afternoon."

"Who saw them?"

"We talked to all the assistant professors—Ursula Barnes, John Pope, Grady Schuyler, Guadalupe Hutchinson, everybody. They were all down there, and one or more of them saw nearly everybody in the English Department—Liz Finley, Guy Peyton, Fred Harper, Gertrude Sergeant, Cliff Kingsley."

He pulled a folded piece of paper from his pocket. "We made a list of them all." He handed it to her. McLeod, the compulsive note taker, began to copy the names into her own notebook.

"Good heavens," said McLeod. "The dean of the college. What was he doing down there?"

"Don't know," said Lyle.

"Margie Kinkaid, Ginger Kingsley, Jim Macy—who's he?" asked McLeod. "Oh, the director of public relations." She read on; a distinguished French professor had been down there, and lots of students.

"Students?" said McLeod. "Do you suppose an angry student could have killed Bob Dewey?"

"The police must think so," said Lyle. "They've called in all the students in his classes this semester one by one and they're working on the ones who had him last semester."

"I thought when a student killed a professor, it was always in a rage over a grade, and they all used guns and gave themselves up, or took a hostage. Isn't that the way students do it? They're not secretive about it. Anyway, students are a possibility that we overlooked," said McLeod.

"We think his murder is connected to the cosmopolitan murders, remember?" said Lyle.

"I suppose so," said McLeod. "Actually our theory is gaining credibility with the faculty, if not the police."

She told him then that Trudy Sergeant wanted to visit

the class and about her chats with Margie Kinkaid, Mystique Alcott, and Liz Finley.

"They were full of revelations," she said. "Margie told me that Alcott's real name is Miriam and that Dexter caught her in plagiarism." McLeod gave him the details, as she had them from Margie.

"Then Mystique told me it was all hogwash—the plagiarism charge," said McLeod. "She said—rather persuasively—that she could show conclusively that she had not quoted any secondary sources. Dexter probably got the idea of plagiarism, she said, from the fact that they had all used the same primary sources."

"She's probably lying," said Lyle. "It would have ruined her if Dexter had lived."

"I'm not so sure," said McLeod. "And anyway, she says she has an ironclad alibi for Wednesday. She was in New York."

Lyle's jaw dropped. "You don't mean it?" he said.

"I do mean it," McLeod said. "And you notice her name was not on that list of people in McCosh basement."

"Well, that list doesn't have to be a hundred percent accurate," said Lyle. "They're not bound to have seen everybody."

"True," said McLeod, "but she says she had lunch with her editor and dinner with her agent."

"Can we check up on that?" asked Lyle.

"Sure," said McLeod, "I even got the names and telephone numbers from her."

"I'll call them," said Lyle. "I'll say it's to settle a bet. I'd like to know. I've always thought Alcott was *the* prime suspect after Bob Dewey was killed."

"Me, too, actually," said McLeod. "She was always the best bet to fix that cosmopolitan at her house."

"I know," said Lyle. "And she's so—well, awful—"

"I know what you mean," said Mcleod. "But she's not so bad when you get to know her." She paused and added, "And she thinks you're cute."

"Jesus," said Lyle.

"That's not all," said McLeod. "I think another suspect is off the hook. Liz Finley came by this morning to tell me that Dexter's criticisms of her book were based on jealousy and groundless, and that the Harvard University Press is going to publish it. She was like a different person."

"Well, do you believe her?"

"I think I do," said McLeod. "She may have been trying to con me, but I don't think so. No, I believe her. It would be too easy to find out that she was lying about the Harvard Press and her book."

Lyle looked very glum. "Who does that leave us?" he asked.

"It leaves us Trudy Sergeant and Margie Kinkaid," said McLeod. "And to tell you the truth, I don't see how Margie Kinkaid could have fixed the drink at Mystique's house. If she had made it after they came, wouldn't Dexter have drunk it right down?"

"That is a puzzler," Lyle agreed. "What about Sergeant?"

"She doesn't seem to have a motive," said McLeod.

"I thought for sure we could solve this thing," said Lyle. "I thought we *ought* to solve it since the police aren't getting anywhere."

"Lyle, let it drop," said McLeod. "I'm convinced it's really dangerous to pursue this. That fire at Ben True's apartment last Saturday made me wonder how far somebody would go to stop us."

"I thought about that, too," Lyle said. "We all did. We talked about it on the way back to the campus."

"And I've been scared to death two other times," McLeod said. "I don't know whether somebody was trying to kill me or not. But I certainly didn't like it."

Lyle asked her what had happened and she told him about the library stacks closing on her and the incident on Faculty Road.

"I can understand," said Lyle. "But I wish we could

keep on. The police are interviewing all these students. They don't have a clue."

"Don't ever underestimate the police," said McLeod. "I was impressed with Captain Perry. But they did go off in the wrong direction when they tried to blame it on Mimi."

"Mimi?" said Lyle.

"Bob Dewey's girl friend from Rome," said McLeod. "Didn't I tell you about her?"

"No," said Lyle.

She filled him in on Mimi as quickly as she could.

"It's a puzzle," said Lyle. "I see you didn't stop asking questions yourself."

"It is a puzzle," said McLeod. "And I was just trying to help Bob's girl friend."

Lyle looked at her doubtfully. "I've got to get back," he said. "I'll call these people from the dorm. I'm taking the Airporter to Newark and I've got to be in front of Dillon Gym at three o'clock. But I'm coming back Friday or Saturday. I'll call you."

"Good," said McLeod. "Have a good holiday."

McLeod rushed out of Small World. She had to get her shopping done in time to meet Rosie at Newark Airport. Horrors. Maybe she wouldn't finish in time. The traffic would be awful on the day before Thanksgiving.

Fifty

※

MCLEOD DIDN'T THINK about murder until Friday. Both her children left that morning. Harry never stayed long, and this time Rosie was eager to get back to Charlotte. She said she wanted to work on her Nadine Gordimer project, but McLeod thought the new beau she had mentioned might also be a factor in her early departure.

Since Harry was dropping Rosie off at Newark Airport on his way to New Haven, McLeod could stretch luxuriously on the sofa, enjoying that feeling familiar to all parents of grown children: It was great when they came and great when they left.

She needed to clean up her apartment and do the laundry—all those dirty sheets and towels—but she did nothing. It was too much fun just to lie on the sofa. Alone. Thanksgiving Day had been a huge success, she thought. The turkey had been fine, and so had her rolls. Everything else was good, too, even though it was "bought." The dahlias had impressed them. "You've made such nice friends here, Mama," Rosie had said on Thanksgiving about the display of flowers.

"Some of them are murderers," said Harry.

And then she had had to tell the whole tale to Rosie and bring Harry up to date. Harry was fascinated with the story about Mimi. "I like her," he said. "Is she still around?"

"No, the police let her go. I think she's going to stay in this country, though, until the funeral."

"Maybe I'll see her in New Haven," Harry said.

Everything had gone well during the children's visit, and they were great, McLeod reflected. Funny and intelligent and standing on their own two feet. Rosie, with her curly black hair and appropriately rosy cheeks, had looked terrific. She had admired the lavender sweater, which was nearly finished. She liked her job and was working hard on her research. Harry's dissertation seemed to be going well and he was, as usual, sunnily sure that he would get a job when he finished his Ph.D., although statistics were against him. "Don't worry, Mama," Harry had said. "If I have to work on Wall Street, I'll probably enjoy that, too."

It had been pleasant to listen to their optimistic chatter.

But now, there were still the murders.

She got up and brought a notebook and pencil back to the sofa, where she sat and made yet another list of all the people who had been at both the crucial parties:

McLeod Dulaney, she wrote.
Margie Kinkaid
Elizabeth Finley
Mystique Alcott
Gertrude Sergeant
Grady Schuyler

She looked at the list critically. Was that all? Only six people. Who else at her party? Dexter and Bob Dewey, eight. Who else? Oh, Cliff and Ginger Kingsley.

She pulled herself up again and got her purse and

looked at the list of people who had been seen in McCosh basement on Wednesday. Every single one of the "suspects" was on that list.

Even Cliff and Ginger Kingsley had been seen in McCosh basement, but everyone had eliminated them from serious consideration early on. No motive. But wait a minute. Cliff, the department chair, probably had an excuse for being in McCosh basement. But Ginger? What on earth was Ginger, whose office was in East Pyne, doing in the basement of McCosh on Wednesday afternoon?

"I'll ask her as soon as I get the chance," McLeod said to herself.

SHE GOT THE chance later that morning. She couldn't remember when Cliff and Ginger were coming back but she decided to call and see if they were at home. If they were, she'd ask them to dinner tonight or tomorrow. They had invited her to their house so many times.

When Ginger answered, McLeod thanked her for the turkey. "It was the best turkey I ever ate," she said.

"You Southerners are always so flattering," said Ginger cheerfully. "I'm so glad you liked it. Lee's turkeys are free-range and organic and not frozen."

"I have something impertinent to ask you," McLeod said. "The police were asking what you were doing in McCosh basement on the Wednesday Bob Dewey was murdered."

Ginger was quiet. "I don't mind your asking, but I have to remember," she said. "Oh, I went to see Guadalupe Hutchinson about this visiting writer we're bringing in after Christmas—you know Guadalupe is our Pan-African person and this is a Nigerian poet. Guadalupe's not too good about returning phone calls, and I thought maybe I could catch her in her office."

"Oh," said McLeod, "I'm glad you have a good excuse. I was worried. Did you catch Guadalupe?"

"What?" said Ginger. "Oh, no, she wasn't there. She lives in New York, you know, and commutes. She's very elusive, really."

"Oh well," said McLeod. "You'll catch up with her eventually." She decided not to mention the students' investigation. After all, she had promised Ginger to drop it. "There seems to be a list of everybody who was seen downstairs in McCosh that Wednesday."

"Well, I was over there," said Ginger. "I'm awfully glad I have a reason."

"Oh yes," said McLeod. "You do have a hard time with all your people, the ones who come in and the ones who stay."

"I do, but I can usually work it out," said Ginger. "Always work it out. Can you come to dinner tonight?"

"Ginger, you're so wonderful to me," said McLeod. "I was planning to ask you and Cliff to come over here, but I have no character. If you ask me, I'll come with my tongue hanging out. I'd love it. I'll bring a bottle of champagne. I seem to drink nothing else these days."

"You seem to drink nothing else anytime," said Ginger.

"Well, there's soda water," said McLeod.

"Oh, sure," said Ginger.

LYLE E-MAILED HER that he had called Mystique's editor and agent. He hadn't reached the agent yet, but had left a message. "Her editor just laughed when I said I was a student at Princeton and was settling a bet. She said she had a long lunch with Alcott. They were at the Four Seasons until three o'clock. So even if Mystique didn't have dinner in New York, it would have been hard for her to get here in time to kill Bob Dewey. I guess she's off our list. I hate it."

• • •

ON HER WAY to the Kingsleys' house, McLeod stopped at the liquor store to buy a cold bottle of Perrier-Jouët. She blanched at the cost, then shrugged. If it was good enough for Mystique, it was good enough for her—and the Kingsleys, who had been so wonderful to her.

Cliff had outdone himself in the short time since they'd been back. There was a spicy crab soup and broiled salmon with hollandaise, a salad of beets and avocado, and flan for dessert.

"How do you do it?" asked McLeod.

"I like to eat," said Cliff. "And I like to cook what I like to eat. It's much more rewarding than teaching English or chairing a department. I'm already tired of that. I dread Monday."

"Cliff," said Ginger. "You can't just throw away a chance like this."

"I can't?" said Cliff.

The Kingsleys seemed strained and McLeod left early—but not before she ate heartily.

IT WAS MIDNIGHT before she woke up, feeling terribly ill. She threw up and then the diarrhea started. Was it something she had eaten? Something she had eaten—with acetaminophen in it?

Fifty-one

❧

AS SHE LAY awake after calling 911, between trips to the bathroom, McLeod thought about the Kingsleys. Either Ginger or Cliff had murdered Archie and Dexter and Bob Dewey. There could be no doubt about it. And now one of them had tried to murder her.

And Ginger—both of them—had always seemed so warm and generous and helpful. In fact, it had been McLeod's first impulse to call Ginger to ask her to take her to the hospital.

She shuddered at the thought. She was getting worse rapidly, but she used the last of her strength to open her laptop and send Lyle an e-mail: "In hospital. Kingsleys poisoned me. Acetaminophen. Be careful. Tell others."

It seemed only seconds—she barely had time to put on her bathrobe and find her purse—before the buzzer rang and a whole crew of uniformed young men and women from the Rescue Squad dashed in.

"Intestinal upset?" one of them asked as he took her

temperature and another her blood pressure. It didn't sound like much of an ailment when they said it like that.

"I've been poisoned," she panted. "I'm sure of it."

They looked at her doubtfully, but unfolded the stretcher, made her lie down on it, and took her to the ambulance that waited outside. She noted that they did not turn on the siren on the way to the hospital.

The dry heaves continued, though she had nothing to throw up anymore, as she registered at the desk in the emergency room. The clerk handed her an enamel dish and directed her to the triage nurse.

"I think I've been poisoned with acetaminophen," McLeod struggled to say.

"Acetaminophen?" said the nurse. "You mean Tylenol?"

Unimpressed, she began the customary routine questions. When did the symptoms start? Why did she think she had been poisoned with acetaminophen?

"A friend of mine died . . . not diagnosed . . . too long a story . . . ," said McLeod, exhausted.

Eventually, she was ushered into a curtained booth and handed a hospital gown. The emergency room doctor examined her and asked a thousand questions. As she grew weaker, they finally admitted her. When they asked her who her doctor was, she roused herself enough to think of Dr. Winchester.

When Dr. Winchester arrived, he remembered Archie Alexander's case very well. "Acetaminophen," said McLeod, who by now found it a terrible effort to speak. ". . . doesn't show up on tests . . ."

"That's right," said Dr. Winchester. "We'll specifically look for it in your case—and look for other things, too, just to be on the safe side. But if it is acetaminophen, there is an antidote."

Fifty-two

❧

IT WAS SOMETIME the next day when McLeod swam up toward consciousness and saw Ginger Kingsley standing by her hospital bed.

"Ginger!" she said.

"McLeod!" said Ginger, mocking her note of surprise.

McLeod shrank away from Ginger, whose curly hair today looked menacing, like lightning bolts. She had always thought Ginger was adorable looking, but today she seemed like some horrible Greek avenger. Medusa.

"What are you doing here?" asked McLeod.

"I'm visiting the sick," said Ginger.

"How did you know I was here?"

"I read your e-mail, *Peaches*," said Ginger. "That's how I kept up with what the Murder Project was doing. Remember, you told me what your password was when I showed you how to use the campus computer network?"

McLeod remembered all the information that had flown over cyberspace—meetings of the Murder Project, her speculations about the murder method, and students telling her about upcoming appointments for interviews—including Marcy's meeting with Bob Dewey, which must have rung an alarm bell in Ginger's twisted mind. She had also kept Cliff and Ginger up to date on the project when she saw them. She writhed in anguish.

"But aren't you glad to see me?" Ginger was saying, and now she did smile, but her mouth was contorted and her eyes were cold.

McLeod stared at her. "Of course I am . . ." she began, but she decided not to lie. "I can't believe it. Why did you do it?"

"Do what?" asked Ginger. "Come here? I told you—it's my good deed for the day." Again the frightening smile. "Actually, I've come to finish the job I started Friday night. I have to do it, since you seem to be recovering so nicely. No, don't reach for that call button. I'll just keep that little device over here." Ginger jerked the call button out of McLeod's bed and held it firmly. "I brought a scarf with me. Another new scarf from K-Mart. Buying from K-Mart is the best way to be anonymous, don't you think? No one *we* know goes to K-Mart, do they?"

"But why me?" asked McLeod. "I thought we were friends."

"You ask too many questions," said Ginger. "When I found out you knew I was in McCosh basement that Wednesday, I knew it was just a matter of time before you or one of those students found out."

"Archie and Dexter?" asked McLeod, wondering if she could possibly gather strength to leap up and grab the call button from Ginger. "Why?"

"You haven't figured it out yet? Those students who you're teaching to be just as inquisitive as you are, they don't know either? None of you figured out why I did it? But then, I don't think Cliff has ever caught on, either. Of course, he always has his nose in a cookbook—or in the steam from a stew pot. So what does he know?"

As she talked, Ginger was pulling a scarf from her purse and twisting it. "I bought an orange scarf for you because I know you like bright colors," she said, smiling her hideous smile.

"Tell me *why* you killed the others, Ginger, before you do me," McLeod said.

"Curious to the last, aren't you?" said Ginger. "This may be the worst punishment you could possibly endure—to die without knowing *why*." She flicked the orange scarf. It looked like a huge adder's tongue, McLeod thought.

"It's been a terrible semester. I'll be glad when it's over," Ginger said as she stepped closer. "You know, I won't even have to use the scarf. I can hold the pillow over your face. You're too weak to do anything about it. I can tell." She dropped the orange scarf and the call button on the floor, jerked the pillow out from under McLeod's head, and put it over McLeod's face. McLeod saw blackness. And she couldn't breathe.

Fifty-three

❦

THEN SHE *COULD* breathe again, after all.

"Oh, no, you don't." It was Lyle Cramer's voice she heard, and when she opened her eyes, she could see daylight.

She could also see Lyle holding Ginger's hands behind her back. Her pillow, she noticed, was on the floor with the scarf and the call button.

"Call the nurse," Lyle said to McLeod, who pulled on the cord until the call button was in her hand. She pressed it. Ginger was trying to break free, and McLeod realized she probably outweighed Lyle. She prayed that Lyle was young and wiry and strong enough to hold her.

"Yes," said a disembodied voice. "Can I help you." Someone from the nurses' station always answered a call over an intercom.

"We need help right now." McLeod's voice was a hoarse whisper.

"What kind of help?" asked the canned-sounding voice of the nurse.

"We need the police!" shouted Lyle. "Or a doctor or an orderly or a security man!"

A nurse came swiftly around the door. "What's going on?" she asked.

"She was trying to smother Ms. Dulaney with her pillow," said Lyle. "I saw her. I got here just in time."

"Nurse, he's not telling the truth," said Ginger, smiling her frightful smile at the nurse. "He's a very bad boy. Let me go, you naughty thing."

The nurse looked at them. McLeod thought it was obvious that Lyle was sane and Ginger was demented, but she was afraid the nurse wouldn't see it that way. Ginger, after all, had always been very persuasive. But that smile gave her away. It wasn't Ginger's old, marvelous smile at all. Even a stranger could see that.

The nurse pressed her beeper, and help appeared. Lots of help. Ginger and Lyle left, in the midst of a good-sized crowd, it seemed, and a nurse and doctor stayed with McLeod to make sure she was all right. When the doctor finally left, the nurse remained.

"Well, this is a bit of excitement," she said.

"Go find out what's going on," McLeod said.

"I don't want to leave you alone," said the nurse. "They're calling the police. You'd better take this." McLeod swallowed the capsule, and saw blackness again.

Fifty-four

❦

WHEN MCLEOD WOKE up again, Lyle was there.

"It was seriously exciting," he said. "I had to go to the police station and sign a statement. I talked to Captain Perry."

"Do they finally connect all the murders?"

"Oh, sure," said Lyle. "They know she did them all."

"How is Ginger?" asked McLeod.

"She is totally crazy," said Lyle. "It's awesome. She's in jail. Without bail. She called Cowboy Tarleton to be her lawyer."

Dr Winchester appeared and Lyle left.

"You're lucky," he told McLeod. "You got an extra big dose of acetaminophen. I can't believe you didn't taste it."

"It was in a spicy crab soup," said McLeod. "And the soup was delicious."

Dr. Winchester shook his head. "It's a good thing you got to the emergency room when you did. It's a good thing

you're not much of a drinker. It's a good thing you knew
what had happened and a good thing we had an antidote. I
just wish Archie Alexander had known what had caused
his illness." He shook his head again.

The police came and took a long statement from her
about the pillow incident and the dinner where she'd been
poisoned. She asked them some of the questions about
Ginger's motive but they said they had no information to
give her.

Late that afternoon, she called her children and told
them the news, but ordered them not to come to Princeton.
They had enough on their plates, she said, and she was
fine.

She checked the messages on her answering machine.
One was from Oliver Hunt, wanting to know if she could
check on the progress of the murder investigation.
She called him immediately to tell him what had happened and he said he would come straight to Princeton to
do the story himself. Shortly, a huge arrangement of
flowers was delivered to her room with Ollie's name on
the card.

Visitors began to arrive the next day— her students,
bearing flowers and candy, and Stephanie West. It was
Stephanie who went to her apartment and gathered up
books, her knitting, and some warm socks and brought
them to the hospital.

The four former women suspects—Mystique, Liz,
Trudy, and Margie—all came by. Margie stayed for quite a
while.

"McLeod, you're a lesson to us all," she said. "I've
learned a lot from you. I've decided not to just sit around
thinking about Dexter. I'm going to get out and do something. I've signed up for art classes at the Community
College. I've always wanted to paint, and I never took the
time. I thought Dexter needed me. And I'm going to
move—I'm tired of that big old house. Oh, I'll wait a

year, like everybody says to do, but I'm going to start getting rid of stuff and looking around. I may even leave Princeton."

"Princeton's awfully nice, Margie," said McLeod. "But I'm glad to see you so perked up. Good for you."

Fifty-five

❦

WHEN MCLEOD GOT out of the hospital, she went to Borough Hall to see Nick Perry. He was looking very pleased with himself.

"You were right," he said. "Bob Dewey's murder was connected to those two deaths from 'liver disease.'"

"It's not that I'm so smart," she said. "I knew them both and I saw Archie Alexander drink that cosmopolitan with my own eyes. But will you answer some of my questions?"

"I'll tell you what I can," he said. "Ms. Kingsley has confessed. Cowboy Tarleton is representing her. I think he'll plead insanity."

"But why?" said McLeod. "What was her motive?"

"Well, like you said, Alexander was an accident. She never meant to kill him. And I think it rattled her when he died. But she was determined to get Kinkaid. They had had an affair and he broke it off, and it was too much for her. She went berserk. It appears she was disgusted with her husband. All he cared about was food; he wasn't even interested in sex anymore. And he isn't ambitious enough for her. She raves about how lazy he is."

"Poor Ginger," said McLeod. "She was frustrated in every way. Princeton wouldn't let her teach. Cliff wanted to cook all the time and wouldn't work to win academic distinction. And then that awful Dexter Kinkaid threw her over. I think that when Cliff got promoted after Kinkaid died, Ginger must have regarded it as a bonus. She gets even with the lover who scorned her and wins a promotion for her husband even if he doesn't want it."

"That's probably right," Perry said.

"And I guess we drove her crazy, my students and I," said McLeod. "We were a big impediment that she hadn't counted on. Did she try to run into me on Faculty Road? Did she try to close the stacks on me at the library?"

"I don't know about those incidents," said Perry. "Tell me."

McLeod described what had happened. "I don't know whether they were accidental, or whether they were real attempts on my life."

"I don't either," said Perry, making notes. "But there's a dent on Professor Kingsley's car that needs looking into."

"And what about the fire on Park Place? When all of us were at Ben True's apartment?"

"I know about that one. When the fire marshall's report on the arson popped up on the computer, I checked it out, because all of you were listed as being in the house. It turned out to be the landlord—trying to burn the house down for insurance. *That* one's unrelated."

"With people asleep in the house? That's sick," said McLeod.

"Another crazy."

"But how did Ginger know about acetominophen? That it would poison somebody?"

"She heard a doctor friend in New York mention it at a party. It has to be a massive dose," Perry said. "She thought about it a long time before she did it. And she had to use it in something that had a strong taste, like cosmopolitans or crab soup."

"What will happen to her?"

"It's in the hands of the prosecutor," Perry said. "But she's practically a serial killer. I don't think there's any way she can go free—ever."

AFTER THE NEXT class, McLeod and all the project members went down to Frist Student Center. McLeod praised their detective work.

"We were awfully slow to figure out that Ginger Kingsley was the murderer," said Lyle.

"That was my fault," said McLeod. "I refused to even consider either one of the Kingsleys. "They were so nice to me." She sighed. "I didn't figure it out until she poisoned me. She had such plausible answers to all my questions. But eventually, when I was at death's door, even I caught on."

"That's right and you e-mailed me," said Lyle. "I never did really figure it out. I guess I didn't believe you until I saw her holding that pillow over your face."

"Ginger could go around fixing cosmopolitans in other people's houses because she was always doing things for people," McLeod said. "Everybody liked her. She even had an excuse for being in the basement of McCosh when Bob Dewey was murdered."

"But why?" the students asked. "Why did she do it?"

McLeod explained what she knew and what she had deduced since her talk with Nick Perry.

They talked endlessly about the case. Of Mystique Alcott, Ben said, "She never reported me to the dean or anybody else. She called me up the other day and invited me to dinner."

"That woman is sex mad," said Lyle.

"Great!" said Ben.

"I thought it was Professor Finley," said Marcy.

"I longed for it to be Sergeant," said Lyle. "Her biceps! She could easily have strangled poor Dewey."

"Everybody forgets Ginger was not a tender weakling," said McLeod. "She was very fit—I should know."

NEXT MCLEOD WENT to see Cliff in his office.

"I'm sorry, McLeod," Cliff said. "I didn't know what she was doing. I guess I didn't want to know."

"I'm sorry, too," said McLeod. "And I'm dreadfully sorry for Ginger. She was a great friend to me."

"Until she tried to kill you," said Cliff.

"She was a very good friend who is now deranged. I don't think she knew what she was doing when she tried to kill me."

"She knew what she was doing, alas," said Cliff. "But I think her lawyers are going to plead insanity."

"How about Miranda?" asked McLeod.

"She's stunned," said Cliff. "She wants to drop out and come home but I told her to stay where she is, for now, anyway. I started to resign, and I may have to. I'd love to get out of this, you know. I never did like academia much. I really want to cook."

"Well, maybe you can quit now," said McLeod.

"I think I'll need every cent I can lay my hands on to pay for Ginger's defense," said Cliff. "I expect the university would rather I quit, but I—" He broke off.

"Maybe they'll pay the lawyers in lieu of a terminal settlement for you," said McLeod.

Cliff brightened. "That's a great idea" he said. "I'll talk to the dean."

Fifty-six

❧

MCLEOD WENT HOME for Christmas, where she was joined briefly by Harry and Rosie. Then she had to go back to Princeton to pack up and to be around for reading period and finals week. There was no final exam in her class, of course, but she had to be available for conferences during reading period and, finally, receive the term papers, the long articles, and grade them.

McLeod turned up the heat in her apartment and read all the students' papers. They were extraordinarily good. Lyle had written an exhaustive account of the Murder Project, drawing on his original article on Archie Alexander; he had interviewed Margie Kinkaid, who had been very helpful, and Nick Perry among others. Ben True had written a revealing profile of Mystique Alcott. These two, McLeod thought, were publishable, but everyone in the class had done a creditable job.

I can't wait to tell Ginger how good they are, she thought, and then realized Ginger was gone from Joseph

Henry House. The university had named an aging German professor as temporary director of the Humanities Council, and McLeod could not see herself talking enthusiastically about her students' work to him. Nobody knew when a permanent replacement for Ginger would be chosen.

Police investigation still could not confirm for certain that Ginger had been behind the wheel the night McLeod was nearly hit on Faculty Road, and the episode in the library stacks seemed likely to remain a mystery. McLeod was content with the confession—and to be assured of her own safety and that of her students.

When she went by to turn in the keys to her office and the grades for the course, she wished Frieda well. Frieda did seem to have thawed.

"We'll miss you," she told McLeod.

"I'll certainly miss Princeton," said McLeod. "This has been the most interesting semester I believe I ever spent anywhere."

"The students adored you," said Frieda.

"Thanks, Frieda," said McLeod. "I hope you get a nice new director to work with."

"I hope so, too," said Frieda. "You know, I always thought that Ginger Kingsley had a mean streak."

McLeod's Faculty Brunch

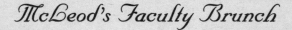

Mimosas

Mix equal parts of champagne and orange juice, and serve icy cold.

McLeod's Mother's "Egg Thing"

8 eggs
6 slices dry white bread
1 cup grated cheddar cheese
1 pound sausage, browned and drained
2 cups milk
1 teaspoon salt
1 teaspoon dry mustard

The night before you plan to serve, trim crusts off dry bread slices and cut slices in pieces. Line a 9 x 13 inch pan with these pieces. Put browned and drained sausage on top of bread. Mix together eggs, milk, salt, dry mustard and 3/4 cup cheese and pour over sausage. Sprinkle remaining cheese on top. Let stand in refrigerator overnight.

Bake the next morning for 30 minutes at 350 degrees, until puffed and brown. Serves 8.

Baked Grits

1 cup uncooked grits
6 slices bacon
1 green pepper, chopped
1 onion, chopped
1 cup chopped tomatoes
1 Tablespoon chopped garlic
salt and pepper

Cook grits according to package directions.

Fry bacon. Use two tablespoons of the bacon fat to saute onions, peppers, and garlic. Add onion, pepper, garlic and tomatoes to cooked grits. Add salt and pepper. Pour into casserole and top with crumbled bacon. Bake 25–30 minutes in 350 degree oven. Serves 6.

Vondelle's Whipping Cream Pound Cake

2 sticks butter
3 cups cake flour
1 cup whipping cream
6 eggs

3 cups sugar
1 teaspoon vanilla

Cream sugar and butter in an electric mixer or by hand. Add eggs one at a time, beating well after each addition. Add vanilla, then alternate adding flour and cream, 1/3 of each at a time, beating after each addition, until all ingredients are thoroughly mixed. Pour into a greased tube pan. Place cake in cold oven, set oven to 325 degrees, and bake 1 hour and 15 minutes.